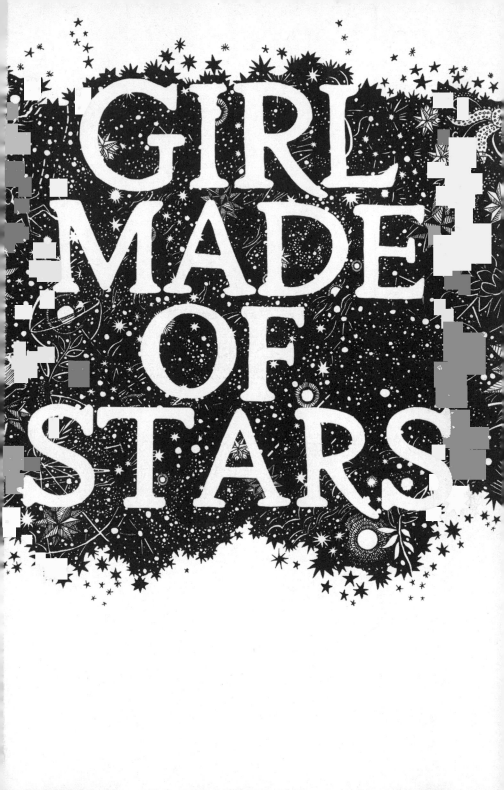

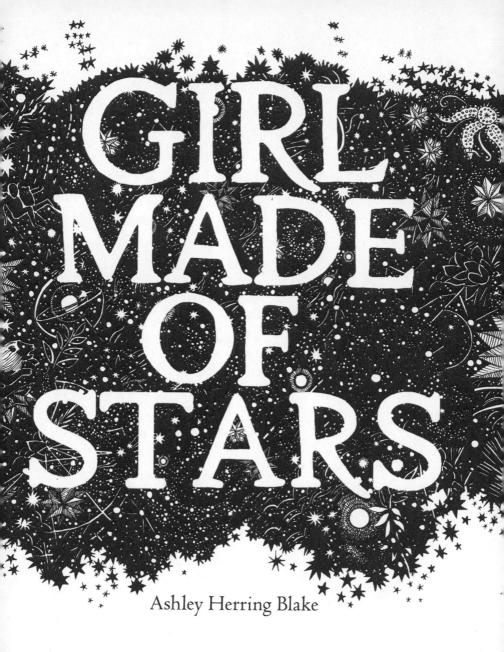

GIRL MADE OF STARS

Ashley Herring Blake

HOUGHTON MIFFLIN HARCOURT
Boston   New York

Also by Ashley Herring Blake

Suffer Love

How to Make a Wish

Copyright © 2018 by Ashley Herring Blake

All rights reserved. For information about permission to reproduce selections from
this book, write to Permissions, Houghton Mifflin Harcourt Publishing Company,
3 Park Avenue, 19th Floor, New York, New York 10016.

hmhco.com

The text was set in Centaur.

Library of Congress Cataloging-in-Publication Data
Names: Blake, Ashley Herring, author.
Title: Girl made of stars / Ashley Herring Blake.
Description: Boston ; New York : Houghton Mifflin Harcourt, [2018] | Summary:
When Mara's twin brother Owen is accused of rape by her friend Hannah,
Mara is forced to confront her feelings about her family, her sense of
right and wrong, a trauma from her past, and the future with her
girlfriend, Charlie. Identifiers: LCCN 2017015661 | ISBN 9781328778239
Subjects: | CYAC: Twins—Fiction. | Brothers and sisters—Fiction. |
Rape—Fiction. | Sexual abuse—Fiction. | Bisexuality—Fiction.
Classification: LCC PZ7.1.B58 Gi 2018 | DDC [Fic]—dc23
LC record available at https://lccn.loc.gov/2017015661

Printed in the United States of America
DOC 10 9 8 7 6 5 4 3 2 1
4500705770

For you. You are worth the telling.

"There was a star riding through clouds one night, and I said to the star, 'Consume me.'"
— Virginia Woolf, *The Waves*

CHAPTER ONE

Charlie refuses to answer my texts. Or she has her phone set on silent. Or she forgot to charge it. Or she had a rare fit of temper and tossed it into a toilet, thereby rendering it unusable.

Whatever the case, this lack of communication between us is decidedly not normal.

I stare at my phone for a few more seconds, analyzing my last text to her. It's a simple question—Will you be at the Empower meeting next week?—so I don't understand why she won't answer it. Yes or no. How hard is that? Then again, Charlie's never missed an Empower meeting, so she probably sees right through my desperate attempt at indifference.

Groaning at the still-blank screen, I toss the phone onto my bed and slide my window open. An early autumn breeze ghosts over my skin and hair, bringing with it the smell of burning leaves and cedar from the rocking chairs on our front porch. Throwing a leg over the sill, I twist my body through the window and onto the porch's flat roof. In the distance, the setting sun drizzles the last bit of color through the sky, lavender fading to darker violet. The first stars are blinking into view and I lie down on the gritty shingles, my eyes already peeling through the almost-dark for Gemini. You can't really see the constellation this time of year, but I know those twins are hiding somewhere in the west.

"There they are," Owen says as he climbs through the window and settles next to me. He waves his hand off toward the east.

"You're so full of shit."

"What, they're right there."

"That's Cancer . . . or something."

"I know my twins, woman."

I laugh and relax into the familiarity of the scene. Owen, messy-haired and clad in flannel and slim-fit jeans, full of astrological pomp and circumstance. We lie quietly for a bit, night sounds growing thicker with the dark.

"Once upon a time . . ." Owen whispers, and I smile. This is familiar too, all of his bravado softening into this: my twin brother spinning stories under a domed sky.

". . . a brother and a sister lived with the stars. They were happy and had wild adventures exploring the sky," I continue, filling in the beginning of our story the way we always have since we were kids.

"One day, they went out searching for true love," Owen says.

"Oh my god, you're such a sap."

"Shut up — my twin does what I want."

"Fine." I stare at a spot of darkening sky, hoping to catch a shooting star. "But Sister Twin didn't care about true love, so —"

"Oh, *I'm* full of shit?"

"—she decided to seek her fortune in a nearby galaxy."

"But on her way, she caught a glimpse of Andromeda and thought, *Screw fortune, give me that ass!*"

"You are a vile human being."

"I'm not a human at all. I'm a *constellation*."

"Half of a constellation."

"The better half."

I groan dramatically and try to shove Owen's shoulder, but he dodges me and hooks his arm around my neck, blowing a raspberry into my hair.

"Speaking of better halves," he says when he releases me, "why isn't Charlie attached to your person right now? Wait, is she in your pocket?"

He leans into me as if he's trying to look into my literal pocket and I push him away. "These leggings don't have any pockets, and you know why she's not here right now."

His mouth forms a little circle. "Right." He squints at me, then shakes his head. "No, sorry. I can't imagine one of you without the other."

My smile fades and I sit up, wrapping a lock of hair around my forefinger. Charlie's always loved playing with my hair and plaiting the ends into little braids. It's a years-old habit, born freshman year when I sat in front of her in American Lit and my nearly waist-length waves spilled over the back of my chair. Starting school that year had me tied into a million little knots, but

Charlie's long fingers weaving through my hair relaxed me, helped me focus and feel like me again. Right now, with my best-friend-turned-girlfriend-turned-ex-girlfriend bricking a wall of silence between us, I feel everything but.

"Which is exactly why I broke up with her now," I say. "Before it's too late."

Owen coughs "bullshit" into his hand, an intimation I decide to ignore.

"We'll be okay," I say. "Remember two years ago when I convinced her I could give her an awesome haircut?"

"Mara, you butchered her hair. It was like a faux hawk on meth."

"Which led to her getting it fixed by a professional the next day, giving rise to her beloved swoop. So really, she should've thanked me."

"Pretty sure she didn't talk to you for a week."

"And we got through it. You're only proving my point."

He tilts his head toward me. "This is a bit different from a haircut, Mar."

I swallow through the sudden ballooning in my throat. My fingers itch for my phone, my mind already forming another text, just to check on her. Maybe I should tell her I'm going to the party at the lake with Owen and Alex. Surely she'd at least grace me with a craughing emoji. Instead, I make myself stay put, literally pressing my butt into the roof.

"We'll be fine," I say. Because we will. We have to be.

Wheels crunch over gravel, pulling our attention to the driveway and Alexander Tan's sunshine-yellow Volkswagen Bug pulling to a stop in front of our house.

"I'm never going to get over his car," I say, getting to my feet and brushing roof grit off my tunic dress.

"He's lucky he's not driving around on a Huffy beach bike. Besides, he loves that thing. Even keeps little flowers in the vase by the steering wheel."

"Only when you put them there. Are you two courting?"

Owen feigns shock as his best friend steps out of his car. Alex's hair is so dark, it blends in with the rest of the night and nearly disappears. The rest of him is very, very visible. Checkered button-up under a snug gray sweater. Slim dark jeans and boots. He's the definition of dapper as hell.

"You ready for this?" Owen asks me, standing and stretching like a cat.

"Oh yeah," I deadpan. "A night of dodging guys with beer breath and perpetual boners. Can't wait."

"Maybe they'll leave you alone if they think you're still with Charlie. I don't think the breakup is common knowledge yet."

I snort a laugh. Thinking I'm not single is the last thing that will keep some of the cretins masquerading as teenage boys at our school from harassing me. It was bad enough when I came out as bisexual last year, but to date a girl? It's nothing but threesome jokes and passive-aggressive slut shaming every time I venture into the hallway. Lucky for me, Empower's monthly newspaper is pretty widely read this year, so I get to eviscerate every last one of those jerks on a regular basis. At least on paper.

"Why are you on the roof?" Alex calls, hooking his thumbs into his jean pockets and peering up at us.

"Thought we'd catapult ourselves into the car tonight," I say. "Sound good to you?"

"Blood and I aren't exactly friends."

"Pansy ass," Owen mutters as he curls his body back through the window. He and Alex have one of those annoying bro-hate-love relationships. The three of us have known one another since the first grade, when we all sat at the same table in Mr. Froman's class and shared a box of crayons and safety scissors. They constantly berate and nag each other but can barely go a few hours without texting. They're like Charlie and me . . . without all the queerness.

And recent and extreme awkwardness. Let's not forget that.

"Um . . . want me to catch you or something?" Alex asks, and I realize I've been staring down at him for a good minute.

I inch toward the ledge, dangling one foot into empty space. "Maybe . . ."

"Mara McHale, don't you dare." He stumbles toward me and holds up his hands, his long violin-playing fingers splayed wide as if he could really break my fall if I took a dive.

"Don't tell me what to do," I say, letting my foot continue to hang over the edge.

"Don't be stupid."

My lip curls involuntarily. "Don't be a brute."

"Don't be so . . . mean."

The tension leaves my body and I can't help but laugh. Alex never could execute a good comeback. It's sort of adorable.

"Good god, Mar, stop antagonizing the entire human population," Owen calls as he bursts out of the front door below me. He claps Alex on the back and peers up at me. "Let's go. We all need a drink."

I don't know about a drink, but I sure as hell need something. Climbing back through the window, I force myself to leave my phone pillowed in my blue down comforter.

Two can play the ignoring game.

CHAPTER TWO

AFTER RIDING IN THE BACK SEAT of the Bug while Owen and Alex babble on and on about orchestra something or other — correction: Owen babbles and Alex *uh-huhs* — I decide that I do, in fact, need a drink.

Alex pulls into the dirt parking lot in front of a large grassy area that circles Lake Bree. Flashlights bob through the dark, and we can see the amber glow of a small fire, the shadows of our peers weaving in and out of the light. A bass line booms, the vibrations knocking against my feet as soon as I step out of the car.

"Ah, smell the pheromones!" Owen says, spreading his arms wide and inhaling deeply.

"I think that's booze," Alex says, pocketing his keys.

"Same thing." My brother grins at the scene before him and I can see all the stress he carries most of the school year lifting off his shoulders. Owen has straight As and works his ass off on the violin. His room at home is freakishly neat and all of his schoolwork is meticulously organized into color-coded binders and notebooks. He's never so much as been tardy to a class, let alone skipped one. He has aspirations for orchestras on Broadway and at Symphony Hall in Boston. But when he gets around his friends, he unfurls. If you ask me, he acts like a total moron at these parties, but it's how he unwinds. Beer and jokes and bass-addled music that you can feel pulsing in your toes and fingertips.

We walk through the pine beds toward the party, Owen all but dragging me along. This is so not my scene. Not that I don't enjoy a good time with my friends, but let's be honest: crowds set me on edge, and dudes full of beer and bravado make me nervous.

It seems like the entirety of our little corner of Pebblebrook High School is here. It's a big public school in Frederick, Tennessee, but it houses the Nicholson County Center for Excellence in the Performing Arts, which is a magnet program any kid can audition for. If accepted, students are bused here to the high school, train in their specific art within the magnet, and take regular academic classes with the nonprogram kids.

Tonight, as usual, everyone splits off into their art sectors. The theater and musical theater crowd, the chorus crowd, the orchestra crowd, the dance crowd, and so on. It's not as though it's some social faux pas to hang out with another group or nonprogram kids — we just spend so much time with our own specialty, there's not room for much else. Between classes and after-school rehearsals for concerts and musicals or plays, we quickly form our own little communes. Owen and Alex are always lovingly at each other's throats for first chair violin (Owen holds that honor this semester, but Alex had it last spring), and the only reason they spend so much time with us show chorus girls is because Owen and I once shared a womb.

"Hey, guys!"

I squint through the dark and spot Hannah edging around some dancing girls I recognize from my music theory class. She's in a loose bohemian dress the colors of a sunrise, cognac-hued leather sandals lacing halfway up her calves. The shoulders are cut out of her dress, the cool night air already purpling up her arms. As usual, her strawberry-gold hair is an unruly tangle. She wears it long with messy braids curling randomly through the locks, which drives her mother completely bonkers, but I think that's half the appeal. Despite her genteel southern parents, Hannah's our little hippie, all laughter and horoscopes, a wild hum running just underneath everything she does and says.

For the past two months, Hannah's channeled her energies into my brother, which has only solidified the friendship between her and me. She was the first person I called when Charlie and I broke up—because I couldn't exactly call *Charlie*—and she took me to Delia's Café downtown to drown my sorrows in lavender macarons and sage tea.

"Babe, you look amazing," Owen says, slipping an arm around her waist and nuzzling her hair.

"Do I?" She grins and winks at me.

"Did you walk here?" I ask.

"Yup." Hannah lives in a nice neighborhood that backs up to the other side of the lake. Her family even has its own dock.

"You know, this week was super exhausting," Owen says, still burrowing into Hannah's neck. "I think we need to walk back to your house and lie down for a while."

Hannah huffs a laugh and shrugs one shoulder, playfully knocking Owen's chin. "Not right now, Romeo."

Owen just grins wider and starts pulling Hannah toward the keg.

"Wait," Hannah says, glancing around. "Where's Charlie?"

"Shhh!" Owen says, clamping a hand onto her mouth. She yanks it off immediately. "Do not speak of She Who Shall Not Be Named."

"Owen, don't be a dick," I say. "It's not like that."

"It *is* like that, actually. Awkwardness abounds and I'm just trying to be a loyal older brother."

"Older, my ass."

"By three minutes!"

"You wish."

He laughs at my habitual insistence that our birth certificates are just plain wrong.

"Besides, I'm more mature," I say.

"How do you figure?"

"Simple observation."

"I'll attest to that," Hannah says. Alex laughs while Owen pinches her side, pulling a playful yelp from her graceful throat.

"For real, is everything okay?" she asks me, stepping away from Owen and leaning closer so only I can hear her. Owen whines like a toddler and Alex shoves his shoulder.

"Yeah," I say.

She lifts that bullshit-detector eyebrow of hers.

"I don't know," I say, shrugging. "She won't answer my texts."

Hannah nods, clearly unsurprised. "Just give her time. You both have to get used to this new thing between you now."

"But it's not new. It's old. Years old. That was the whole point of the breakup."

"Was it?" Hannah tilts her head and smiles at me and I sort of hate it. It's an *Oh, you poor sad little thing* kind of smile.

"Oh, shut up," I say, and Hannah laughs, nudging my shoulder with hers.

Before we can talk any more about everything I'd rather not talk about anyway, Owen hooks his arm around Hannah's waist and pulls her to his side. "Babe, let's go."

"I'll see you later?" she says while Owen presses his face against her neck again.

I wave her off and force another smile. "Yeah, sure. Go make out or whatever."

Owen tousles my hair as they pass, no doubt to get a drink before slipping onto the trail that meanders in and out of the woods alongside the lake. Also known as Make-Out Maze. His hand is tucked into one of the loose pockets of Hannah's dress.

"They're sort of disgusting," I say with a laugh.

"To say the least," Alex says. "Want to get a drink?"

"I thought you were the DD?"

"I am. A soda for me, nasty vodka punch for you."

"Sounds irresistible."

We head toward the water and the keg of beer. Next to that, there's a table full of red Solo cups and a huge blue water jug containing, as Alex accurately guessed, some amalgam of fruit punch and vodka. It's pretty gross but it forces my knotted stomach to unclench a little.

We wander around for a bit, talking to kids from school as I plaster a smile on my face, trying not to think about my phone lying on my bed at home, most likely textless. Depressingly textless. My peers offer up confused glances, eyes circling the space around me and then frowning when the only person they see is Alex. It's annoying as hell. They wrinkle their noses when I'm holding Charlie's hand and they wrinkle their noses when I'm not.

About an hour in, I spot Owen walking off with Hannah toward the trail, one hand all over her ass and the other lifted into the air, cup sloshing red liquid all over his arm. He yells and whoops while Hannah tries to get him to shut up with a hand on his mouth. He's totally smashed.

"Called it," I say to Alex, gesturing toward my brother as he and Hannah disappear into the trees.

"The man loves his vodka punch."

"A little too much, if you ask me."

"Speaking of," Alex says, peering into my empty cup, "refill?"

"Eh, why not? But if I start grabbing your ass and hollering like an idiot, cut me off."

He laughs and then blushes and it's sort of cute. We make our way back toward the keg, which looks as if it's edged even closer to the lake, the grass below the barrel all trampled and muddy.

"How long till someone topples into the water while trying to refill their cup?" Alex asks, cracking open a Sprite from a cooler.

"An hour, tops."

He maneuvers around the boy-surrounded keg, looking at the lake gently lapping at the tall grasses and brush. "It's not the smartest spot to store the liquor."

"It's probably not the smartest spot to hang out—"

Someone knocks into my back, shoving me forward to collide with Alex's chest. His hands brace around my arms, but my punch splashes all over his sweater anyway.

"Oh, shit, sorry," I say, turning to see who else is already trashed at eight thirty at night.

"My bad," Greta Christiansen croons. Her blond hair falls into her heavily made-up eyes.

"Oh, absolutely no problem," I say, injecting as much saccharine as I can into my voice. I refuse to let Greta get to me. She's a kick-ass alto—consequently playing Lucille in the fall musical, *No, No, Nanette*—and one of my compatriots in Empower. Also, she believes that my leadership of the group is weak, thinks that I sing perpetually flat in chorus (I absolutely do not), and is basically bitter that I wouldn't put in a good word for her with Owen when she was crushing on him last year. For the sake of female camaraderie, we're sweet to each other—the kind of sweet that could give you a massive cavity.

"I'll get you another drink, Mara," she says, grabbing a cup. She fills it with about a centimeter of liquid and hands it over.

"Thank you so much. You're so considerate." I knock the swallow of punch back in one gulp, then push past her in search of some paper towels. Alex is still standing there, watching us passive-aggressively claw at each other while his sweater suffers the consequences.

"Hey, I have some napkins in my car," he says, tapping my elbow. "Come on."

Without another glance at Greta, I follow Alex back to the car, glad to get away from the melee. He opens the passenger door and roots around in the glove compartment before pulling out a pile of Sonic napkins. He dabs fruitlessly at his sweater. Soon he gives up, tossing the pink-tinted mess into the back seat. He leans against the car and runs his hand through his hair.

"Not really your kind of party?" I ask.

"Not really, no. I come because Owen annoys the hell out of me until I agree."

"I don't believe that for a second."

He laughs. "Plus, I try to make sure he doesn't make an ass of himself."

"I do believe that. For many seconds."

Alex's smile widens and he looks down, scuffing one boot-clad foot against the other.

"So what is your scene?" I ask. Alex has always been something of a puzzle. Well, not so much a puzzle as an anomaly among teenage boys, especially considering his best friend is Owen. Where my brother is all wind and noise, Alex is the smooth surface of a lake.

Pebblebrook can get pretty competitive, especially for people in leadership roles like Owen and Alex, but Alex never gets ruffled. He's a quiet Korean-American kid who shrugs when Owen takes over first chair, almost as if he's relieved, frequents the gym at least three times a week because his arms are oh-my-god gorgeous, and reads tattered Stephen King novels in his spare time.

Alex shrugs and glances away, a tiny smile settling on his mouth. This wordless gesture is nothing new, which is exactly why after years of friendship by proxy, I still don't know Alex all that well. He's beyond economical with his words. Weirdly, he doesn't come off as aloof or as though he doesn't want to talk to you. More like he hasn't figured out the right words yet and he refuses to waste your time.

"What's the story with this car?" I ask when it's clear he's not going to offer anything else. I pat the butter-yellow hood.

"Oh, god." He releases a single laugh and drags his hand down his face. "Um. My sister won it."

"Really? Like at a raffle or something?"

"No . . . on *The Price Is Right*?"

I try to swallow a laugh and fail, choking a little. "Is that a question?"

"It's an I-can't-believe-I'm-actually-speaking-these-words declarative sentence."

"She was really on *The Price Is Right*?"

"Yep. A couple of months ago, she and a bunch of her college friends took a bus to LA for the weekend and waited in line for hours. I'm pretty sure they were still drunk from the night before. Who knew she was such a price-guessing savant?"

"And she didn't want to keep it?"

"Not really any use for a car in Berkeley, so my parents made her drive it all the way here and voilà: I have a car the color of some douche bag's polo shirt, which your brother keeps stuffing with flowers and insists on calling The Lightning Bug. TLB for short."

"This is my favorite story. Like, ever. You realize that, right?"

"Just tell Owen I prefer wildflowers, okay?"

"I'll write it in lipstick on our bathroom mirror."

"Much appreciated." Alex pushes off from TLB and nods his head toward the party. "So, do you wanna . . ."

His voice trails off as a peal of loud laughter drowns him out. My heart gallops into my throat at the familiar sound, my body alert and seeking the source.

And I find it.

Holding the hand of a girl I've never seen before. Granted, Frederick, which is only twenty minutes south of Nashville, isn't so small a town that I know everyone. But I know everyone Charlie knows and I sure as hell don't know this girl.

"Okay, this party probably sucks, so don't say I didn't warn you. Whenever you want to leave, just—"

Charlie cuts herself off as she and Girl edge around a couple of parked cars, and her gaze locks on to me. Literally snaps into place—*click*. She's in a fitted black T-shirt and black jeans, the skinny Gryffindor red-and-gold silk tie I gave her for Christmas loosely knotted around her neck. Her short dark hair is wild, sticking up everywhere and reaching for the stars.

She thrusts out her pointy chin, her expression almost defiant, but then my own face must look pathetically wounded and shocked, because the confidence wanes, pulling all of her features and shoulders down. But her hand doesn't move. It stays twined with Girl's. Girl with dark red hair. Girl with short denim skirt. Girl with soft curves and full lips.

She and Girl pause, but only for a second. Charlie flicks her eyes to Alex and then back to me again, her mouth still open, words poised. But then Girl says something about hearing her favorite song and pulls Charlie away until they're swallowed by dancing bodies and the pulsing music.

Part of me wants to follow them. Part of me wants to grab Alex and kiss him. Part of me wants another drink, filled to the cup's brim. Part of me wants to dive into the lake and float away. Part of me this, part of me that, so many splits and divisions.

Next to me, Alex clears his throat, but I barely react. I feel numb and on fire all at once.

"Do . . . do you want me to take you home?" Alex asks quietly.

"Could you?"

"Yeah. I'll text Owen and let him know." He pulls out his phone and presses the home button, a soft white glow lighting his face. "Damn, no signal in these woods. Let me go find him, okay? Can you wait here? You all right?"

"Yeah." I shrug and swallow and smile and nod and too many things at once. "I'm fine."

He tilts his head toward me, an infuriating amount of pity spilling out of his expression. Before he leaves, he unlocks TLB again and opens the door for me. I fall into the passenger seat, happy to sit in the dark for a while.

Alex's form fades into the trees and that's when it hits—the deafening quiet. There's the dull pound of the party's music, but not enough to drown out the stillness. I press my head against the back of the seat, breathing in through my nose and trying to control how fast I release the exhalation, but it all comes out in a rush of panic. My fingertips tingle and my chest feels tighter and tighter, my mouth dry.

Calm down, Mara, I tell myself, digging my nails into my leggings.

Stupid little bitch.

The voice comes out of nowhere, a startling sneer in my head. I squeeze my eyes shut and try to control my breath and ignore the words knocking around in my head.

Stupid little bitch.

Stupid little bitch.

Breathe in, two, three, four . . .

Breathe out, two, three, four, five, six, seven, eight . . .

Slowly, the voice fades, and blood flows back into my fingers and chest. I glide both of my hands down my hair, feeling the curls, the silk, the locks that have frizzed in the Tennessee humidity, remembering that I'm at a party and sitting in a yellow car, that hand holding doesn't have to mean anything. Charlie and I held hands for years before anything romantic burgeoned between us. Even if it *does* mean something, so what? Charlie and I are just friends. Best friends.

I'm not stupid.

I'm not a fool.

The phrases roll through my head and I keep breathing steadily until I see Alex cross in front of the car and open the driver's door. I take one last deep inhale and pull the seat belt around my hips to secure it. Alex drops heavily into the seat, one leg still dangling out of the car and onto the dirt. I close my eyes and wait for him to start the engine, ready to get home and take a scalding shower to burn away this whole night.

Images of Charlie and Girl filter in and out and I feel my chest tightening again.

"Can we go please?" I ask, an unintentional edge to my voice. Still, Alex doesn't notice, doesn't move. I glance over at him. He still has a leg in the parking lot, his gaze turned toward the lake. "Alex?"

Nothing.

"Alex!"

He startles and jerks his head toward me. "Um . . . sorry."

"You okay?"

Dragging his leg into the car, he closes the door and slides his hands over the steering wheel. Even in the dark, I can see him blinking rapidly, his throat bobbing with a hard swallow.

"Alex, what—"

"Yeah, I'm fine. Sorry. Just . . . nothing. It's fine."

"Did you find Owen?"

"Yeah. He's fine. He's fine, he's with Hannah."

"Okay."

He laughs and rubs his eyes. "God, I'm more tired than I thought. It's been a crappy week. Senior year sucks so far."

"I agree, so let's get the hell out of here and sleep all weekend, shall we?"

"Yeah. Yeah, sounds like a plan."

He jabs the key into his ignition and the engine rumbles to life. Music rushes into the space, some strings-driven bluegrass song I've never heard before. Without thinking, I glance toward the lake one more time, looking for Charlie.

Always looking for Charlie. Except this time, I don't find her.

CHAPTER THREE

THE REST OF THE WEEKEND passes in a haze of sleep, binge watching shows on Netflix, and subsisting on bowl after bowl of cereal. My phone hasn't made a peep. I figured Alex would've told Owen why we left early and then Owen would've told Hannah and she'd at least text and try to coax me out of my carefully controlled cave, but nope. Not a word. And call me naive, but I really expected Charlie to call and explain the Girl. Again, a colossal nope. On top of that, my parents were busy with the furniture store they own downtown and I'm pretty sure Owen was sleeping off a legendary hangover, so I caught only glimpses of anyone on my way to and from the kitchen until Monday morning.

"How are you, my daughter?" Mom asks as I drag myself to the refrigerator for some yogurt.

"Grunt."

"What's new? Your dad and I haven't seen you all weekend."

"Grunt and groan."

She laughs and hands me a spoon. I peel back the foil lid on a Greek blueberry.

"How are things with Charlie?" she asks.

"Grumble grumble."

"Mara Lynn."

"They're fine, Mom. Just . . . still weird."

She pushes a stray curl behind my ear. "I'm sorry, honey."

I wait for a little more comfort, but it doesn't come. My parents are pretty cool parents. They trust Owen and me. They have a sense of humor. They know when to back off and when to push. They don't freak out when we bring home a grade lower than an A minus. And they were generally chill when I came out to my family during breakfast one morning last Thanksgiving break. But "Oh" and "Okay" and "We want you to be happy" are about the extent of their support. And hey, that's more than a lot of kids get, especially in the South, where going out in public as a queer person can be like tiptoeing through a minefield.

Still, when I started dating Charlie, Mom got a little squirrelly. She'd stare at Charlie's and my joined hands a little too long and she asked way too many questions about how things had *changed* between us. To her credit, I don't think she cares what gender I date or who I like. With Charlie, she was honest-to-god worried about romance ruining things with my best friend.

A best friend is an irreplaceable person in a girl's life, Mara, she said more than once.

It was annoying, but eventually, I agreed. At least that's what

I told her. In truth, I was worried about Charlie and me because I was incapable of being a normal girlfriend. A good girlfriend. I was defective, and ultimately, I knew Charlie would figure that out.

Not that I'd ever tell Mom any of that. My mother and I . . . well, we operate on a need-to-know basis. When I was younger, we were the kind of close that meant a phone call home at midnight whenever I tried to sleep over at a friend's house. She'd come pick me up and I'd spend the rest of the night snuggled in between her and my dad. Owen would join us in the morning, bashing through their bedroom door and hurling himself onto the mattress. I was happy there. I had friends, but I just didn't like being away from home, being away from the people I trusted the most.

The people I knew would never let anything bad happen to me.

All that changed after eighth grade. I tried to act like I always had, tried to make myself feel close to my mother again, telling her little things about my life in a desperate attempt to connect. But it all felt hollow. I know she felt it too — felt it and was completely confused and hurt by it.

"So have you picked out your outfits?" Mom asks now, a smile on her face while she pours herself another cup of coffee. The subject change is glaringly obvious, but it's better than an *I told you so*. Still, I can't help but smile a little, thinking about Empower's newest mission, taking on Pebblebrook's violently inequitable dress code. Empower is the feminist group and newspaper I founded freshman year, and my plan is to push every possible limit of the dress code without actually violating it. I'll get hauled in to the office, probably more than once, and despite Principal Carr's inability to find any infringement according to his handy-dandy measuring tape, he will demand that I change. I'm a distraction, he'll say. Boys will be boys, he'll say. If I'm a nice girl, I should know better, he'll say. Because that's what he says to any girl who shows a deltoid or has naturally long legs under her skirt or has to wear anything above a AA-cup.

And that's when I'll breathe fire.

For a second, I get lost in the simple beauty of it. The way I'll take him down with words, with defiance, with cool logic and reasoned arguments. Just thinking about it calms me down, makes me feel as though I'm in control. Charlie says I'm obsessed with it —control. And she's a little right, though she doesn't know why.

The Dress Code Takedown is one of the few things I've shared with Mom. I knew she'd love the idea, and honestly, I wanted to make sure she wouldn't ground me for all eternity if I end up in detention.

As expected, she literally squealed when I told her about it. The woman has two great passions in life: refinishing old furniture to look even older, and feminism. Before she and my dad opened the store five years ago, she wrote op-eds for *Ms.* magazine and still does a few times a year. She's always tried to let Owen and me make up our own minds about stuff, and when I started Empower, she cried. Actual tears that required a tissue.

"Nothing's final, but yeah, I've got a few ideas," I say, licking my yogurt spoon clean and tossing it into the sink.

"Let me know if you need help. I pushed quite a few boundaries back in my day."

"You didn't burn your bra on the quad, did you?"

"No, I rather liked my bra. Although I did retaliate against my cheating boyfriend in high school by filling his locker with water balloons."

"Water balloons?"

"They were very special balloons." She winks at me and I can't help but laugh.

Mom laughs with me, the golden-brown curls I inherited springing into her face, but then her expression sobers. She sets down her mug and comes over to me, cupping my face in her hands. "You know I'm very proud of you. It takes a brave person to challenge the institutional misogyny of the patriarchal system."

Even though I want to roll my eyes at Mom's verbose dramatics, a flicker of warmth spreads through my chest. But it blinks out with the next breath. Mom doesn't know how much of a coward I really am. She'd write one hell of a cautionary op-ed if she knew the real reason I started Empower.

"Ugh, why are Mondays a thing?" Owen asks as he walks into the kitchen pulling on a dark-green Pebblebrook sweatshirt.

"Inevitable consequence of the weekend," I say as Mom pats my cheeks once and releases me.

"Good morning, son of mine," she says.

"Grunt."

I bust up laughing while Mom whacks Owen on the back of the head with a rolled-up magazine. "Go to school. Be good."

"Always am," he says, chipper as usual, even though he still looks half hung-over and exhausted. Must've been some party.

Mom forces us to endure kisses to our foreheads and we grab our bags, heading outside at the same time. Owen frowns at his phone as I unlock the Civic and toss my stuff into the back seat.

"What's wrong?" I ask.

Owen's frown deepens. "Nothing. Just . . . Hannah's not answering my texts or calls."

"Did you guys have a fight?"

He glances up at me, his eyebrows knotted in the middle. "No."

"Maybe her phone's dead. I haven't heard from her either."

"Yeah." His lips form a thin line as he pockets his phone. "Anyway, can I bum a ride?"

"It's your car too."

We don't talk all the way to school, which is rare but kind of nice. I need the minutes to run through what I'm going to say to Charlie. On top of Empower, we have three classes together. I've decided to play it totally cool and ask about Girl because that's what friends do. We *ooh* and *aah* over new crushes and tease each other about that inevitably weird first kiss.

Girl's full mouth flashes through my mind and I swallow against the tangle in my throat. "This is what friends do," I whisper to myself as I pull into the school parking lot.

"Huh?" Owen asks.

"Nothing."

"You sound so convincing."

"Really, it's nothing."

"Is this 'nothing' the redhead with Charlie on Friday night?"

I wince. "You saw them together?"

He waves a hand. "I vaguely remember something crimson-hued in Charlie's vicinity. Then again, maybe it was just a giant Solo cup."

"Were you really that trashed?"

He rubs his forehead with both hands. "Do you have to scream all your questions?"

I laugh and turn down the music a little. "Good thing you had Hannah to take care of you."

He sighs, dropping his hands into his lap and turning toward the window. "Yeah."

Some alarm in me goes off — some twin sense. "What's wrong? You sure you aren't fighting?"

But he just shakes his head and turns up the music. I can't help but roll my eyes. Clearly, yes, they are fighting and probably about Owen acting like a total miscreant frat boy when he drinks. Hannah's ridden his ass about it more than once.

"Good luck with Charlie," he says when we walk into school, parting ways in the main hall to head to our separate homerooms.

"Thanks. Good luck with Hannah."

He frowns but waves me off, disappearing into a crowd of his perpetually laughing orchestra friends.

I watch him, but my eyes don't focus on him for long. Almost immediately, they start a search for Charlie. I run through my even-toned questions about Girl in my head over and over, determined to be a good best friend.

Except I never get to prove that I'm a good best friend, because Charlie is absent from school. So is Hannah, and neither of them responds to my messages. Consequently, not only do I spend the entire day obsessing over what I would've said to Charlie, I don't even get to hash it out with Hannah at lunch or through texts, leaving me feeling like a dormant volcano about to erupt by the end of the day.

To top it all off with an irritating cherry, Greta accosts me on the way to my car.

"Hey, is Owen okay?" she asks.

"What do you mean?"

"He got called out of calculus and never came back."

I frown. "He didn't?"

"Hope he's not sick. Tell him hey for me."

I roll my eyes as we reach my car and she leaves, and then I take out my phone to text him. The cars around me clear out and still no Owen and no returned text.

"What the hell is with everyone today?" I whisper-yell as I drop myself into the front seat. I suddenly feel marooned on a desert island, all my friends nowhere to be found. Before I leave the parking lot, I text Alex and ask if he knows what happened to Owen. Surprise, surprise, he doesn't respond either. I power down my phone, sick of looking at its stupid textless screen.

When I pull into my driveway back home, my stomach immediately goes twitchy. Both of my parents' cars are in the garage, which is totally unheard of at three thirty in the afternoon.

I throw the car in park and jog through my dad's myriad of carefully stored tools and furniture polish and paints, opening the garage door that enters the house through the kitchen. Out of habit, I kick my shoes off, and my gray flats have barely joined Owen's ratty Chucks before I hear him.

"—swear to god, Mom. This is . . . I don't get it." His voice filters in from the living room. Our house doesn't have one of those fancy open-concept designs. Each room is neatly in its little box, so a giant wall of cabinets blocks my view of my brother, but I don't need to see him to hear the tremble in his words. The sound of it pulls my feet to a stop.

"He said the state attorney might press charges, Owen," Mom says evenly, but there's an edge to her voice, the kind she gets when dealing with an irate customer. "And you're telling me you have no idea why?"

"No! I swear. I'd had a few drinks, yeah, but . . ." A sob cuts his words off and I hear him gasping for breath. I feel my own lungs shrink and gulp at the air.

Dad murmurs something I can't make out, his voice soft as always. Still, there's something off about the sound of that, too.

"Owen," Mom says, "are you sure you asked—"

"She wanted to," Owen chokes out. "I swear to god she wanted to."

"Honey," Mom says, and I hear the squeak of a body moving

over our ancient leather couch. "We'll figure it out. I'm sure it's just a misunderstanding. It has to be, right?"

"I'd never do that," Owen says, his voice raised to a fever pitch. "I didn't . . ."

"Of course not, sweetheart," Mom says softly, trying to calm him down, but I doubt it works. I'm the only one who can get Owen to simmer down when he's stressed or drunk. Well, me and Hannah.

"I'll call the Priors again," Dad says, his voice coming closer. "Surely we can work this out quietly."

"It's not only up to them, Chris," Mom says. "It's the state's decision."

"Well, I still think I should call."

"Thanks, Dad," Owen says, and he sounds so small, I can't hold myself still anymore. I drop my bag onto the kitchen tile and nearly run into my dad on my way to the living room.

"Mara," Dad says, eyes widening behind his black-rimmed glasses. His salt-and-pepper hair is sticking up in all directions, as though he's been dragging his hands through it over and over. "When did you get—"

"What's wrong?" I ask. "What's going on?"

I don't wait for my father to answer. Instead I circle around him, needing to see that Owen's okay. He's huddled in one corner of the couch, my mother's arms wrapped around his back and his chest, joining at his shoulder. He leans into her, his messy hair messier than ever and his eyes red-rimmed.

"What happened?" I ask.

His gaze snaps to mine, something like fear blooming in his expression.

"Nothing," Mom says emphatically. "Just a misunderstanding."

"About what? Why is Dad calling the Priors?" Prior is Hannah's last name. "Is Hannah sick or something?"

Owen's mouth drops open and I wait for a joke to roll out of it like always when things get serious. When Grammy, Mom's mom, had a stroke, he spent the entire four-hour drive to Kentucky quoting *Monty Python and the Holy Grail*. To an outsider, it would seem insensitive, ill-timed, totally uncouth. But I know Owen. He did it to make me laugh. Make Mom laugh. Make us all breathe a little easier until we had to deal with reality.

But a joke doesn't come. He watches me for a few more seconds before looking down at his lap, picking at a loose thread on his shirt.

"Mom?" I say, taking a step closer to them. "Please. You're scaring me."

She sighs, releasing Owen long enough to rub at one eye before looping her arm around him again. "Like I said, honey. It's a misunderstanding. Apparently . . . Hannah feels like . . . she thinks . . ." Mom blinks rapidly, the color slowly draining from her face.

"Thinks what?" I tell my feet to move, to go sit on the couch, to take Owen's hand, but something keeps me cemented in place.

Mom presses her eyes closed and inhales a huge breath. "Hannah feels that Owen . . . took advantage of her at the lake the other night."

"Wait. She thinks that Owen . . ." But my words trail off as the entire scene clicks into place.

He said the state attorney might press charges, Owen.

She wanted to. I swear to god she wanted to.

"Took advantage?" I whisper, and Owen lifts his head to meet my eyes.

"I didn't, Mar. You know I didn't."

"Took . . . *advantage?*"

But we all know that's not the right word. The word we should be using lunges into my throat, trying to unfurl on my tongue. "Did you . . ." I shove the word back down. There's no way in hell I can say it. There's no way it's really the right word. "Owen, did you . . . force yourself on her?"

"Mara!" Mom springs to her feet, her eyes blazing, her curls wild.

On the couch, Owen flinches, recoiling farther into the cushions. "No! Hell no. You know I would never do that, Mar."

"I know you wouldn't. I know that. So why would she say you did?"

"That's enough, Mara," Mom says, but it's not. And I can't stop. I have to understand. I need Owen to explain this. Because, yes, I do know Owen would never do that, but I also know Hannah would never lie about something like that. She loves Owen, so why would she lie?

"We had a fight, that's all," Owen says, raking both hands through his hair. He leaves them there, resting his forehead in his palms.

"You told me this morning that you *weren't* fighting," I say. Unshed tears sting my eyes; my thoughts tangle and scatter and I can't hold on to one long enough to make sense of any of this. It has to make sense somehow.

"All right, enough," Mom says. "Go to your room, Mara."

I blink at her. "What?"

"You're not helping. Go to your room and cool down."

"No. I need . . . we have to . . . Owen, just tell me what happened."

He keeps his face pressed into his hands.

"Owen!"

"Go," Mom says. "Right now." She places her hand on my shoulder and pushes me gently toward the hall. I feel boneless, weightless, so I go.

"It'll be all right, honey," she says. "You know your brother. It's just a misunderstanding."

She leaves me at the bottom of the stairs, a light squeeze to my hand the only other comfort offered. In the kitchen, I hear Dad mumbling into the phone. In the living room, I hear Owen start to cry again, Mom whispering support.

I stand by myself in the hallway, the unspoken word echoing through my mind as though it's another language. The stairs unfold in front of me, but I can't seem to push myself up. Instead, I find my keys and ghost toward the front door.

Open.

Close.

Car door. Key into the ignition. My body moves through the motions but my thoughts . . . where are they? My eyes drift toward the still-blue sky.

Not a star in sight.

Ten minutes later, I pull up outside Charlie's house.

CHAPTER FOUR

IT TAKES ME ANOTHER TEN MINUTES to get out of the car, and even then, only because Charlie comes out of her house and taps on my window. I turn my head slowly toward the sound, my eyes taking in Charlie's tattered Nirvana T-shirt and concerned face. I'm underwater, drowning in that unspoken word, and I need air.

Unbuckling, I push the door open. Charlie moves out of the way, all grace and indifference.

"Where were you today?" I ask. My feet scrape across the grit of the asphalt and I wince.

Charlie frowns down at my feet. "Where the hell are your shoes?"

"Gee, I guess I left them at home," I spit back, pushing forward. "Where were you? Were you with her? That girl? Who is she? Where did you meet her?"

Charlie tilts her head, her expression part curiosity and part sadness. "Is that really what you want to talk about right now?"

"Yes." I slam the car door shut. "Yes. That's what friends do, right? We talk about our dates and what it felt like to kiss them and how so-and-so made us feel all giddy and how you didn't even need a drink at that party because Girl was enough of a high for you and oh, isn't she hot? Wow, so hot. I can't believe how hot she is. Damn, Charlotte, you're so lucky—"

Cold sears through my back as Charlie presses me gently against the metal of the car, her hand on my stomach and her eyes glaring into mine. "Stop."

"Just tell me."

"I'm going to let this go, because I know you're upset right now. But just so we're clear, I don't owe you an explanation or a story or even one juicy detail. *You* put this in motion, Mara. I'm only doing what you said we should."

Her hand drops away and all my cells feel too loose, as though they're seconds from drifting off in different directions.

"And don't call me Charlotte," she adds, taking my hand and pulling me toward her front door.

I let her lead me and I focus on the familiar feel of her hand in mine, all of my molecules slowly coming back together.

Inside Charlie's house, more familiarity calms my breaths. The faint smell of her dad's after-shave, the modern furniture, about a million pictures of Charlie as a baby, as a toddler, as a kid, as a tween, and so on. She's everywhere, her parents' miracle child after years of fertility treatments.

She drops my hand as we head upstairs. Once in her room, she immediately clicks on some gloomy music via her laptop. She knows I can't stand the stark silence. I sit on her bed, careful not to disturb her guitar resting on the pillow. A notebook lies open on the plain navy blue comforter, her slanted half-cursive, half-print handwriting spilling over the page.

"Are you writing a new song?" I ask, resisting the urge to pull the notebook closer and devour her words. Charlie's an incredible songwriter. An incredible singer. An incredible guitar player.

"Yeah." She flips the notebook closed and places her guitar on the stand in the corner. The rest of her room is pretty messy. Clothes everywhere and posters taped to the wall, showing off singers I know about only because of Charlie. Her knitting supplies are piled into a laundry basket in the corner, needles and half-finished scarves and beanie hats overflowing and dripping onto the floor, yarn hued in mostly blues and silvers, golds and reds—her and my Hogwarts house colors. Her room is a type A personality's nightmare.

"Have your parents heard it?" I ask.

"Heard what?"

"The song."

She just stares at me, that crinkle between her eyes that makes me want to smooth my thumb over it. Charlie's parents send her to the Nicholson County Center at Pebblebrook because she's been singing—and singing well—since she was five years old. They think she adores arias and big choral pieces meant for giant concert halls. And it's not that she doesn't like all that. It's just that she loves the guitar, a tiny stage, soft lighting on a single stool, a whole lot more.

"I'm sorry," I say, running my finger over an almost-hole in my jeans.

Charlie lifts her dark eyebrows. "Why?"

"For calling you Charlotte."

A sigh escapes her throat, and the bed depresses as she sits down next to me. I wait for her hand to reach out and start playing with my hair or to gently squeeze the back of my neck like she'll sometimes do when she can tell I'm getting worked up. I'd even take a playful shoulder shove. Anything to connect me to her, to feel like us.

But nothing comes. She just sits there, picking at a peeling callus on her middle fingertip.

"Where were you today?" I ask again, and she lifts her dark eyes to mine. "Are you sick? You don't seem sick."

"I'm not sick."

"So you skipped?" Charlie never skips, calls skipping a wasted lie. Her parents are administrators at two different middle schools in the next county over and are nearly impossible to bullshit about school stuff. They wrangle hormonal seventh-graders all day for a reason. Still, Charlie works hard to craft this certain picture of herself when she's around them, full of half-truths and half smiles. "I lie with loving care," Charlie joked once when I asked her why she doesn't tell her parents how much she hates it when they call her Charlotte. Which they always, always do.

"I didn't skip," she says. "I was —"

"You weren't in school. You aren't sick, so you skipped. Why didn't—"

"Mara."

"I don't get this. Is it because we broke up? I told you why. You agreed that our friendship was more important."

"I agreed in part."

"In part is still agreeing."

"Mara, sit down."

I hadn't realized I'd stood up, but I don't comply and pace across the worn maroon rug spread across the hardwood floor. I need answers. I need this to make sense. I need to somehow hold all of this in my hand and see the whole picture, the what and why and how.

"You were with her, weren't you? That redhead. Just say it, Charlie."

She rubs her forehead, then tangles her fingers into her hair. A short lock drops into her eyes and she leaves it there. "I was with Hannah."

Her voice is soft, as if she's coaxing a wild animal out of a cave, but it doesn't matter. The name is still an explosion in my ears.

"Why?" The tiny syllable comes out on a breath and my knees go rubbery. I must be swaying, because Charlie grabs my hand and pulls me back down onto the bed.

"Because she's upset and scared and her parents are pretty much smothering her right now and she just wanted to be with someone who wasn't going to shove more chicken soup down her throat."

"Why?" I ask again. Charlie still has my hand in hers and I

will her not to let go. If she does, surely this time I'll splinter into pieces.

"Have you been home?" she asks. "Have you talked to your mom? Or . . . or your brother?"

I stare at her, blinking.

"Mara—"

"It's not true. It can't be. There has to be some—"

"It's true, Mara."

My throat tightens at the soft way she says my name, the vowels almost musical. Part of me realizes she's trying to keep me calm. Part of me doesn't care.

"How?" I ask. Tears bloom but don't fall. "Owen wouldn't. He would never."

"I saw Owen at the lake and he was hammered."

"I know. I saw him too."

"He was acting like a total dumb-ass with his orchestra friends."

"That's what he does at parties, Charlie. It doesn't mean he—"

"Just let me talk." She says it gently, reaches out a hand to squeeze my knee. All it does is make me feel wild, but I force my words behind my teeth.

Charlie takes a deep breath. "Hannah wasn't with him, and when I asked him where she was, he just stared at me and mumbled something about getting another beer. You were nowhere to be found and my phone didn't have a signal, so Tess and I went looking for Hannah."

I vaguely register the unfamiliar name. It seems so silly now. "I went home," I whisper, but I'm not sure Charlie even hears me.

"I found her on the trail," she goes on, pulling her hand from mine. She takes a few more big breaths, her gaze going hazy. "She was just sitting on a bench at one of those cement overlooks about half a mile from the party, staring at the water. Her dress was all stretched out over her shoulders and I couldn't get her to talk to me for, like, ten minutes. Finally, she mumbled something I couldn't make out about Owen, and I half carried her to my car. I was going to take her home, but after I dropped off Tess, Hannah still wouldn't say anything and she was holding her arm weirdly, like it hurt. I was totally freaking out. I tried calling my parents, but they were at a fundraiser for my dad's school and weren't answering so I took her to Memorial. I didn't know what else to do."

"And they said she was okay, right? She wasn't hurt?"

Charlie looks away and presses the heels of both hands into her eyes. "She *is* hurt, Mara. She has a sprained wrist. Her parents showed up and wanted her to do one of those rape kits, and it was fucking awful. She screamed the entire time. It took hours."

I flinch at the word. At all the words.

"After that, the hospital called the police."

"The police?" Every word coming out of Charlie's mouth seems foreign. Strange and guttural syllables, unfamiliar vocabulary, cryptic context clues. My own voice sounds odd repeating the words, a child trying out a new language she's not sure she wants to learn.

I squeeze my eyes shut until color spirals out behind my lids.

My fingers curl around the comforter, blood pulsing into the tips. The mattress moves as Charlie shifts. Next thing I know, there's a warm weight on my thighs. I look down to see Charlie kneeling on the floor in front of me, her forearms resting on my legs.

"Talk to me," she says. "Tell me what you're thinking."

But I can't. I need command of that foreign language, words to explain this black thing leaking into my blood. I'm not even sure what it's made of. I can't think about Owen. I can't attach his name to Hannah on a hospital bed, bandages on her wrist, tears on her lovely face.

I can't. Every name in this horror story is a separate thing, each a disconnected vignette. So I close Owen's chapter and flip to Hannah's, to Charlie's.

My hands find hers resting lightly on my hips and I tangle our fingers together. "I'm so sorry."

She tilts her head, and her eyes have a rare sheen to them.

"I should've been there," I say. "I should've been with you, with Hannah. I'm sorry I left. I'm sorry you had to help her alone."

"Hey." She pushes herself to her knees so we're eye level. She leans into my space, her fingers tightening on mine, our foreheads inches from resting against each other. "This is not your fault. It's not like any of us had any clue this would happen. Owen is—"

"He's *my* brother. He didn't do this and I'm the one who should've been there. Not Tess."

Charlie frowns and puts some space between us. "Is that what this is about?"

"What do you mean?"

"Tess."

"No. I'm just saying, I wish I had been there."

She shakes her head and untangles her hands from mine before pulling herself to her feet. "Well, yeah, I wish a lot of things."

"Are you mad at me?"

"I'm always a little mad at you, aren't I?"

I search for a smile on her lips, but it's not there. They're pressed into a colorless line. Since the first hour of our meeting freshman year, Charlie's always considered me adorably infuriating. Every time we argue — over what music we play in the car, what movie to watch, what topping to order on our pizza — she usually relents because I make a point of being a pain in the ass. *I'm always a little mad at you* has become a theme in our relationship.

But this time there's no humor in it, no flirty wink, no affectionate grin.

"This isn't about you and me or Tess or whoever," she says. "I mean, do you get this? Do you understand what's happening, Mara?"

I open my mouth to say yes, but I can't, because I don't. There's no way this happened, no way my brother did this. He's not even capable of it and I can't understand how anyone could think he is.

"Fuck," Charlie sighs out, shoving her hands into her hair. "I'm sorry. This is . . . I don't know what to say."

I nod and stand up, a helplessness settling on my bones like age. "I guess I should go."

"Mara—"

But whatever she was about to say, she swallows it. I wait for her to go on, to stop me from leaving, but she doesn't. At her door, I pause, keeping my eyes fixed on the painted white wood.

"Is Hannah okay?" I ask.

A beat. "No. She's not."

We let the question and answer settle between us, the dark and clouded sounds finally giving way to a shimmer of meaning.

CHAPTER FIVE

I NEARLY SLAM INTO CHARLIE'S DAD on my way down the stairs, my feet tangling together in an attempt to avoid collision. He wraps his huge hands around my arms to steady me. Instantly, I go rigid, pretty much jerking away from him and retreating back two steps.

"Whoa there, Mara," he says, presenting his palms. "You okay?"

"Yeah. Yeah, sorry. You just startled me."

"No problem." He smiles and loosens his tie. Mr. Koenig is a big guy. Tall and broad and generally imposing, sure to scare the hell out of all the kids he educates on a daily basis. He's got a head full of dark hair, and a beard covers half of his face. He's handsome, for a dad, and has always been super nice to me, welcoming and gentle. He's just so huge that my first instinct is always to shrink up and disappear.

"You girls headed out?" he asks, moving around me on the stairs on his way to his room.

"I'm sorry, what?"

He turns back, his brows furrowed. "It's Monday. Don't you and Charlotte always go to the bowling alley? I know it's been a couple weeks. We've missed you around here."

I blink at him, his smile totally at ease and normal. "Oh. Oh, right." Charlie and I have gone to the bowling alley every Monday for the past couple of years. It's smoke-free and neon-lit, full of old people with personalized bowling-ball bags and monogrammed shirts. We people-watch while we gorge on nachos and soda and candy and, yes, hit the shit out of some bowling pins. I usually kick her ass, and I crave my favorite swirly pink ball that I manage to find every week exploding against the pins.

The ritual started pretty early on in our friendship. One Monday, we were riding our bikes through downtown Frederick, found out it was two-for-one games at the Queen Pin, and that was that. Except for the past three Mondays, when one of us has begged off with stupid excuses like homework and lack of sleep the night before. Last week I had a plan to tell her I couldn't go because I thought I was getting sick, except I never got the chance. She beat me to it, claiming a sore throat. Now that I think about it, she was probably busy with Tess.

"You two should get going," Mr. Koenig says now, glancing at his watch. "Deirdre will be home soon and you know she'll talk your ear off."

Before I can answer or figure out how to excuse myself from the house without his daughter in tow, Charlie's bedroom door opens. "Dad, who are you talking—oh." Her eyes widen when she sees me. "I thought you'd gone."

"I did. I mean, I was. I am."

"Hi, honey," Mr. Koenig says, running his hand over Charlie's short hair.

"Hey," she says to him, but she's looking at me.

"Have fun, you two. Don't be too late. And try to eat something other than junk." Then he drifts off down the hall toward his room, fingers tugging at his tie.

Charlie squints at me. "Bowling?"

I nod. "Bowling."

"We don't have to go," Charlie says, folding her arms over her chest.

I nod and take a step down the stairs, but then my mind fills with images, fuzzy at the edges and too bright all at once, like a dream. Owen, sitting on the couch, crying. My mother, baffled and trying to comfort him. Hannah's accusation, a quiet whisper trailing all of us through the rooms.

"No, I think we should," I say.

Charlie's eyes narrow, but I just nod my head toward the front door.

"Let's go—I'll drive."

"Are you sure?"

I huff out a breath. "If we wait any longer, your mom will come home and then we'll be stuck here for an hour."

She laughs. Charlie's mom could talk the paint off the walls of an empty room. "Truth. Let me grab my shoes."

"Can you get me some?"

She glances at my bare feet and rolls her eyes, but nods.

Soon we're in my car, windows down, wind loud. I can't tell if it's because we want it like that or we're avoiding conversation, avoiding eye contact as the twilight dims into night.

At the Queen Pin, we exchange our shoes and stock up on licorice whips, Cherry Cokes, Whoppers, peanut M&M's, and a bag of popcorn as big as my torso. We don't usually get this much crap to eat, but we pile it all onto a chair at lane five. I search for my pink ball in the racks lined with colorful spheres while Charlie taps our names into the computer. My ball tucked under one arm, I spot a black ball exactly Charlie's size. She doesn't usually care what ball she uses as long as her fingers don't get stuck and it won't fall on her toes when she swings it back to hurl it down the lane. But this ball — this ball is Charlie. Blackest black with gold and silver swirls. I grab it and make my way over to her.

Her mouth ticks up in one corner when she sees the ball, but she says nothing. Soon, we're bowling, stuffing our faces with sugar and greasy popcorn and laughing at Mr. Hannigan, a middle-aged pet-store owner in town who is here every Monday night and can never seem to keep his pants above his crack.

"Can I ask you something?" I say. We're six frames in and the only things we've really talked about so far are candy and the fall concert coming up in November.

Charlie grabs her ball from the ball rack. "Sure."

"You haven't told them, have you?"

She pauses, her black ball balanced on her fingertips. "What?"

"Your parents. You haven't told them. About us."

Her mouth drops open but then snaps shut. "I . . . I didn't—"

"Are you for real? Your parents have no clue we broke up? I knew your dad seemed super friendly."

"He's a super friendly guy."

"Have you told them or not?"

Her jaw tightens and she turns, throwing her ball down the alley sloppily, like she's tossing a blanket onto a mattress. The ball clatters toward the gutter and disappears behind the pins.

"That's a zero, you know," I say, like a total smart-ass. "Let's hope your second ball is a little better."

Charlie walks back to where I'm sitting and falls into the chair next to me. "No. I haven't told them."

"Why?"

"Because . . ." She trails off, her eyes blinking at the flashing neon red-and-white bowling pins on the back wall of the alley.

Talking to her parents about herself—all of herself—has always been a sort of land mine for Charlie. They know she likes girls, only because four years ago, her mom sat her down, handed her a salted-caramel brownie—Charlie's favorite—and flat out asked her. Charlie would never have told them on her own. Consequently, her relationships are the one aspect of her life that's wide open to them, and they've always been super cool about everything. When we started dating—which they knew about only because they came home early one Friday night and found us wrapped up on the couch watching a movie—Mrs. Koenig just grinned and said it was about time.

Charlie hated that they knew. When I asked her why one night while we were curled together on her bed, she just shrugged and said the reason didn't matter now anyway.

"Bullshit," I'd said. Then I pulled a blanket over us, creating a tent. "Secrets are safe in here. It's our own little world, just you and me."

She sighed and looked away. "It's just . . . my parents wanted a kid so bad, you know? Tried for years and it never happened. Until it did. Now they've got me and I just . . . god, it sounds stupid."

"Nothing that comes out of this brain can be stupid," I said, kissing her on the forehead.

"I'm not a normal girl, I know that."

"Me either. What the hell's normal?"

"No, I know. But, I guess what I mean is that I'm not really the kind of daughter parents dream of having, you know? I just wonder sometimes . . ."

"Charlie. You like girls. That's normal for you. It's not a deal breaker. And your parents are totally cool with it. Hell, they even seem happy about it."

"I know, but all the other stuff." She waved a hand down her body. "I mean, gender issues freak people the hell out."

"That's because some people are assholes. Your parents aren't. And all this"—I tapped her forehead and then drifted my hand down her arm— "is who you are too and your parents love you."

She frowned at that but nodded. "I guess part of me is always waiting for my parents to figure it out."

"Figure what out?"

"That I'm not the daughter they dreamed about."

I couldn't say anything to that. My heart broke for her, for all the things she was scared to tell her parents. Basically, Charlie will have to come out twice to her parents. They pretty much helped her along about liking girls, but eventually, she'll have to do it all over again about being genderqueer. Coming out once was hard enough for me, so I just tangled my legs with hers and kissed her until she stopped shaking.

"Can I ask you a question?" I said when she seemed a little calmer.

"Yeah, of course."

"Do you . . . I mean, do you like it when people use *she* and *her* when they talk about you?"

Her eyebrows knitted in the center. "Honestly, not always. But *he* doesn't really fit right now either."

"What does?"

She sighed. "I'm not sure. Both? Neither? Something else altogether? Maybe *they* and *them*, eventually, after I tell my parents. *She* and *her* work for now. They feel okay. I've been reading a lot about it all lately. There's this term—nonbinary. It means someone who doesn't identify as only male or female or maybe identifies as both or neither. So . . . I guess that's me? For now, at least."

"Nonbinary." I rolled the term around in my mouth. "Sounds kind of badass."

She laughed and nudged closer to me. "I know how I feel, but putting that into words is hard."

"And that's okay. You know that, right?"

She nodded, but that little pucker remained between her eyebrows.

The memory makes my stomach hurt and I release a huge sigh.

"I'll tell them, okay?" Charlie says now. "I will. It's just—"

"It's another change," I say.

"Yeah. I'd just gotten used to them knowing about us. And then they'll ask me *why*."

She bites off the word like it tastes bad. Even wrinkles her nose a bit.

"Charlie, we're fine."

She nods, rubbing her palms on her jeans. "Of course we are. Best friends forever." Then she gets up and grabs her ball from the rack. She hurls it down the lane, nothing sloppy about it, and decimates all ten pins.

"Spare," she says as she sits down in the chair in front of the computer. As if I don't know.

We bowl through our next few frames in silence. I'm playing like crap, pitching it into the gutter more times than not. Anger sparks in my gut every time her sparkly black ball hits a pin, and I let it ignite and grow into a flicker and then into a flame. Because this is exactly what I *didn't* want to happen when we broke up. All this . . . fuck, all this awkward, passive-aggressive bullshit. And being angry with Charlie about how our relationship is going down makes sense.

It becomes clear that Charlie's going to win. We barely talk for the rest of the game and I hate the silence. For once, I want to hear my own voice, the edge to it as I scream. I feel something building, rising up in a heated rush through my toes to my legs and up my middle. When the game is over— 187 to 162—Charlie must see the red settling into my cheeks as she ties on her Converse. She yanks up both of our pairs of bowling shoes and turns them in at the counter without a word. I come up behind her, holding out her leftover licorice whips, and she yanks those from me too.

"What the hell, Charlie?"

"I am not the one you're mad at," Charlie says, chucking the candy into the trash. "I know you've had a crappy day and it sucks, but even if all this shit with Owen and Hannah wasn't happening, I am *not* the one you're mad at."

"What does that mean?"

"You know what it means. This is all you, Mara."

"I have no idea what you're talking about."

She closes her eyes and bites her lower lip. "Look. We should just go. I'm tired and so are you and you probably need to go home and talk to your mom."

"I don't want to talk to my mom. I want to talk to my *best friend*."

It slips out before I can stop it, this cold, callous tone I've never used with Charlie before. Not even in the first few days after we broke up.

She narrows her eyes at me, but her glare is more hurt than

pissed. I feel a prick of guilt underneath my burning skin, but the heat is just too damn good right now. Too damn distracting. I fold my arms and wait her out. This is Charlie and me. We don't fight. Neither of us can stand it for very long, and dammit, I do not want to be the one to break. Not tonight.

Just when I think she's going to crack, to soften and take my hand like she always does, she moves past me and out the door without another word.

CHAPTER SIX

Driving has always calmed me down. I love the steady movement, the sound of the tires on the road, whatever music I want playing and filling my thoughts. When Charlie and I leave the bowling alley, I drive until her words stop echoing so loudly between my ears, until I'm not so angry. Still, I don't care what Charlie says—I have no idea *who* I'm angry with.

She sits next to me, quiet and perpetually fiddling with her phone, changing from one song to the next, something she always does when she's nervous. Or pissed off. Or worried. Hard to tell with Charlie and music sometimes. It holds every emotion for her, cradling each one until she can sort them all out.

When my car finally comes to a stop, I'm in a familiar neighborhood near the lake, at a familiar park, a familiar house with softly glowing windows across the street. I tell my body to move, to get out and ring the doorbell and talk to Hannah. See with my own eyes that she's okay.

"Mara?" Charlie asks, peering through the window into the dark. "What are we doing here?"

I blink at Hannah's house. Blink again. Behind the seat, my phone buzzes in my bag.

"Mara?"

"What if you're right?" I ask. "What if she's not okay?"

Her fingertips press against my arm and I immediately tense. Then I relax and tense again. It's amazing how many feelings you can go through in only a few seconds, all because of someone's fingertips.

"We can call her," Charlie says softly. "See if she's up for some company."

Across the park, Hannah's house looks warm and inviting, and I'm weirdly surprised. Like it should've darkened to a cold blue, a shell of its former self. I stare at the windows, imagining Hannah inside and breathing, curled up in her big room with its own fireplace, that huge tapestry with the rainbow-colored peace sign set against a star-packed night sky she got at the folk art festival downtown last spring spanning the entire wall in front of her bed. Her mom hates that thing, but Hannah adores it. Says she bought it because it reminded her of us — of me and Charlie and herself.

In my mind, I separate her from Owen again, tucking them into their own worlds. They don't even know each other. Whatever Hannah's feeling, Owen wasn't the cause. They're two strangers dealing with different issues, with different stories and different outcomes. I think about everything I want to say to Hannah, but I can't make sense of any of it, can't sift through what I've been told and what I believe and what I feel. My thoughts are all a mess.

Before I even register what I'm doing, I'm throwing the car back into drive and pulling out of the park's gravel lot.

"Mara, wait." Charlie turns in her seat, watching Hannah's house fade from the back window. "I thought you wanted to —"

"I need to go home." My fingers go bloodless on the steering wheel. "Isn't that what you said? That I need to go home?"

The night flies past, a blur of swirled-amber streetlights and silhouettes. I feel Charlie's eyes on me, her slow inhalation and even slower exhalation. Finally, she turns away, staring out the window while she lets a whole song play out, a velvety voice crooning sadly through my speakers.

✳★✳.

The house is quiet when I get home. Too quiet, not even the hum of my mother's favorite prime-time shows interrupting the silence. I rush upstairs, heading to my bedroom and not bothering to check if anyone is still awake, but Mom finds me in the hallway.

"There you are." She has a cup of tea in her hands and she's still in her jeans and sweater. Usually, my mother's in her pajamas the second dinner is over.

"Here I am."

"Don't disappear like that, Mara. You can't just leave and then not answer your phone. I was about to send your father after you."

"Sorry," I say, even though I'm not sure if I really am.

"You okay?"

I nod, but it's so half assed, she lets out a sigh.

"Sweetie, this will blow over. It's a misunderstanding. You know your brother."

"You keep saying that."

"Saying what?"

"That it's a misunderstanding. That I know Owen. But . . . Mom, I know Hannah, too."

She presses her eyes closed and inhales slowly. "I know."

I wait for her to go on, but she doesn't. Just stares into her teacup.

"He couldn't have done this, could he?" I ask. I need her to tell me. She's my mom, the parent, the grownup, the one who always reminds me, whenever I whine about curfew or summer jobs, that she has years of experience behind her.

"Of course not," she says, and everything in me lets up, just a little. But not enough. My stomach is still coiled like a sleeping snake.

"So . . . what do we do?"

Her eyes snap to mine. "What do you mean?"

"I mean . . . what do we *do?* What's going to happen to Owen? And Hannah . . . we can't just not listen to her. You've always said that we have to listen to girls no matter—"

"He's ours, Mara," Mom says, a kind of quiet fury edging her words. "He's my son. And we love him. That's what we do."

I nod and she presses a kiss to my cheek as she moves past me and down the stairs. I watch her go, my feet aching to follow her, to make this simple for me, too. But I can't move toward her. Instead, I close myself in my room. I check my phone and find a voice mail from Mom and three missed texts from Owen.

Where are you?

Mom's freaking out & Dad's gone totally comatose. Come and save me.

Mar? Please.

I stare at the screen, a cold numbness spreading through my limbs. Then I power down the phone and toss it on top of my dresser. After I change and get into bed, I flip over onto my stomach and pull the curtain back from the window, searching for the stars. They're dim tonight, dulled by the bright moon.

Several feet down on the porch roof, a dark form blocks out a few distant trees.

Owen.

He sits with his arms resting on his knees, head arced to the sky until he turns toward me. At first I'm not sure if he can see me through my window, but then our eyes catch, the moon reflecting off the glasses he wears at night after he takes out his contacts. I have a matching pair perched on my nose right now. We share horrible eyesight, inherited from Dad. Owen inclines his head, a clear invitation. He looks so small, like a kid stuffed into a teenage boy's body. Even from here, I can feel him asking, waiting, needing me to come spin him a story.

And I want to. I want to hug his neck and let him blow a teasing raspberry into my hair. I want to go back to a few days ago when he made me laugh. When we found ourselves in the sky.

60

Owen has always been loud and kind of crude with his friends, but that's not who he is with me. With me, he's a boy made of stars, soft and light and safe. He always has been.

Mom used to tell us stories at bedtime. One of my first memories is snuggling with her while she ran her fingers through my hair, my floppy pink stuffed bunny clutched to my chest. Owen was curled against Mom's other side and we were all piled on our parents' giant bed. Our skin was bath-fresh and our pajamas matched —yellow stars and comets streaking across a navy background. We were the star twins, ready for our next adventure.

"Once upon a time," Mom said, "a brother and a sister lived with the stars. They were happy and had wild adventures exploring the sky . . ."

For as long as I could remember, the stories were a thing with our family. The twins born in June, Gemini soaring through the sky. There were even several years when Mom put *Happy Birthday, Gemini* on our cake, little yellow icing stars dotting the chocolate. Time passed, we got older and too big and cool to snuggle with Mom for bedtime tales, but we never let go of those stories. They were—are—part of our blood. Owen and I took them over, told new stories for laughs, as passive-aggressive jabs at each other when we argued, as comfort, as a way to remember we weren't alone.

I pull the curtain back a little more, my eyes locked with my twin's.

I believe him, I do, but my body won't let me move any closer. I tell myself I'm just tired, exhausted from everything with Charlie and wondering *why why why* Hannah would say something like this. I press my hand against the window. He lifts his hand too, mirroring mine. I offer him a weary smile.

And then I let the curtain fall back into place.

CHAPTER SEVEN

BLUISH MORNING LIGHT splays across my face. I reach out my hand, hoping for something warm and soft, but I find only a handful of wrinkled sheets.

I sit up alone in my bed, tank top damp against my skin, and try to press the disappointment that Charlie didn't sleep over away from my eyes. Of course she didn't. After we started dating, our parents put a stop to sleepovers pretty quickly, but we'd push our curfews to the limit and send gooey good-morning texts as soon as the sun split the dark.

It took forever for me to fall asleep last night, half terrified I'd dream about Owen and Hannah and something I didn't want to see. I don't remember dreaming at all, but the ache in the center of my chest is still thin and sharp.

Tossing my covers back, I throw on a pair of leggings and the first tunic dress I wrap my hands around in my closet. It's still early, the sun low and winking through my window, and the house is quiet as I tiptoe downstairs. Too quiet. I stand in the kitchen, the coffeemaker still idle, everything in its place.

And nothing in its place. Nothing like my house should feel.

I shiver, finding my school bag in the hall, my keys, my jacket. I take Owen's and my car and drive to school an hour before I'm supposed to be there. Mom texts me not long after and I tell her I have a project to finish up.

I don't think she buys it.

Family meeting tonight, no excuses is the only response I get.

I cut the engine but leave the music blaring, some female songwriter Charlie introduced me to, with a smooth voice and a name I can't remember right now. "She's the perfect blend of gloom and pop," Charlie had said a few months ago. We had just decided to try dating, and even though we'd been best friends for almost three years, everything was new and stomach-fluttering and wild.

I lean my head against the seat and close my eyes, trying not to think about her. But every time I succeed, my mind goes places that are dark and covered up and knotted instead. Not exactly what I was going for.

I'd rather have the Charlie thoughts. I'd always rather have Charlie. Best friends forever, after all.

Owen used to say Charlie and I were always going to end up as more than friends. He'd been saying it for close to three years, even before I'd really claimed the word *bisexual*. Charlie had known she liked girls since she was twelve, so that was no secret. And I knew I did as well, but I liked boys, too, and it took me a while to figure out I could like both in different ways and for different reasons and that was actually a thing.

The year I met Charlie, I was nowhere near ready to own that.

64

I'd just had the worst summer of my life, eight weeks stuck in a barely air-conditioned classroom repeating prealgebra because I failed the class the last semester of eighth grade.

Only I didn't fail the class. My teacher, Mr. Knoll, failed me.

Regardless, I was in summer school, my parents completely shocked and disappointed that I had *earned* an F. Consequently, during the hours I wasn't suffering through material I already knew, I was grounded. I would close myself in my bedroom, mulling over that rainy day in Mr. Knoll's classroom at Butler Middle School, reliving the scene over and over. How quiet the room was. The smell of the dry-erase markers and teenage sweat. The summer weeks passed slowly, a heart-shrinking routine. My parents assumed I was just being petulant. Owen knew better. Nearly every day, he tried coaxing me onto the roof, promising stories, but nothing really helped change my mood.

Everything I knew seemed to change after that last day of eighth grade. I changed. Mr. Knoll, looking at me with that smirk on his face, stripped me of my choices, my control, the safety of school and teachers and my own body.

By the time I started ninth grade at Pebblebrook, the mirror always reflected limp hair, purple crescents under my eyes, a blank stare and a flat-lined mouth.

On the first day of school, I met Charlie in American Lit. She sat behind me, told me her name and how much she liked my hair. Asked if she could braid it. I'll never forget how shocked I was by her question, almost scandalized. I turned in my seat, my eyes searching hers, and she just grinned. She seemed so sure of herself.

Still, there was a weariness to her smile and I clung to it, pulled it into my own emotional exhaustion.

Charlie was wearing a plaid shirt with a lace-trimmed tank top peeking out from the bottom and skinny jeans. Her legs were splayed wide under the desk. "Knock yourself out," I'd said, and my permission shocked me too. I hadn't let anyone touch me all summer. My mom would squeeze my arm or try to hug me good night and I'd stiffen, all my senses instantly on alert. I knew it hurt her, but I couldn't tell her why. Not even Owen's playful shoulder bumps when we passed in the hall were allowed. I'd arc away from everyone. My dad didn't even try, but the sad look on his face every time I shrank away from him was clear.

But when Charlie started lacing her fingers through my hair, I instantly relaxed. Breathed easier. I still don't really understand why. Later, Charlie and I laughed over our first meeting, joking about what a creeper she was.

"I like hair, okay?" she'd said, twisting a lock of mine around her finger. "Yours in particular."

"So you have a hair fetish. That's what you're saying, right?"

She'd laughed and tugged the lock gently, but something serious spilled into her eyes.

Almost a year later, when our friendship had blossomed into something neither of us could live without, lying together in my bed, limbs entangled and still under the guise of *just friends*, she'd confessed that she hated her own long hair.

"I don't know what it is about it," she'd whispered in the dark of my bedroom. We spent at least one weekend night together at one of our houses, binging on pizza and watching eighties movies. "When I look in the mirror, it just doesn't look like me."

"I think you look beautiful."

She'd smiled, but it was a sad sort of smile.

"If you don't like it," I said, "you should cut it."

"I don't know if my mom would let me. I want it really short."

"Have you asked her?"

She pressed her lips flat and shook her head softly, looking away from me.

"I'll cut it for you," I said. I just wanted her to smile again.

She'd laughed. "Really?"

"Sure—how hard can it be?"

She smiled, her foot brushing up against my calf. A week later, I totally butchered her hair.

Slowly, I slipped into my own skin again. Slowly, the memory of Mr. Knoll faded to a dull buzz in the back of my head. Slowly, I started to need more. Do more. Fight more. I'd spent months feeling small and inconsequential. I won't say that Charlie was completely responsible for the change, but she definitely helped. She made me feel safe, like it was okay to be whoever or whatever I needed to be. Charlie dealt with so much inside her head, hid so much from her parents, but she never hid herself from me. She let me see just how hard life hit her, just how confusing it was some-times for her. All of the assholes in our school who'd bump into her in the halls, wondering aloud and obnoxiously if she was a girl or a guy. Every time her mom wanted to take her dress shopping. Every time her dad pulled her into his arms and whispered how thankful he was for his beautiful daughter. She wore it all with a lifted chin and steely eyes, with a grace I envied. I still kept so much from her at that time, but she made me feel like, someday, I wouldn't anymore—she made me feel so many *somedays*.

Empower was my idea, but Charlie and I really started it together. A place to talk about the shit that girls and queer kids deal with every day. A medium to write about it. We got school approval and convinced our chorus teacher, Ms. Rodriguez, to be our faculty advisor, and for the first time in months I felt as if I was holding the reins on my own life. Steering it the way *I* wanted it to go. There was no topic I'd shy away from, and I quickly became known as Queen Bitch at school, which just fueled every flame I had in me. I devoted an entire article to why I found the term delightfully empowering, and the piece ended up being a pretty hilarious and scathing commentary, one of my favorites I've ever written. I remember typing it up furiously on my laptop in Charlie's room. She sat on her bed, ankles crossed lazily as she attempted to knit a Ravenclaw beanie hat out of blue and gray yarn, which I knew was for me because she was a Gryffindor through and through. Every now and then the clack of her needles would still and our gazes would snag. Her proud grin was like kindling for my fingers.

Near the end of junior year, we had just put the finishing touches on a kick-ass issue tackling the double standard when it comes to sex: guys were sex-crazed animals; girls just did it for an emotional connection. We interviewed a ton of students—all genders, all orientations, different races and ethnicities. Some owned being virgins; some talked proudly about one-night hookups; some discussed how much the idea of sex stressed them out; some confessed a total lack of interest in sex. It was the best issue all year and I knew people would talk about it for months. Principal Carr got sort of pissed when he read the draft for approval and almost didn't let us put the issue out, but Ms. Rodriguez calmed him down. I don't know what she said to him, but I felt almost high that day in her choir room as I hit print.

"This is really amazing," Charlie had said as she read over the articles on the computer. We'd done a chat piece together, where she and I discussed her liking girls and me being bi and our general thoughts about sex. I wanted to add in some stuff about Charlie's gender identity, but she hadn't wanted to get into it publicly. Unless she brought it up, we rarely talked about it, even though I knew it was something she dealt with every day.

"I think so too," I'd said. "Thanks for your help." I beamed at her, adrenaline flooding my veins, the paper in my hands still warm from the printer. She peered at me over the laptop, her hair almost impossibly tall.

"Your cheeks are flushed." She got up and made her way toward me, glancing toward Ms. Rodriquez's empty office as she crossed the room.

I laughed. "It just feels good."

"What does?"

"*Doing* something. Anything."

She'd looked at me, a question in her eyes, but it didn't make its way to her mouth. Instead, she reached out her hand to cup my chin. "I'm really proud of you."

Such a simple statement. But something in those words pulled me over the slowly blurring line in our relationship. Maybe it was the adrenaline. Maybe it was the fact that we'd created something powerful and beautiful, said something important, and we'd done it together. Maybe it was always going to happen, like Owen said.

Whatever it was, the distance between us kept shrinking, smaller and smaller, until our lips met. Immediately, she smiled against my mouth and hooked her arm around my waist, her other hand soft on my cheek. My own hands were more unsure. She was only the second girl I'd ever kissed. The first girl was a one-time thing at a party near the end of sophomore year, and even then it was anxiety-laced. With that girl, I faked a headache and proceeded to have a panic attack in the bathroom that lasted fifteen minutes. I wasn't sure I could ever kiss anyone again. It was supposed to be so fun and it ended up being so terrifying.

But with Charlie, it was different. When I finally registered what was happening, I locked up and she pulled back, worried eyes searching mine. I was dizzy and nervous, but I also felt safe and turned on as hell. So I smiled at her and my fingers found their way to her slim hips and I pulled her back to me, deepening the kiss. She tasted like cinnamon gum, her lips soft against mine, tongue gentle and slow, seeking and finding mine over and over. For the first time in a long time—maybe ever—I really wanted someone.

And that was the beginning, such a natural transition from what we had been to what we were always becoming. For a while it was good. So good. I was shocked by how good it was. And then my mom kept casting us worried glances and Owen would crack a joke about how the world would theoretically end if we ever broke up. But the real problem wasn't that our friendship was changing. Not really. Charlie was absolutely fine with whatever we did or didn't do physically, but I know she must have wondered why I never let her hands wander below my waist and why I never touched her like that either. I couldn't be her girlfriend the way I wanted to be. The way she deserved. I felt my control slipping, the worry that I'd ruin everything a palpable weight on my chest.

Because who was I without Charlie? Who was she? How did we get so entangled that I couldn't imagine a life without her? And how fair was it to her that I couldn't touch her, couldn't be touched?

Three weeks ago, the ship went down, and I'm the one who blew a hole in the port side.

We were eating tacos at my house, the evening light fading from a vibrant orange to a delicate lavender, the night growing soft around the edges. Mom and Dad were on an overnight trip to Chattanooga, hoping to descend upon some estate sale at the crack of dawn and acquire yet another four-poster bed or antique desk for their furniture shop. Owen was probably at the lake with Hannah, soaking in the last of the warm sun. I don't even remember now. I do remember glancing up at Charlie, her pretty pale skin almost violet in the twilight, and all of those worries finally overflowed.

So I told her I missed my best friend.

She said the same, even though she had to know there was more to it.

But I miss her even more now.

❦★∗.

Pebblebrook is a big school, but in our tiny little program full of dramatic artistes, it doesn't take long for a whisper to snake through the halls, eating everything in its path until it's a shout. I'm halfway through a notation in second-period music theory when the murmuring starts.

I spent the first ninety minutes of school forcing my eyes straight ahead in the halls and on my own papers in class. I'm on a different schedule than both Owen and Hannah, so I don't know if either of them came to school. I'm not sure what I'd do with that information even if I did know.

Now Beethoven's "Moonlight Sonata" plays gloomily through Dr. Baylor's sound system while I scribble on my composition paper, straining to catch every chord and quarter rest. I've just added a crescendo symbol when I hear them.

Voices, whispering.

"For real?"

"That's what I heard."

"What a bitch."

I turn my head toward the hissing. A group of orchestra kids huddle over their desks, heads bent together, notation paper forgotten between them. All of them are wearing matching disgusted expressions, a tinge of hunger underneath.

"This morning, Owen told me they had a fight after they . . . you know," Jaden Abbot says, waggling his eyebrows. I want to rip them off. "Then he told her maybe they should take a break. Just a breather, you know? She freaked and now she's crying rape."

My heart stutters and my eyes instinctively look for Charlie. She's a few rows over, already staring at me, her mouth a little circle of shock.

"No way," Rachel Nix says. "They've been together for months. You're telling me they haven't already done it?"

Jaden grins. "That's exactly what I'm not telling you."

"There's no way he hasn't already been in her very tiny skirt," says Peter Muldano.

"Multiple times," Jaden adds, and the group devolves into laughter.

"Enough," Dr. Baylor snaps as she circles the room. "This assignment is due at the end of class. I suggest you listen and write."

"Yes, ma'am," Peter says, saluting like the ass hat he is.

Dr. Baylor rolls her eyes and I catch her as she comes up my row.

"May I have a bathroom pass?" I whisper.

She leans toward me, her glasses slipping down her nose. "I'm sorry, what?"

I clear my throat, swallow, try to force some audibility into my voice. "Um . . . the bathroom? Please?"

"Make it fast." She glances at my half-completed paper while waving me toward the classroom door.

The classroom door all the way on the other side of the room.

I slide out of my desk, feeling Jaden's and his crew's eyes slide over me like curious fingers for the entire trek across the shiny tiled floor.

"She must hate Hannah," Rachel whispers to Peter as I pass. The words are a firework in my ears, and my feet nearly tangle together. I brace one hand on a desk near the exit—I don't even know whose—and then all but fling myself into the quiet hallway.

I take off running. Lockers blur in my periphery, a teacher on his planning period calls out to me from down the hall, but I don't stop until I'm in the restroom, my gasps for breath fogging up the mirror above the sinks.

"Are you okay, Mara?"

I startle, but more from the syrupy tone of the voice than the voice itself. Greta stands two sinks down from me, calmly drying her hands on a brown paper towel.

"Fine," I say, and run the water in my own sink.

"You don't have to pretend with me."

"I'm not doing anything with you, Greta. I'm washing my damn hands."

"Okay. But we need to figure out how we're going to handle this at the Empower meeting tomorrow."

I just stare at her, fighting to keep my expression blank, but something like panic begins a slow crawl up my throat.

"Handle . . . what?"

She lifts her perfectly defined eyebrows. "Interesting."

"*What's* interesting?" I snap off the faucet, my fingers dripping water onto the floor.

She puts up her palms. "I know this has to be really weird for you."

"Oh my god, Greta, you don't know what you're talking about."

"One of us sure as hell doesn't."

"Look, I don't—"

The main restroom door squeaks open, shutting me up. Charlie stands in the entryway, long legs in gray jeans. Her eyes dart between Greta and me.

"Everything good in here?" she asks.

"I was just leaving," Greta says, catching my eye once more in the mirror. "See you girls in chorus."

Charlie winces but manages a smile as Greta leaves.

When she disappears into the hallway, my knees buckle. I let myself go down, squatting so my feet are still on the floor and wrapping my arms around my legs. My hands are still wet, slippery hooks on my elbows.

"Shit," I hear Charlie mutter. Then she's in front of me, her hands on my shoulders as I gasp for breath again.

"Is it . . . is it true?" I ask. "Did Owen really try to break up with Hannah? He told me they fought. I mean . . . he said they didn't, but then he said they did, and I don't . . . I don't know . . ."

"Hey, hey, just breathe." Charlie pulls me back against a wall, forcing me to sit on my butt. She settles on the other side of me, her legs blocking the restroom door. She rubs circles on my back, pulls her hands through my hair before moving to my back again. "Breathe."

So I do. Over and over, measured and steady, until my fingertips are no longer tingling, until the waves of nausea pass. "Is it true?" I ask again.

"Mara. You know the answer to that."

"I don't. Maybe something happened at the party. Something we don't know about."

Charlie shifts so she's facing me. "Owen isn't telling the truth. How can you not see that? Hannah told me what happened: They were messing around on the trail. It got pretty heavy. She changed her mind. He didn't let her. End of story."

"But they've . . . they've had sex before."

Charlie doesn't have to say it for me to hear how ridiculous I sound. How unlike myself. How full of excuses and provisos. But they're not excuses to me. This is my brother we're talking about.

"This doesn't make any sense. This isn't . . ." *This isn't my brother,* I want to say. He would never have hurt Hannah. But that would make Hannah a liar and that's not her, either. I know her. Sat beside her during Empower meetings, listened to her talk about getting boobs in the fourth grade and how it made her feel self-conscious and foreign in her own body. How the first time she got her period, she figured it out all by herself because her mom hadn't told her about it yet. I remember nodding in reluctant agreement when she told me to be patient with Greta, even when Greta acted like a power-hungry harpy.

"It's us against the world, Mara," Hannah said one time. "If we're not on each other's side, who will be?"

"I can't believe it," I say to Charlie, locked-up tears strangling my voice. "I physically *can't*. How can I believe either one of them? How can I *not* believe them?"

"I don't know," Charlie says softly, her hands on my back stilling. "He's your brother, I get that. But I . . ." She breathes out heavily, her cinnamon breath fanning into the space between us. "I need you to know that I do believe Hannah. And it sucks. Everything about this is shitty. I mean, I loved Owen too."

Loved. Past tense. Charlie's made up her mind, picked a side and marched onward, and I'm still trying to wake up from a nightmare.

"I'll help you work through this," she says. "I'll do whatever I can, Mara. Just . . ."

"Just what?"

"Don't forget about Hannah. Okay? She's totally devastated."

"She loved Owen," I whisper, and Charlie nods. Her hands slide to the back of my neck, thumb right on a pulse point. I can feel my blood pounding against her skin. Hannah did love my brother. He loved her too.

"I can't be here today," I say, moving Charlie's hands away and pulling myself to my feet.

"Where will you go?"

"I don't know . . . I just can't."

"I'll come with you. I don't want you to be alone."

"No. No, I need to be."

"Mara—"

But I nudge her legs out of the way and open the door. Instantly, I'm swept into a throng of students in the middle of a class change, Hannah's name a constant whisper in the air.

CHAPTER EIGHT

I END UP AT THE CEMETERY on Orange Street. It's a weird obsession of mine, but I've always loved the eerie sort of peace you can find only in graveyards. All the lives already lived, done toiling, hopefully resting. It's sad and hopeful all at once, and I can spend hours wandering among the century-old tombstones, wondering at the sleepers under my feet. This particular cemetery backs up to the Harpeth River, so it's never completely quiet, even on a windless day. The sound of the water rolling gently over the rocks is a continual hush in the background.

I drift among the rows of stones, the long grass dying around them as winter gets closer. The air smells like fall and I breathe in the scent of burned leaves and river water—a rocky, mineral scent. There aren't many flowers or other tributes adorning the graves, most of the inhabitants having died so long ago they're barely a memory in the world anymore.

I stop at one ancient stone, the carved writing nearly faded from the surface. Bending down, I find a young girl's name.

Elizabeth Ruby Duncan

Beloved daughter and brave sister

May 3, 1879–November 26, 1897

She was eighteen, barely older than me. A sister. I wonder if she had a brother, if they were close, why *brave* is the adjective her family chose to put on her final resting place. I wonder how she died, why so young. I wonder if anyone she trusted ever made her feel small and powerless.

If she fought back.

In my mind, I see a girl in a white dress, dark curls and a fierce smile. She's soft and lovely. She speaks the truth, and the world took her anyway.

I run my fingers over Elizabeth's name. "Brave sister," I whisper. Suddenly, I want to find more. More girls, more sisters, more proof of lives lived boldly no matter how short or long. I cut through the grass, eyes scanning the stones, a desperate hunt, stopping to read every girl's epitaph. I'm near the riverbank and I've just found *Valiant mother* Virginia Howard, when I hear my name over the swirling water.

"Mara!"

Turning, I see Alex walking quickly toward me from the newer section of the cemetery, the graves marked with fake flowers and plaques stuck into the ground. His hands are stuffed into the pockets of his dark jeans, his nearly black hair windblown, a gray cardigan buttoned over an azure-blue shirt.

"Hi," I say, slightly out of breath from running around the cemetery for the past hour.

"Hey." He stops in front of me, a question on his straight brows. "What are you doing? Are you okay?"

I try to say an automatic yes, but I can't seem to form the word. Instead the past few days tangle in my throat, a giant knot of *not okay*.

He must see it all coalescing in my eyes, because he blows out a long breath and rakes his hand through his hair. Then suddenly his arms are circling me and my face is pressed to his chest, inhaling some kind of herbal scent, neither manly nor girly. Just clean. Just Alex.

"Yeah," he says softly. "Me too."

My arms hook under his, clinging to him. Or maybe he's clinging to me. Either way, I can feel how tired he is, like all his weariness is leaking from his bones to his skin and into my fingertips.

"Sorry," he says, pulling back.

"Don't be. Oh shit, sorry." I wipe at a wet circle on his sweater, a swirl of black mascara mixed in with the tearstain.

"Eh, whatever," he says, not even dabbing at the spot while I wipe under my eyes.

"I seem to have a habit of ruining your sweaters."

He gives me a small smile. "So what are you doing running around here in the middle of the day?"

"What are *you* doing spotting me running around here in the middle of the day?"

"Fair enough." He starts a slow amble toward the river and I follow. "I saw you leave school. You seemed upset."

"You followed me?"

"Not in a creepy way. Just . . . wanted to check on you. Plus, I do come here sometimes, just to clear my head. I like reading the tombstones. It's interesting."

"Alex Tan, communing with the dead."

He grins. "Oh, you know me. Usually I bring my violin and play them a little song."

I laugh, which makes him smile even wider. "Also, my parents work at our house, so I can't really go home yet. I couldn't deal with school today."

"Yeah," I say through a sigh. "Me neither."

Silence falls between us, but I can't handle it for long. "Alex, what happened? Have you talked to him?"

He bites at his lower lip. "Not today."

"Since the party, though? Did he say anything about Hannah?"

"No."

"But you saw him and Hannah at the lake, when you went back to tell him you were taking me home?"

Alex bends down to pick up a wayward twig and tosses it into the water. "Yeah, I saw him."

"And he was fine, right? Hannah was fine?"

He sighs and is quiet for a long minute. "They . . . they were pretty wrapped up in each other. I didn't want to interrupt them."

82

I stop him with a hand on his arm. "Do you believe her? You know him almost as well as I do. Owen wouldn't do this."

"No way. I mean . . . I never would've thought . . ." He sighs again and rubs both of his eyes. "I fucking don't know what to think right now. He's my best friend, but . . ."

He trails off. That *but* hangs heavily between us, his exhaustion and confusion so familiar that it makes my stomach hurt. We want everyone to be right and no one to be right.

"Let's go do something," I say.

"Huh?"

"Something fun."

"It looks like you're having plenty of fun frolicking among the dead."

"You're one to talk."

He fights a smile. "I was most certainly not frolicking."

I laugh. "Well, while I have enjoyed my time with the residents of Orange Street Cemetery, I'm thinking something a little less . . ."

"Deceased?"

"Yes, exactly. Something silly where we don't have to think about anything for an hour or two."

Alex watches me for a few seconds, his eyes running up my galaxy-print leggings so intently I feel myself blushing. Then a smile splits his smooth lips. "I think I know just the place."

✹★*.

"You're kidding me, right?" I say, peering up at the neon bubble letters on the front of the building.

"Hey, you said silly and fun. I'm just delivering."

I laugh and we climb out of TLB. "Fun is yet to be determined."

"Oh, just you wait."

Inside, Glow Galaxy smells like industrial-strength sanitizer and rubber. A bored-looking lady behind the counter plays a loud game on her phone. Behind her, doors lead into the main room, the windows in the center completely dark.

"Hello," Alex says, and the lady snaps up her head, surprised. "Two, please."

She flicks her gaze between us, and I can see her mind guessing at our ages and whether or not she should question our presence here in the middle of the day on a Tuesday. Finally she shrugs and types something on the computer next to her.

"Nineteen fifty. You can put your shoes in the cubby just inside the door." She chin-nods toward the main room. "No shoving, no hitting, no spitting."

Alex raises his brows while he hands her a twenty from his wallet. "Spitting?"

"You'd be surprised." She drops two quarters into his palm, then gestures for us to hold out our arms. She fastens two neon-green paper bracelets around our wrists. "Have a glowing time."

"Ah," Alex says. "I see what you did there."

She just stares at him and then goes back to her game.

"Cheery," I say as we head toward the main room.

"We interrupted her game — have some sympathy."

I smile as he holds open the door for me, surprised by his quick and easy humor. Usually, Alex is quiet, always a little dimmed next to all of Owen's bright. I'm not sure if he's compensating for all the shit that's going on around us or if this is who he really is when you separate him from my brother. Alex undiluted.

There's not much time to think on it because we're immediately swallowed by darkness and the bass line of a Taylor Swift song. The room is huge and cold, and the black lights ignite the entire space with glowing reds and blues, greens and oranges.

"Holy shit," I say, taking in the tiny glowing putt-putt course, the glowing bouncy house, the glowing inflatable slide, the glowing ball pit, the glowing basketball court.

"Right?" Alex says, slipping off his black Converse and stashing them in the glowing shoe cubby. "A veritable galaxy."

I store my own boots. "What should we do first?"

"I'm not sure, but I think we need to talk about your teeth."

My hand flies to my mouth. "My teeth?"

He bares his own and I laugh. They're radioactive white.

"At least I'll be able to find you in the dark," I say. I'm in a navy tunic dress, and his sweater is dark enough that the black light doesn't pick it up very much. The only things visible are our teeth and socks.

"Where to?" he asks, waiting for me to take the lead.

I squint through the neon gloom. We seem to have the run of

the place. With most kids in school, I can't imagine Glow Galaxy sees much action on a weekday.

"Bouncy house," I say, slipping my hand into his and starting toward the giant glowing structure.

"I think you mean bouncy *castle*."

We slip under the net that apparently doubles as a drawbridge. At first we both sort of hop around on the tight vinyl fabric. I'd be lying if I said I didn't feel a little ridiculous. Without the conversation and with my body moving too slowly, the day creeps back in. Owen. Hannah. All the whispers at school. Charlie's dark eyes so intent on mine as she tries to figure out how to help me.

Squeezing my eyes shut, I hurl my body into the air and throw my legs out in front of me so I land on my butt. I ricochet against the vinyl, getting tossed sideways and landing in a heap in the corner.

"Wow," Alex says. "Complete abandon — I like it."

"Go big or go back to school, I guess."

Alex teeters around while I get to my feet. This time I jump a little higher and a little longer, until finally I'm a foot off the surface, my hair flying around my face. Soon Alex is jumping too, gravity pulling the laughter out of us.

"Don't spit on me," I say.

"I'll try not to."

He backs up to the netted wall and gains some height. Then he throws himself forward, arms out like Superman. He lands on his stomach and bounces back up into the air, turning onto his back before hitting the sloped surface again.

"All I saw was a set of flying teeth," I say, and Alex lets out a long laugh.

We take on the slide next. It's at least three stories high, and I can barely climb the inflatable stairs because I'm laughing so hard.

"Your socks are my light in dark places," Alex says from behind me. I have to pause in my climb, more laughter sapping me of all my strength.

The slide is exhilarating. We climb up and shoot down at least ten times, sometimes on our backs, sometimes on our stomachs, forward and backwards. The last time, Alex somersaults down and all I see are his socks flashing as he rolls down in a little ball. It's silly and fun.

It's perfect.

We hit the putt-putt course and Alex pretty much kicks my ass, but then I annihilate him on the small basketball court, so we call it square.

"There's no way in hell I'm going in that ball pit," I say as we catch our breath.

"Oh, come on, I'm sure they clean each individual ball every hour with a toothbrush."

"No way in hell," I repeat, and he grins, looking around the room.

"Ah, the planetarium."

"The what?"

He takes my hand and leads me to a little alcove in the far corner of the room. It's about the size of my bedroom, glowing beanbag chairs spread across the floor. He settles into a fluorescent orange one, pulling me into a green one.

Above us a neon night sky swirls.

"Isn't this cool?" he says, snuggling deeper into his beanbag.

"Yeah," I say vaguely, my eyes on the sky. I find it right away, connect the lines in my mind to form that upside-down U shape. The brightest star in the constellation, Pollux, blinks at me with a soft orange hue. I'm not sure if I've ever seen Gemini without Owen next to me. Anytime I'm outside with someone else, I never even look. Plus, this time of year, the twins hide in the west, waiting for winter and spring.

My head feels light and floaty, so I look down for a few seconds, blinking at the glowing fabric of my beanbag. It's silly—I know these stars aren't real, but they look real. They look alive.

"You okay?" Alex asks, nudging my bag with his foot.

I nod. Alex doesn't know about Owen and me and Gemini. Neither does Charlie or Hannah. The constellation is ours, Owen's and mine. It's always been only ours, our retreat from the world, our respite from annoying parents or a bad grade or a bunked audition or a breakup.

Glancing back up at the sky, I try to see Gemini as Alex would —a constellation that's sort of hard to pick out, a row of stars connected by others. A pattern in the sky, no more, no less. But I can't do it. Those stars, they're Owen and me. They always will be.

"Hey," I say to Alex, and he leans toward me. "Can we go?"

"Yeah, sure."

We dig ourselves out of the beanbag chairs and collect our shoes. The lady at the front counter has been replaced by a very chipper dude with a handlebar mustache, who tells us to have a glowing day as we leave.

Outside, the sun is absurdly bright after spending an hour in the dark. We blink against the light as we walk to the car. Once on the road, Alex turns down the music. "So . . . what happened in there? You okay?"

"Yeah. I just . . ." I turn to look at him. His long fingers move over the wheel as he makes the turn onto Orange Street. "Thanks for this. It was exactly what I needed."

"Me too."

"I just need to go home, you know?"

He glances at me and nods, his mouth pressed into a line. He pulls into the cemetery and throws the car into park next to my Civic. The sun is just starting to touch the tops of the trees, the late afternoon light thick and lazy.

"You want me to come with you?" he asks as I unbuckle my seat belt.

I shake my head. "Mom wants a family meeting."

"God."

"I know." My stomach flutters with nerves. I haven't really talked to Owen since Friday night, since I saw him saunter off happily, his arm around Hannah's waist. I know it's time, but that doesn't make facing him any easier.

"Thank you," I say again. Then, before I know what I'm doing,

I lean forward and kiss Alex on the cheek. His hand comes up and tucks a lock of hair behind my ear, his touch there and then gone.

"You're welcome," he whispers as I pull away. He closes his hands around the steering wheel, a blush spilling into his cheeks.

"See you tomorrow?" I ask, and he nods.

We go our separate ways as we turn out of the cemetery, leaving all the brave girls behind us.

CHAPTER NINE

AFTER A DAY OF TRYING not to look at my brother, I can't stop staring at him now. His wavy mop of golden-brown hair, the way he's spread himself over the couch, legs splayed and one arm thrown over the back cushions. That scared little boy curling into his mother from yesterday afternoon is gone, replaced with all of his usual confidence and ease. This is the boy I know. The boy I love, the boy I believe. The boy I *have* to believe.

"Why'd you leave school today?" he asks. I'm tucked into the armchair across from him while we wait for our parents, who are whispering in the kitchen but pretending that all they're really doing is making tea. They both love hot tea. Dad thinks it solves just about anything.

"Were you there?" I ask, even though I know he was. How else would Jaden have heard about this supposed breakup?

Owen nods. "I won't tell Mom. That you left."

"Thanks." I lace my sweaty palms together in my lap just as Dad comes into the room carrying a tray. A sweet peppermint scent fills the room. He sets the tray on the ottoman and starts handing out smooth white mugs.

"With a little drop of honey, just how you like it," he says, holding out my tea.

"Thanks, Dad," I whisper, and close my hands around the warm cup.

Mom settles on the couch next to Owen, tucking her jean-clad legs underneath her. Her hair is straight today, a golden sheet around her face. Owen and I look exactly like her—gray-blue eyes, straight brows, hair that takes on a life of its own unless we take care to tame it. She seems a lot calmer today, a determined set to her chin.

"All right," she says as Dad sits in the chair next to me. "This has been a rough couple of days, so your father and I wanted to touch base with both of you and make sure we're all on the same page."

"Same page?" I ask.

"Just let me finish, Mara."

I press my lips together and she inhales slowly through her nose.

"We've spoken with Owen and he's told us what happened, but I think you need to hear his side, Mara, because people will start talking at school once this gets out."

Owen studies me and I can almost feel him trying to burrow into my thoughts.

"So . . . what happened?" I ask him.

He clears his throat and leans forward, arms resting on his knees. "Hannah's just pissed off, Mara. She'll calm down."

"Owen, what *happened?*"

"Please don't take that tone," Mom says. Dad reaches over and squeezes my knee once. "Just listen."

"I'm trying—he's not saying anything."

Owen sits back, digging his thumb and forefinger into his eyes. "This is weird, okay? I'm basically baring my sex life to my parents and sister."

"Fine. I'm listening."

"We were on the trail," Owen says, meeting my eyes head-on. "We stopped at that overlook—you know, the one with the benches and that plaque about some Civil War battle that happened nearby that no one ever reads. Anyway, we sat down and started . . . well, you know, kissing and stuff, and then we . . . you know."

"Do I?"

"Don't make me say it."

"I think you need to."

"Mara, for god's sake," Mom says.

"We had sex, all right?" Owen says. "Not like you didn't know what I was saying."

I swallow hard, my throat tightening. Everything he's saying makes sense. Still, something's not settling right, like a greasy meal on an empty stomach. "So . . . how did her wrist get hurt?"

"We were on a freaking stone bench, Mar. It wasn't exactly a feather bed. It was awkward and uncomfortable, to be honest."

Dad shifts next to me, sighing and running his hand through his hair.

"Then . . . well, she got really pissed," Owen says.

"About what?"

His fingers fiddle with his bottom lip, even while he talks. "About her wrist. She just . . . leaned on it weird or something. She had a piano test coming up and she sort of freaked out about it. I told her I was sorry, that maybe we should've thought it through better, but I swear to god she said yes before. But she just kept at me. You know how she gets. She's passionate. And honestly, I'm a little sick of her drama. So I got pissed, and yeah, I was sort of buzzed, and I told her maybe we needed a break and she agreed and I left while she fumed and that's it. Next thing I know, she's ignoring my texts and Mom's picking me up from school telling me she got a call from Hannah's parents."

Throughout his story, Owen keeps messing with his lip. His elbow is propped on his knee and he's picking at the bottom corner of his mouth. It's such a subtle gesture, my parents don't notice. I don't think even he realizes he's doing it. He looks straight at me, voice steady, expression the perfect mix of embarrassed and confident. Mom nods along with his story, sipping tea, like we're talking about some childish playground scuffle.

But as I listen to him, watch him, it's as if my skin is peeling away, struggling to reveal this new girl I'm not sure I want to be. It's as though the stars are breaking apart in the sky, nothing but dark underneath.

Because I know my brother is lying. The best lies are layered in between solid truths—I know that better than anyone. And Owen is a careful storyteller, blanketing every falsehood with a truth. But he's not careful enough. I know him too well, share too much blood, and for the first time in my life, I wish I didn't. I'm not even sure what it *is* exactly, this nebulous certainty that he's lying—at least about some part of all of this—in my gut. Maybe it's a twin thing, that almost supernatural inability to bull-shit each other.

Finally, Owen goes quiet. I know I should say something, but all I can do is flick my eyes down to his fingers on his lip and back again. He sees me do it and calmly lets his hand fall into his lap.

"So that's our story," Mom says, curling her hands around her mug.

"Our *story?*" I say, and Mom winces, realizing how her words sounded.

"That's what happened," she amends. "The Priors haven't contacted us again since yesterday, so I'm hoping the state attorney realizes how ridiculous this is after he talks with Owen tomorrow afternoon. Whatever happens, we need to be united. As a family."

"What does that mean?" I ask.

"It means you don't talk to anyone about this," Dad says quietly. "Kids are going to gossip, but we need you to refrain, Mara. Just ignore it. Support your brother."

I can't seem to drag my eyes away from Owen. *You want me to lie* is on the tip of my tongue, but to my parents, it's not a lie. It can't be. Not for them. He's their kid and they've swallowed his story whole. It's part of them now.

The panic rises fast, a lightning bolt ripping up my middle and splitting me in two. Daughter and sister versus the frantic pump of my blood in the center of my chest.

My family watches me, waits for me to say, *Okay, of course, whatever you need*, but I can't form the words.

I won't.

"I need a minute," I say, jumping to my feet so fast, my hip collides with the end table next to my chair, disrupting my cup and splashing tea all over the polished wood.

"Mara, sit down," Mom says. Dad heads to the kitchen for a towel.

"I just need a minute, Mom. This is a lot, okay? Hannah's my friend." Truths, hiding everything I can't say.

"Owen is your *brother*."

"I know that," I say, but my voice is a cracked whisper.

"Let her go, Mom," Owen says, his eyes on me. Something brews just underneath them, something pained and lonely. I look away. "You know Mar—she needs time to process. Remember when you changed our toothpaste to that natural stuff a couple years ago? She boycotted brushing her teeth for a week."

Mom laughs, but it's short and shallow. "Okay, you're right. I know this is the last thing any of us expected to happen." She glances up at me. "We've always adored Hannah, Mara. You know that."

Dad comes back into the room, towel in hand, and mops up my spill. He's even more quiet than usual and I wish I could read his mind. I know he'll stand with my mother, with Owen, but Dad's always been a little philosophical. He strives to see all sides, taught us that nothing is ever black and white.

Owen rubs circles on Mom's back. "I'm sorry, Mom."

"Oh, honey, me too. I know you must be so hurt that Hannah is saying all of these awful things. I wish we could talk to her."

I blink, trying to reconcile this woman in front of me with the woman whose eyes gleamed at the mere thought of Empower pissing off the patriarchy just yesterday. The possibility that Hannah is telling the truth never entered my mother's mind, but she's not exactly demonizing Hannah either. There's been a *misunderstanding.* Any doubt about that was fleeting and flimsy, quickly buried under a mountain of unconditional trust.

This. This is why I never said anything.

Because no one ever believes the girl.

My brother shrugs but looks down and away, the picture of putting on a brave face. Mom sets her cup on the coffee table and wraps her arms around him. I bite my lip hard and back up toward the hallway stairs to stop myself from joining them. My hands itch to hold my family — hold them together.

But we're already in pieces.

✷★✻.

Later, I sneak downstairs for some water. It's late and the house is dark and quiet, the amber glow over the kitchen sink the only thing lighting my way. I fill a glass and gulp it down.

That's when I hear it.

Thump. Thump. Thump-thump-thump.

I lean over the sink, peering out the window and through the dark outside to where the garage floodlight shines onto the driveway. There, my brother dribbles a basketball in lazy circles, pausing every now and then to try and *swoosh* it through the net.

My feet carry me out the side door, that constant, unseen thread between Owen and me pulled taut and slowly shortening. And I miss my brother. I'm used to daily jokes and shared glances. I'm used to so much more than this silence, this avoidance and doubt. The air is cool and damp against my face and arms, my tank top doing little to guard against the autumn chill. I walk slowly, my feet on the pebbled cement, my heart a rock in my throat.

Owen shoots the ball toward the basket and it bounces off the rim, rolling toward me over the ground. I stop it with my heel and slide it closer with my foot before I pick it up.

When I straighten, his eyes are already on me.

"Hey," he says, so normal.

"Hey."

"Can't sleep?"

I shake my head.

"I had too much Mountain Dew at dinner," he says, a sheepish smile on his face.

"Really? Too much caffeine is the only thing keeping you up?"

He sighs and tilts his head upward. There's a blanket of clouds over the stars, making the whole sky blurry and fathomless.

"Alex is acting weird," he says. "And Hannah . . . god, I don't even know what's happening." He lowers his head to look me in the eye. "Can you believe all this?"

I shift the basketball from hand to hand, hating his tone, as though we're the only two levelheaded people left on the earth and everyone else is full of shit. The ball's tread is almost completely smoothed out, but there's still enough for a bit of a grip. I tighten my fingers in place, plant my feet, and hurl the ball through the dark air. It hits the backboard with a bang and falls through the net.

"Nice shot," he says.

"Yeah, well, I've always been better than you at basketball."

He laughs and I swear there's a hint of relief in the sound. He retrieves the ball, dribbling around me before sinking a shot from the hand-painted line on the driveway we long ago deemed the top of the key.

"*Lucky* shot," I say.

After that, we fall into a rhythm. A too-easy rhythm. Too familiar, too natural, probably too good to be true. Summer nights, crickets chirping, barbecue smells drifting through the air while a brother and sister play horse. Because here, under the empty sky, he *is* just my brother. My twin who would never hurt me, whom I could never imagine hurting anyone. In between passes and dribbles, I find myself watching him, looking for signs that he's not that lying boy from our family meeting earlier. Or that I imagined it all, conjured up some twin sense because I felt us slipping away, the him and me I've always known and counted on. Maybe that fear—that I never really knew him at all—was stronger than anything else.

Out here, maybe he's not a liar. Maybe I just need to trust him. Trust *us*.

"So," he says after a few more shots. "How's Charlie?"

Her name brings everything back into sharp focus, the whole cluster fuck of this day—everyone whispering at school, that sham of a family meeting. Everything is too bright and loud and rough.

Everything except Alex, his hand in mine as we ran through a neon galaxy.

"She's fine," I say, gesturing for the ball from Owen. My voice sounds dead, a bad actor spitting out badly written lines.

He frowns, pausing in midthrow, arms outstretched in front of him. "You still haven't kissed and made up?"

"There's nothing to make up about. We're just . . . we're fine."

He tucks the ball under his arm. "Okay. Sure."

"Don't give me that."

"Give you what?"

"That *okay, Mara, whatever you say* bullshit."

"What should I say? That I think you're full of crap for breaking up with her?"

He tosses me the ball and I catch it, but not before it slams into my chest, his throw too hard and too fast.

"What about Alex?" I ask.

"What do you mean?"

I take a deep breath, my chest hot and tight. "You said he's acting weird. Why's that?"

"I don't know — ask him."

"Are you serious?"

He throws his hands into the air. "Yes. Jesus. What the fuck is with everyone?"

His words, his tone, everything about him right now infuriates me. As if everything is just *happening* to him. "Again, *are you serious?*"

"I thought we were talking about you and Charlie."

"Well, you think I'm lying to her and myself, so it sounds like we're talking about truthfulness."

His eyes narrow on me, his mouth dropping open a little. I throw him the ball and he catches it neatly.

"You don't believe me, do you?" he asks. "This whole ridiculous thing with Hannah. You believe *her* over me?"

Hurt spills into his voice, but it clouds into *my* throat, as though we share it.

"I want to," I whisper.

"Want to what?" He drops the ball and it bounces away, colliding with the bushes.

"Believe you," I say.

"But you . . . but you don't."

I shrug and it feels so inadequate, Atlas suddenly too weak, the world crushing his shoulders.

"Why?" he asks, hands balling into fists. "Why? What the hell did I do? I told you what happened. She just . . . read the whole thing wrong, Mar. She's pissed off. I can't control that. That's her issue, not mine."

Each one of his words is a gunshot to the chest. "I'm just trying to make sense of it, Owen. None of this matches up with the Hannah I know."

"But it matches up with the *me* you know? So, you have no trouble believing I'm some kind of sexual predator? That I'd do that to Hannah? It's really that easy for you?"

I flinch, all the air sucked out of my lungs. "No. No, it's not easy. I don't . . . want . . ."

To believe that either is what I mean to say. But I don't have the oxygen for it. Owen's tone of voice is wounded and loud, but a cold calmness hums underneath all of that and it makes me feel small and stupid and awful.

Stupid little bitch.

My head is pounding, or maybe it's my heart, maybe it's my blood, my veins. All of me. My fingertips fizz and crackle, my ribs feel like they're about to splinter, bone dust filling me up.

"Shit." Owen is suddenly in front of me, his hands on my elbows, his body bent over to look me in the eye. "Breathe, Mara."

"I . . . can't . . ."

"Don't talk, just breathe."

He turns me gently and presses my back to his chest, wrapping both of his arms around my shoulders and holding me against him.

"Breathe with me," he says. "Feel my breaths, try to match them." His chest rises and falls, steady and deep. I grip his forearms, nails digging into his skin. He doesn't protest. Just holds me, breathes with me, until our breaths sync up.

This has happened before. A few times that summer before freshman year and maybe once or twice since. Panic attacks, sudden and earthshattering. Most of the time, I can get control, breathe through them, but every now and then, they fall like a huge hammer on a very tiny nail. And every time, Owen gets me through them.

"You haven't had one of those in a while," he says after a few moments of steady breathing.

I nod, my eyes wet with the inevitable tears the attacks always pull up.

"You ever gonna tell me why they started?"

"I . . . they just did."

He goes to release me, but I tighten my grip on his forearms. I need this—this tiny moment where he's my brother and I'm his sister and he helps me from getting bulldozed by this unseen anxiety.

He sighs and rests his cheek on the top of my head. "It's me, Mara," he says, reading my mind as usual. "Please. It's still me. I'm just me."

The desperation in his voice makes my breath stutter and jerk again. A thousand thoughts and doubts bloom to the surface of my skin, trickling out like blood. And I don't understand *why*. Why Owen needs to sound so desperate. Why we're even here, standing in our driveway in the middle of the night, belief and disbelief all tangled up with a connection I can never break.

"I love you, Owen," I say, my voice a dry whisper. I say it because it's true, because I need to say it. Because I know he needs to hear it.

"I love you too, Mar."

I nod, and behind me, I feel his whole body relax. But my own muscles are tense, like those of a spooked animal, our reassurances to each other only adding to the mottled mess of truth and lies in my head.

CHAPTER TEN

THE NEXT DAY, Charlie slides into the chair next to mine, her guitar case *thwunking* onto the floor, but I don't look up from my laptop. I've been sitting in Ms. Rodriguez's choir room since the final bell, prepping for the Empower meeting. I successfully dragged myself through the day, avoiding Charlie, hiding in the library at lunch, and trying to close my ears and eyes to the incessant whispers and nosy glances.

"Hey," she says.

"Hey."

And that's it. That's literally it. She doesn't ask how things are going. She doesn't ask me anything. I can't seem to push any questions out of my throat either, and we just sit there in a cloud of weird while I pretend to type on my computer and she pulls out the novel we're reading for AP lit.

"Shmerda?" she asks after a few minutes.

"Huh?" I glance over at her to find her peering at my computer screen, where I have indeed typed *shmerda*. And also *frenisk* and *mywot*. "Oh." I hit the delete button, the clacking echoing between the acoustic-paneled walls.

"Trying to multitask?" she asks.

"Something like that," I mutter, hating this bullshit small talk.

She makes a *hmm* noise and goes back to her book, but she can't have read more than a few sentences before she smacks it shut and drops it into her lap. "So, I need to ask you something." She doesn't turn to face me, just stares straight ahead and twists her fingers together.

"What is it?"

She blinks at the floor, filling her lungs with several deep breaths before releasing them.

"I'm playing a show at 3rd and Lindsley. Tomorrow night."

"Oh my god. Really? Charlie, that's huge!" 3rd and Lindsley is a pretty major music venue in Nashville.

She nods. "They're having this young artists series where a few musicians play every night this month. You have to be between sixteen and twenty-two to do it, and I sent their booking person my demo a few months ago. I guess she liked it."

"'Guess'? Of course she did. It's *you*."

Charlie waves off the compliment, but crimson spills into her cheeks and she smiles. "I found out a couple weeks ago. Will you come with me?"

"Oh. Really?"

"Of course. Who else would I ask?"

"Are your parents going?"

She frowns and looks down.

"Charlie—"

"I'm not ready for that, Mara. You know I'm not."

"But your songs are *you*. They'd love to hear them—I know they would."

"Yeah. They're me. Too much me."

I sit back, rubbing at my eyes. I wish I had the right words to say to her, words that calm all of these fears about her songwriting, but I don't. I can sing and I can sing well. It's why I'm at Pebblebrook, though I'm a pair of clanging cymbals next to Charlie, so I get being nervous about performing. But I can't write songs. I can't manipulate guitar strings so they seem like an extension of my voice. Then again, maybe I've never really tried. All that . . . *me*, just falling into people's ears. I shiver thinking about it. Still, my issues about putting myself out there are completely different from Charlie's. I have no idea what she's really going through.

"Please, Mara," she says. "I need you with me. We're best friends, right? Isn't that what all of this is about?"

I'm not exactly sure what *all of this* means, but I can take a wild guess. "Yeah, of course."

"Then, please. Come with me."

I watch her, desperation spilling into her eyes as she watches me back.

"You know I wouldn't miss seeing you on that stage," I say.

Her shoulders visibly descend. "Thank you."

After that, we maneuver around each other—Charlie pulls choir chairs into a circle, I turn on the floor lamp near the piano and flick off the fluorescents so the light is softer—everything we're not saying like a *friends forever* necklace around our throats.

＊★＊.

Naturally, Greta's the first person to arrive at the meeting. Her fountain of blond hair is twisted into a side fishtail braid and she takes a seat next to me, a navy notebook in her lap and a closed-mouth smile her only greeting.

Empower is a small group. Our numbers vary every week, but our committed regulars are Hannah, Charlie, Greta, Jasmine Fuentes (Greta's best friend), a willowy ballet dancer named Ellie Branson, and Hudson Slavovsky, Empower's only dude, who I'm pretty sure comes only because he's dating Jasmine. Still, he's a good guy and he contributes a hilarious comic for our monthly issues called *Well, Actually.*

My stomach flutters as I take in Hannah's absence. Everyone else is here, including a drama major, Leah Lawrence. Or maybe it's Landon. She comes so rarely, I forget her last name half the time. I'm pretty sure she wanders in only once every few months to meet some sort of quota for extracurriculars on her college applications.

Everyone gets settled, pulling out water bottles and granola bars, and I use the time to stall, half hoping and half dreading that Hannah will walk through the door.

"She's not back at school yet," Charlie whispers, squeezing my arm.

"I know." And I know why Hannah's not here. But part of me still hopes this whole situation is some elaborate dream that we'll all wake up from any minute. I open my laptop, pretending to scan my notes for the hundredth time while I get my breath under control.

"Okay. Welcome, everyone." I blink at the group, trying to force some life into my voice. This is usually a pretty casual meeting, everyone laughing and talking about their week so far, happy just to be together in a safe space. But right now everyone is silent and fidgeting. On edge. "So, um, this week, our first item on the agenda is to make some decisions about the Dress Code Take —"

"I have an urgent matter that carries precedence over our skirts and tank tops, Mara," Greta says, her posture snapping straight. "May I?"

"Sure, Greta, go right ahead," I say saccharinely.

She doesn't even half-ass a fake smile. She's gone totally stoic, all business and determination. "I know we've all heard about what happened to Hannah and I know we all feel horrible. A few of you have asked me what we can do to help."

My stomach lurches. I can't even process what she's saying before she barrels onward.

"And I don't want this group to fall apart because of this," she says. "You're all really important to me. When my parents were getting a divorce last year, our meetings were the only time during the week that I didn't feel like pulling out my hair. But I . . ." She sucks in a shaky breath. Is she . . . nervous? "I don't think Mara is able to effectively lead us during this time."

I feel all the color bleed from my face. "I'm sorry . . . what?"

"Come on, Mara," she says. "Don't make it harder than it has to be."

"I'm not making anything anything."

"You had to know this was coming," Jasmine says. Hudson leans forward with his elbows on his knees, eyes glued to the floor.

Greta sighs, her voice softening. "Look, I know this is hard for you. I'm not trying to be a bitch about this. But Hannah is one of us and this school is already becoming a cesspool of Team Owen."

"Team . . . Team Owen?" My palms instantly start to sweat and my pulse throbs in my temples. Because I don't even need an explanation for what she means. Owen is talking, and talking loudly, spreading his story throughout every corner of the school.

"I assume that you're Team Owen too," Greta says.

More silence. Not even Charlie speaks up on this one. Everyone's eyes are on me, waiting.

Waiting for the form of my allegiance. For me to pick a side.

"You don't know what you're talking about," I say, my voice a brittle whisper.

"Even if I don't," Greta says just as softly, "we need to help Hannah. We're her family at this school, some of her only supporters, and you leading that charge is a conflict of interest."

I glance around the circle, looking for anyone who might disagree. No one speaks. Ellie avoids my gaze, her ridiculously long eyelashes fanning over her cheeks. Leah just looks uncomfortable, as though she's really wishing she hadn't chosen today of all days to attend a meeting. Hudson doesn't make eye contact with anyone, his shoulders up around his ears.

"I move that we put the dress code project on hold and talk about what we can do to help Hannah, her family, and her experience when she comes back to school," Greta says. "And that I temporarily replace Mara as Empower's leader."

A beat. Then, a familiar voice. "Seconded."

I turn my head, meeting Charlie's gaze. She doesn't look away. She doesn't smile. Just reaches out and puts her hand on my back. I'm so shocked, I can't even arc away from her touch.

"All in favor?" Greta asks.

Six *ayes* echo through the room.

I stand up slowly, clutching my useless laptop to my chest.

"You don't have to leave, Mara," Greta says.

"No, it's okay. I should . . . you're right. I'm not . . . I should go."

I stumble out of the room, my eyes already blurring. Getting deposed is not a huge deal. And dammit, Greta's right. I'm not the right person to lead the group. Hannah is the focus right now and she should be. I know that. But it's just one more thing screaming at me that I have no clue what the hell I think, who I am, where I stand, why I stand there.

It's one more thing taking my voice away from me.

I wait for Charlie to follow me, chase after me like we've always done for each other no matter what, but the hall is silent, the stale air-conditioned air stinging my eyes. I walk toward the exit, ready to leave, but I can't. I don't want to go home. Not like this, when it feels as if something new and raw is trying to break through my skin.

Please come out here, I text Charlie. The words drip with desperation and maybe that's totally pathetic, but I need her.

Barely thirty seconds pass before Charlie comes out into the hallway. When she gets close, I turn and lead her out the front doors and into the late afternoon light. The setting sun spills over her hair, pulling up hints of red in all the dark. She faces me, silent, her head tilted and her eyes soft—too damn soft—on mine.

"You voted me out," I say.

She sighs. "That's not what I did and you know it."

I nod, trying to parse out what I do know. What is true. What isn't.

"Hey," she says, a whisper. Her hands reach out and wrap around my elbows, fingertips so gentle on the delicate skin.

And suddenly it's too much. Standing on the vast brick porch, columns rising up on either side of us, Charlie soft and strong in front of me, I can't hold it in anymore. The dam bursts, releasing days' worth of tears.

"I think he's lying," I choke out through a clogged throat. "Owen's lying about something or everything and I don't know what to do. I don't know how to do this."

Charlie's face crumples. She never cries her own tears. Not really. Even on her worst days, when she swears her voice doesn't fit who she is and she has no idea how to tell her parents how she feels or thinks about herself, she never cries. Her eyes may well up, but the tears never fall. At least, not in front of me. Only when I break down does she fall to pieces too. Now she bridges the already small space between us, slowly, as though she's trying not to scare me. But I'm not scared. Not of her. I'm desperate. Desperate for this feeling to go away, and the only solution is Charlie. I slide my arms around her waist and bury my face in her neck, inhaling raggedly. I feel her tense at first, but then her hands are in my hair, smoothing and enclosing.

"I know you don't," she says. "I'm so sorry."

"What do I do? Tell me what to do."

"I wish I could."

The tears keep coming, my nose pressed against her throat. They're almost a relief, warm and gentle, and their motion down my face feels like being rocked to sleep. Slowly, I relax, but I don't let go of Charlie. Her cheek rests against my forehead. All I'd have to do is tip my chin a little and our mouths would touch. I press my fingers into her back, pulling her closer. Pulling me closer.

Obliterating any space between us. I can feel her heart pound against mine, and for the first time in days, I feel *right*. I lift my head, settle my eyes on her lips.

And then she clears her throat and releases me. She keeps one of my hands, but now there's so much space between us. Too much.

"How do you know?" she asks.

"How . . . how do I know what?"

"That Owen's lying."

I take a deep breath and try to clear my head. "We had a family meeting last night, and Mom wanted him to tell me what happened so we were all on the *same page*." I hook finger quotes around the last two words. "He just . . . I just know. His whole story makes no sense. Hannah wouldn't have been pissed about her wrist if she'd wanted to have sex. She would've been angry at herself, not him."

Charlie nods. "I know."

We stand there in silence, staring at each other. I'm breathing hard, as if I've been running laps around the school.

"But it's more than that. It was like . . . god, I could *feel* the lie on his tongue or something." I grip my stomach, trying to hold myself together. "And then later, we played basketball, and it just felt so . . . so . . . normal, and at the same time, it was all wrong. And I couldn't figure out *why* and the only thing I can think of is that he actually did . . . that he . . ."

"Shhh," she says, squeezing my fingers. "It's okay. Breathe."

I do, slowly, just like last night during my panic attack, but this time on my own, Charlie's thumb rubbing circles on the back of my hand.

"He's my brother," I say when my chest feels loose enough. "I love him, Charlie."

She doesn't say anything, just looks at me, sadness a physical thing between us.

I press my eyes closed. *My brother.* He's the boy who smiled softly at me from across the table when I told our parents I was bi, as though he'd always known. He dogged my steps during that horrible summer before freshman year, refusing to let me wallow even when I snarled and screamed at him. I've never been without him, could never imagine he'd hurt anyone. I've always trusted him.

But the boy from the woods by the lake, the boy strutting through the school halls these past few days, a new sort of story trailing in his wake, a horrible story — that boy isn't my brother. He's not anyone I could ever trust.

"I need to see her," I say. "I need to see Hannah."

Charlie lifts an eyebrow. "Are you ready for that?"

My heart slams into my ribs. *Ready* is the wrong word. I'm not ready for any of this. But Hannah wasn't either. "Do you think she wants to see me?"

"She does. She's asked about you more than once."

"Really?"

"She's been worried. I mean, she's worried about a lot of shit, but she's also worried about your friendship."

"God."

"Let's go now. I'll go with you. I just need to get my stuff."

"What about the meeting?"

"The meeting is about how to help Hannah." Charlie twines my fingers with hers. "Let's go actually help her."

CHAPTER ELEVEN

HANNAH LIVES in a big white house with a huge wraparound porch. It pretty much begs you to drink sweet tea at twilight while your feet dangle off the green-painted bench swing and fireflies flicker through the hazy air. Her father is a lawyer, and her mother spends half of her time curating a small art gallery in Nashville and the other half reliving her misspent youth through her daughter. Consequently, Hannah savors—to a comic degree—making sure she's pretty much a nail raked over the chalkboard of her mother's nerves. She wears nothing but bohemian dresses Mrs. Prior says look like "something in which you'd smoke marijuana" and brightly colored tights under denim shorts, going braless whenever possible. Regardless, there's rarely an event at Pebblebrook that doesn't have Mrs. Prior in attendance. She even came to an Empower meeting once. Hannah spent the entire hour slumped in her chair with her arms folded while the rest of us smiled politely at her mother's stories about how she met and married Hannah's dad when she was nineteen. It was beyond awkward.

As Charlie pulls her truck to a stop in front of the Priors' sprawling front porch, I think about the first time I met Hannah. It was right here, two weeks after school started in ninth grade. Her dad wanted to throw a Labor Day barbecue for the entire freshman class. Charlie and I came together and pretty much kept to ourselves.

But Hannah found us anyway.

We'd ventured into the backyard, the sparkling lake filling our vision. Kids we'd just met flung themselves off the dock and into the water, screaming with a kind of glee that made something in me ache. The memory is so sharp. Standing there, the manicured grass soft under my feet, wondering if I'd ever feel as wild and happy as those swanning into the lake.

"It's even better close up," a voice had said. Right into my ear. I turned, meeting a pair of flashing green eyes and hair so light red it almost looked pink. Hannah grinned and took my hand. I barely had time to grab Charlie's arm before Hannah started running toward the dock, her fingers still gripping mine.

She didn't stop running until all three of us were in the lake, the clothes still covering our swimsuits be damned.

I smile at the memory but it fades as soon as I step out of the car. The house is as inviting as ever—the porch swept clean of autumn leaves, a wreath woven with purple and orange flowers hanging from the door, a few windows already lit. So normal.

Still, nerves coil in my gut. Because this is anything but normal.

"This is a bad idea," I say.

Charlie doesn't respond, just rounds the car and links her arm with mine, gently leading me up the steps. She presses a finger to the doorbell.

"She knows we're coming," she says.

"She does?"

"I texted her. She's not a big fan of surprises lately."

I suck in a breath, focus my attention on the twirl of ivy lacing through the fake flowers in the wreath.

"Sorry," Charlie says, looking at me. "I shouldn't have said that."

"It's true, isn't it?"

She nods as footsteps sound inside. I tighten my grip on Charlie's arm, but then loosen it and release her. The dead bolt slides free on the door and suddenly I'm all arms and legs, with no clue what to do with my hands or my feet or my face.

The heavy wooden door swings open and Hannah steps into the soft glow of the porch light. She flicks the lock on the glass storm door and opens that, too.

"Hey," Charlie says.

"Hi," she says back, and her voice is so . . . *Hannah*, but thin, like it's splintering at the edges.

I try to say hello, my mouth opening and closing, but I can't get the sounds out. I can't even look at her. I stare at her silver-painted toenails and then the slim ankles emerging from her black yoga pants as we follow her into the house.

"My parents went to run some errands and pick up dinner," she says as she weaves through rooms that have always looked like something right out of a Pottery Barn catalog.

"I'm surprised they left you alone," Charlie says.

We start climbing the glossy hardwood stairs to the second floor and Hannah huffs a dry-sounding laugh. "I had to promise I'd take a nap."

"How's that going?"

"Excellent," Hannah deadpans. "Can't you tell?"

Charlie offers a small laugh. My face splits into a smile, but god, it feels so strange on my face right now, it almost hurts.

We reach Hannah's room — the last door at the end of a long hallway. Inside, a fire blazes over fake gas-infused logs, and signs of Hannah's hibernation are everywhere. Her bed is a four-poster canopy with sheer, coral-hued curtains tied back with gold ribbon. The duvet is more coral and gold and crimson swirled together in a mandala pattern, matching pillows and sheets covering the mattress in a messy wrinkle. Books litter the end of the bed, some of them open and face-down. Her laptop sits propped on a pillow, the screen paused on some superhero's grimace in midbattle. The entire room smells like a mixture of jasmine tea and Vicks Vapo-Rub, a tub of which sits on her nightstand. Hannah's mom uses that stuff for everything from headaches to paper cuts to stomach viruses.

Hannah walks over to her bed and pushes everything to the side. A few books slide off the edge and onto the floor, but she doesn't pick them up. Instead, she climbs onto the mattress. I hear a soft *wap-wap* sound and I know she's patting the space next to her in invitation, but the motion is a blur in my peripheral vision. Charlie presses her fingers to the small of my back—my feet move closer and closer.

Charlie settles in next to Hannah and I sit in front of them, tucking one leg under me while the other dangles off the side. Silence blankets over us, the occasional *pop-crack* of the fire the only sound. I stare at my jeans, at the individual threads forming the whole.

"Mara."

A whisper, too gentle.

"Mara, please."

Slowly, I lift my eyes to her. I have to. For whatever reason, she wants me to look at her and I can't deny her that. I can't deny her anything ever again. My gaze finds her face, the sting of tears instantaneous.

She's my Hannah—my best friend next to Charlie—but she's not. There are dark swaths of color under her eyes, and her cheeks sink in more than they should, throwing her already high cheekbones into too-sharp focus.

Even with all that, she's still beautiful. She's still *her*. I want to tell her that, but I'm not even sure what I mean. It's not about how she looks, not really. It's the way she looks at *me*. The way she holds Charlie's hand. The way she invited me into her house in the first place.

Her red-rimmed eyes look a little wet and she lifts her free hand to wipe underneath them, her wrist wrapped in a beige bandage.

"God, I'm so sorry," she says, continuing to swipe at tears. But they're too fast for her, hurtling down her cheeks.

"What?" I ask, shocked into speaking. "Hannah, why?"

She shrugs. "Just . . . maybe if I . . ." Her eyes flutter closed and I don't know what to say, if anything. Charlie just waits, patient, while Hannah squeezes the blood from Charlie's hand.

Finally, Hannah takes a deep breath. "He was so drunk."

Everything in me seizes up as I realize she's about to tell me what happened. A burning cold spreads through my chest, half terrified of what's about to come out of her mouth and half relieved I don't have to ask.

"Everything was fine," she says, glancing at me and then away. "I mean, you saw us. We got a drink and danced a little, but he just kept going back for more of that punch until I finally convinced him to go on a walk. We got to that overlook, and we've had this inside joke for a while now that it would be a funny place to have . . . to have . . ." She swallows and licks her lips. "To have sex. So we started making out, and next thing I know, we're lying on a bench and it was about to happen and I freaked out. I was cold and uncomfortable and I kept imagining someone walking by. I told him to stop."

Her eyes glaze over and I reach out a hand, placing it softly on her knee. She drags her eyes to mine.

"I told him to stop, Mara."

My eyes well with tears, but I let them come. They feel right. So do the words in my head, so I let them come too. "I know you did."

My belief seems to break her. It breaks me, too. To believe one person is to disbelieve another. Panic clouds my mind and suddenly I just want my mom, want to talk this through, get her to hear me, let her make me hear her. But then Hannah starts sobbing, dropping forward until her head is in my lap, and I know my belief belongs with her. I can't think about the other side of this belief right now — all that stark disbelief left in its wake.

"I'm sorry, I'm sorry, I'm sorry," she says, all in one ragged breath.

I cry with her, smoothing my hands through her hair.

"I'm sorry it was him," she says. "I'm sorry it was Owen."

God, she's apologizing to *me*, because he's my brother.

"Shhh," I say, covering her with my body so I can hold her. Charlie leans over too, her hands sliding up my arms so all three of us are tangled up.

I'm not sure how long we stay like that, a little knot of friends and tears. Finally, we unravel our arms and legs and Charlie grabs a box of tissues from Hannah's bedside table.

"Maybe if I'd said no louder," Hannah says. "Or . . . I don't know. Maybe if we hadn't already had sex, or—"

"Stop," Charlie says, her voice tense. "That puts the blame on you, Hannah, and that's bullshit. Even if he was drunk. You said no, plain and simple."

"But it's not," Hannah says almost dreamily, as if she's talking to herself. "It's not simple. I loved him. I trusted him. I never thought he would . . ." Her voice trails off and she shakes her head before going on. "Then, at the hospital, everything happened so fast once my parents got there. The hospital called the police without even asking me and then Mom wanted me to do a rape kit and I . . ." She swallows and looks down. "It was so awful. It was the worst thing I've ever experienced and it took hours. And then the state attorney was so . . . god, I don't know. He was just so matter-of-fact. It was a nightmare, over and over again. And he kept asking my parents if *I* was sure it had actually happened. Why does no one ask *me?*"

"Honey," Charlie says, wiping a tissue under Hannah's eyes. "Your parents were just scared. And really pissed off."

Hannah nods.

"Wait," I say. "You don't want to press charges?"

"I don't know," Hannah says. "It doesn't matter, anyway— my parents want to. I don't know if I would've even told anyone if Charlie hadn't found me. But it's not up to my parents in the end. My dad says the state attorney decides if they think they have a case. So I don't know. I don't know what I want to happen. I just . . . I wish it hadn't . . ." She heaves a shaky breath. "This is such a mess. People at school already hate me, don't they?"

Charlie and I glance at each other, eyes touching and then darting away, but it's enough to tell Hannah everything we'd never tell her with words.

"Owen's the only one talking right now," Charlie says. His

name sounds strange in my ears, like when you repeat a word over and over again until it loses all meaning. "That's all."

"He does love to talk," Hannah says flatly.

"Okay," Charlie says, inhaling deeply. "Let's talk about something else, just for a little while."

"Good idea," I say.

But then the three of us sit there in silence. Hannah lays her head in my lap, and my fingers move through her hair, pulling gently at her strawberry strands. They're knot free and smooth, nearly straight with slick grooming, as though her mother took a vigorous brush through them.

And Hannah let her.

Somehow, my sadness doubles.

"Let's watch something," I say. I pull Hannah's computer closer. "What've you been watching?"

The Avengers," Hannah says. She moves off my lap and scoots her butt down, burrowing into her covers and sighing heavily as she tucks the comforter up to her chin.

"Perfect."

The three of us pile closer together, Hannah in the middle, and I hit play on the movie. It picks up midexplosion, trucks flying through the air and some guy in a red suit zipping around the sky and babbling sarcastically. I try to let the bright colors and pretty people numb my thoughts, but I can't stop thinking.

I don't know if I would've even told anyone if Charlie hadn't found me.

Emotions collide — relief that maybe the state won't press

charges, because then we can all move on from this sooner than later. And then I hate myself for that thought, because if you separate the person who did this to Hannah from my family, I'd be calling for his blood.

And then there's my own silence, my own fear, my own story. Mr. Knoll and his smug smile, the way he just stood there, totally invulnerable. He held all the power. He could call me a stupid little bitch, and I couldn't do one damn thing about it.

How different would the past three years of my life have been if someone had walked in, if someone had found me as I ran out of that classroom, tears a blinding mess all over my face?

If I'd confided in the mother who's always been there.

I feel a tap on my shoulder and glance over Hannah, who is burrowed deep in the covers half asleep. Charlie smiles at me, her arm stretched underneath Hannah's neck to reach my shoulders, her fingers fiddling with the ends of my hair.

I could tell her. I could tell Charlie anything. I *have* told her everything. Everything except this. But it's been so long, and the only thing that can come of a confession like that is embarrassment that I waited three years to open my mouth.

The ending credits are just starting to roll when a knock sounds on Hannah's door. Hannah jerks beside me, then relaxes, sitting up a little as her mom sticks her sandy blond head into the room.

"Hannah, is that Charlie's car? Ask her if she wants to stay for —"

Mrs. Prior's voice chokes off as her gaze finds me. She stands completely frozen in the doorway, perfectly pressed into her pencil skirt and tailored blouse. She's the epitome of put-together. Expect for her expression, which can be described only as horrified, her mouth a wide chasm and growing wider. Then, suddenly, it snaps shut, the clack of her teeth colliding echoing through the quiet room.

"Everything all right, Melanie?" Mr. Prior says, coming up behind his wife and peering into the room. Whereas Mrs. Prior's face went white, crimson spills up Mr. Prior's neck and over his cheeks, bulging out his eyes.

Hannah kicks down the covers and climbs over Charlie and off the bed. "Dad. Don't."

"Get out," Mr. Prior says through gritted teeth. He pushes the door open and Mrs. Prior moves out of his way, her face still wan and her arms curled around herself.

I blink at him, confused, while Hannah shakes her head. "Dad—"

"I said, get out of my house!" Mr. Prior's eyes are still pinned on me.

Oh, god.

He's talking to me.

Hands shaking, I push the covers off my body and swing my feet to the floor. I expect my legs to crumple underneath me, but somehow they hold me up and drag me closer to the door.

"How dare you come here," Mr. Prior says.

"Holy shit, Dad!" Hannah says, pulling at her father's arm. "It's not her fault."

"Hasn't your family done enough?" Mr. Prior continues, not even acknowledging Hannah's language. "You have to come here and make her relive it? Your brother is lucky I haven't come over there and kicked his ass to kingdom come."

"Hang on, Mr. Prior," Charlie says at my side. When she crossed the room, I have no idea. I'm numb, snared in a hurting, hateful glare. "Mara wanted to see Hannah. She's not—"

"Oh, I'm sure she did. But I'm afraid that's not appropriate at this time. You have to know that, Charlie." Mr. Prior never looks away from me. "Please leave my daughter alone."

"I'm sorry," I say. I'm not sure why, but it seems like the only thing to say.

"Mara, don't go," Hannah says, her voice thick. "This is ridiculous. Dad, she believes me! You can't just kick her out. Mom, tell him."

"Hannah," Mrs. Prior says, gliding her hand down Hannah's smooth hair. "Please, calm down."

"Honey, you've been through so much," Mr. Prior says, his voice instantly going soft. "But Mara cannot be here right now. He's her *brother*."

My head bobbles in a nod as I try to slip past Mr. Prior into the hallway, but Hannah stops me with a hand on my arm. "Mara."

"I don't want to make this harder," I say softly. I feel an unbearable need to whisper, to hide.

"You're not," she says, tears spilling freely. It used to take so much to get Hannah to cry. She and Charlie are alike in that way. They keep things close until they can't do anything else but boil over. Maybe we were all like that, before. Now she just looks so tired, water ready to leak out of her at any given moment.

Mr. Prior says nothing else, just moves into Hannah's room and begins straightening the bed, slapping at the pillows as if he's trying to remove all traces of me.

"I'm sorry," Hannah says. "They're just . . ."

"It's all right." I try to smile at her, because I really *don't* want to make this harder for her. Charlie says something to Hannah I can't make out as I back away down the hall, and Hannah nods. Soon, Charlie's at my side, my hand in hers. Always, my hand in hers.

We make it outside and I throw myself into Charlie's truck.

"I don't want to talk about it," I say, before Charlie can offer platitudes. Before she can say, *It's not your fault* or *Her parents are just upset* or *It's not you they're really angry with.* All true statements, on the surface. But somewhere under my skin, I know they aren't the whole truth.

No, none of us ever thought Owen would do something like this. But maybe signs were there, some hidden darkness that I explained away as spirit or passion or drive. Owen's never been violent with me or with anyone, for that matter. He's never been in a physical fight. He's never talked about girls like they're just pieces of ass, at least not around me. So what did I miss? Because I had to have missed something, somewhere. Didn't I? I'm his twin. He's half of me, I'm half of him.

I close my eyes and let the gentle hum of the tires over asphalt calm me down. I didn't miss anything. I couldn't have.

Because that guy who hurt Hannah?

I don't know him at all.

CHAPTER TWELVE

I'M SITTING ON THE BOTTOM STEP leading up to my porch, putting off the moment I have to walk inside my house, when the front door opens. My mother's voice drifts into the night air, her words so soft that I catch only a few.

"... thank you for stopping by ... needs you right now ... such a good friend ..."

Soon, the door closes and footsteps sound above me and I turn around, meeting Alex's dark eyes.

He makes his way down the stairs and sits next to me.

"Hey," he says.

"Hey. You leaving already?"

"I just came by to give Owen some sheet music for this piece in orchestra and his iPad. He left it at my house last week." His mouth twists when he speaks, as if he's swallowing a grimace.

"Where's your car?" I glance around the driveway again. I was so out of it when Charlie dropped me off, I wouldn't be surprised if I'd totally missed it, bright yellow notwithstanding.

"I walked."

"You walked? It's three miles."

"So?"

He picks at a loose thread on his jeans. Picks and picks until it breaks free in a long, unraveling strand. He flicks it off his finger and onto the sidewalk. I watch him for a few more seconds, wondering why he's not staying for dinner. He usually eats with us a couple times a week, same as Charlie. They're an extension of Owen and me, our neighboring stars. But I'm not sure Charlie will ever step foot in my house again. It fills me up slowly, the idea that nothing will ever be the same.

"Are you and Owen fighting?" I ask.

Alex doesn't move, but the skin around his eyes tightens. "Of course not. I mean, I'm such a *good friend*, right?"

He pushes himself to his feet and starts to walk away.

"Hey, wait," I say, standing too. I glance back at my house, the warmth-filled windows, the dinner my parents are probably putting on the table, four place settings all in the right spots. The perfect little family. "You want a ride?"

The porch light hits just shy of his face, and his hands are stuffed into his pockets. Alex has never been easy to read, but I can almost feel something in him bending toward me, just like I am to him.

"Yeah, okay," he says.

I dig my keys out of my bag and soon we're closed inside the car I share with Owen, tires squealing as I pull out of the driveway too fast. My house fades out of my rearview and it's like a tether snapping free. I put the windows down and hold out my free hand, letting the cool night air drizzle through my fingers and hair. Alex does the same, resting his head against the seat, his arm hanging out the window.

Near downtown, Alex's street comes up on the right and I flick on the blinker, slowing the car to make the turn. Slower . . . slower . . .

Over the console, our gazes lock. He doesn't say anything, doesn't even blink, but the tiniest smile ghosts over his mouth, softening all those tight features he wore at my house. It's enough to make me accelerate right past his street.

We drive around for a while, content just to listen to music and feel ourselves moving over the earth. When I pull into the parking lot of Orange Street Cemetery, Alex laughs.

"I do have other places I like to go, you know," he says.

"Really?" I slip my keys from the ignition. "I thought it was all tombstones, all the time, with you."

He snaps his fingers dramatically. "Dammit, I forgot my violin again."

I laugh, happy to see the Alex from Glow Galaxy, the Owen-free Alex I'm starting to suspect is the real Alex. Light from the full moon spears through the windows and the silvery beams make his eyes dance.

"Well, it's not about the tombstones for me," I say. "It's about the stories."

He follows me out of the car, and we walk up the small hill

that crests before dipping down into a sort of valley, tombstones almost glowing in the dark. The river shines beyond them, its surface sparkling under the moon.

"Wow," Alex breathes.

"Yeah. It's beautiful."

"In a really creepy sort of way."

"It's more gloomy than creepy. Gloomy can be beautiful."

"You've been hanging around Charlie too long."

I try to laugh at that, but it gets stuck in my throat. Instead, I slide my fingers between his and start down the hill. He doesn't pull away, just folds his hand around mine, nearly swallowing it.

When we reach the bottom, I unlace our fingers. The feeling of a hand in mine is so familiar, but so different with Alex. It's intense and scary, and a flare of guilt sparks somewhere in my chest. I step away from him, catching my breath as I read the nearest epitaph.

We wander among the graves for a while, and pretty soon Alex catches on that I'm looking for girls with more than just *daughter* or *mother* or *wife* on their stone.

"Here's *Beautiful friend*," he says, squatting in front of an ancient-looking marker.

I join him, kneeling in the silvery grass. "*Naomi Lark, 1899–1920*. God, there are so many young women in here."

He nods, swiping his fingers so gently over the engraved words on the stone, it pulls a knot into my throat.

"I'd like that on my stone someday," he says, standing up and dusting his hands off. "*Beautiful friend*. It's simple, but . . . damn, what a legacy."

I smile at him, but my thoughts are with Charlie and Hannah and me earlier today, how there was a sort of beauty in the three of us huddled and crying on Hannah's bed, holding one another together. A sort of beauty, but also a sort of ugliness because of why we were there, who I was there for. Because of the *undoing* I felt going on somewhere underneath my skin, like a constellation being split apart.

"Mr. Prior kicked me out of his house today," I say.

Alex raises his eyebrows. "You went to see Hannah?"

I nod.

"How . . . how is she?"

I start walking toward the river and Alex follows. I don't answer for a while — it suddenly seems like such a difficult question. The water rolls over itself, beckoning us closer, the moon glinting off its surface. The scene looks like something out of an old black-and-white movie.

"She's sad," I finally say, stopping where the bank dips and the grasses get longer along the river's edge. "And angry."

Next to me Alex sighs. "And her dad kicked you out?"

"Yeah. He's sad and angry too."

"But you didn't do anything. Owen's the one who —"

My eyes connecting with his cut him off. He looks away, but even in the dark, I can see the confusion thick on his face. His hand finds mine and our fingers tangle clumsily in a desperate attempt to grab hold.

We stand there for a few minutes, silent, the dead resting behind us and the pulsing life of the river in front of us. It flows gently, as though it's trying to make peace of all the chaos. Suddenly, everything feels too heavy. I sink into the grass, my legs folded underneath me.

"Why have we never done this before?" I ask. Alex sits down next to me, resting his elbows on his knees.

"What, frolic through a cemetery? We just did that yesterday."

I shove his shoulder and he laughs. "I was talking about hanging out."

"We've hung out."

"Not just us."

He shrugs. "I don't know why. We should've. We are now, at least."

I look up at the clear sky. The cemetery is far enough away from downtown Frederick that the stars look like a thousand tiny night-lights plugged into the dark.

Though we've known each other forever, taken classes together, performed in the same holiday concerts for years, Alex and I have never belonged to each other, never sought each other out.

And I've never felt so desperate to change that, for both of us.

"Tell me something," I say.

"Like what?"

"Something I don't know about you."

He purses his lips, a little smile playing on the edge.

"Oh god," I say. "Walking around the cemetery with your violin is your only hobby, isn't it?"

A laugh bursts from his mouth, but he nods. "Found me out."

A chilly breeze swings in between us and I scoot a little closer to him. "Seriously."

He sighs. "Seriously? I hate performing."

"Oh. We're just talking."

He nudges my shoulder but then doesn't move it away. "No. I mean, that's what I'm telling you. I hate performing, playing the violin in public."

"Really? But . . . you're amazing."

He shrugs. "I like playing, don't get me wrong. In my room. Or during practices with just the orchestra. But I hate concerts. All those eyes on me while I offer them bits of my soul. It stresses me out."

"Wow, bits of your soul?" I tease, but I understand what he's saying. It's why I've never learned to play the guitar or write songs, even though I've wanted to since the first time Charlie offered to teach me back in ninth grade. It's just too much . . . *me.* Articles for Empower are different—parts of my mind and opinions I need to say because I can't say so much else. But music . . . it's raw emotion.

He shrugs. "I go out for first chair because it's something I feel I should do, you know? I'm at the performing arts school because my parents like the academics there too and it's good for college transcripts. I'm capable of first chair. Therefore, I do it."

"What do you *want* to do?"

He rubs the back of his neck. "Honestly? Study history. Maybe teach it one day. I really love Ms. Cabrero's class. She has fun with it, you know?"

"For real? Charlie's mom was a history teacher before she became a principal."

Immediately, I wish I could take back the comparison. Why am I talking about Charlie right now? Lucky for me, Alex just smiles and nods.

"I like the stories," he says. "The way one event can influence the next hundreds of years, the way we can just . . . *know* these lives that were lived and how much we're changed by them."

"Wow."

"That's the actual reason I come to the cemetery sometimes. I mean, I do like the quiet, but you're right: it's about the stories, lives already lived. It makes me feel . . ." He trails off, eyes going distant.

"What? What does it make you feel?"

He locks his eyes with mine. "Brave. Not so alone."

My throat thickens and all I can do is bobble my head in agreement.

"What about you?" he asks, leaning closer. I could graze his forehead with mine if I moved an inch.

"What about me?"

"Do you like singing? Is that what you want to do?"

"Honestly? I don't know. I do like it. I even love it sometimes, but I feel sort of like you do. The performance part of it is hard for me. That's why I never go out for concert solos or big roles in the musicals."

"You should," he says. "I've heard you sing. You're incredible."

My stomach flutters. "Well, you're incredible at violin too.

Doesn't mean that's what we're supposed to do. I think you'd make an amazing historian."

He smiles.

"But," I go on, "I don't know what else I'd do."

"Your Empower articles are really good. What about journalism or writing books or something like that?"

"You read my Empower articles?"

"Every single one since the day you started it."

"Really? Owen thinks they're ridiculous, like it's all this big joke."

Alex shakes his head. Then he reaches out a hand and smoothes a lock of hair off my cheek. He doesn't tug on it, or run his finger down its length. Just tucks it behind my ear. Goose bumps break out on my arms and I can't tell if I like them or not.

"They're not ridiculous. They're *you*, Mara. That one about the double standards and sex last year? I sent it to my sister. She loved it, made all of her friends read it. And everyone in school talked about it for weeks. It was important."

I just stare at him, tears stinging my eyes.

Because he's right. Those articles are what I want to say — the words I *can* say, because I'm too scared and small to say other words. The right words.

"Greta took my place in Empower," I tell him.

"What? Like, you quit?"

"Not exactly. More like . . . cajoled into leaving."

"Oh. Wow. Can she do that?"

I shrug. "It was the right thing to do. For now."

Realization dawns on his face. "Oh."

"Yeah."

"I'm sorry."

"It's not your fault."

He nods and a beat passes before he speaks again. "It's somebody's fault, though." His cheeks and lips twitch, his voice thick and low, and I realize he's trying not to cry.

My heart feels thin and fragile in my chest, because we both know who that somebody is. I push up to my knees and cut through the few inches between us.

"Alex." I slide my hands up his arms, his sweater soft and fuzzy under my fingers. He presses his eyes closed and inhales a ragged breath. I grip his shoulders, then move my hands to his neck, then to his face. I don't know why. I don't know what I'm doing. I'm scared and memories threaten to creep in and chew me up, but there's something I need here. Something that needs me. Something about this feels right, and dammit if I don't need something to feel right.

He lifts himself to his knees too and his arms come around me, slipping around my waist slowly as if he's waiting for me to move away. I don't. Instead, I pull his face to mine until our foreheads touch. Then our noses.

"Are you . . . are you sure?" he whispers, his breath warm over my mouth.

There's a split second when I'm not, when I remember that my heart is miles away with a dark-haired guitar player and probably always will be. There's another split second when all of my senses take in his expression, consider the press of his fingers, search for a threat. But I don't find one, and all of those split seconds taper down to a deep pit of need in my gut.

I kiss him. A single sweep of my lips over his. The light scruff on his cheeks scrapes my skin and makes me crave a smoother face, but it's also intoxicating. Different. I press my mouth to his, opening his lips with mine. He responds, sighing into my mouth and sliding one hand up to cup the back of my head. Everything starts so gently, but then our kiss grows fevered, desperate, hands in a mad rush for a kind of contact that I've almost never let myself have in the past four years unless it was with Charlie. There's a sadness to this kiss, and that feels right too.

A glow of panic hovers on all of my edges, but it doesn't sink in. That panic is *me*, it's not him, and I really do want this. I want to be able to want it and, more than that, to actually have it. I press myself closer to him and his mouth moves from mine to just below my ear, trailing down my throat and igniting my skin, even with the cool air around us. The flat plane of his chest, the rasp of his jaw over my skin—he feels incredible. I haven't kissed a guy since sophomore year, when I went out with Mathias Dole for a few months. He was boring and safe, let me pick where we went on dates, let me initiate anything physical between us, which I almost never did. Nothing other than kissing. I haven't even been out with another guy since.

I was too wrapped up in Charlie by then.

Alex's hands move up my ribs and some part of me knows I still am. The larger part of me doesn't care. I made my choice and she let me.

I press my face to his neck, inhaling his smell that reminds me of fall and camping and running. Gradually, our movements slow, our kisses fade, but I'm still curled around him and we stay like that for a long while, kneeling in the grass. My face tucked into his shoulder, his hands smoothing down my back, we create our own little warm pocket in the world. We don't kiss again. We don't need to. We just need this.

Here, there is no Owen. No twin brother. There's not even a Charlie or a Tess. There's only Alex and me. All of our confusion and hurt melting into comfort.

And for now, that's enough.

CHAPTER THIRTEEN

BY THE TIME I DROP ALEX OFF and pull up to my house, it's nearly nine o'clock. I check my phone for the first time all night after I park in the driveway. Mom has texted and called about five times, so I know I'm probably in deep shit with her.

Stepping out of the car, I have a sudden urge to talk to Charlie. There's some feeling here in my chest I can't parse — part relief, part guilt. I know that last one has absolutely no reason to be there, but it continues to pick at me as I walk up the steps. Maybe if I just talk to her, tell her I've been hanging out with Alex for a couple hours, maybe even tell her that we kissed, because that's what best friends do. I need her to tell me it's okay.

Before I can second-guess myself, I tap her name on my screen. Charlie hates talking on the phone, but I need her voice. She'll just have to get over the actual phone call. It rings several times before the telltale click sounds in my ear, but there's no greeting on the other end, just some rustling sounds.

"Hello?" I say.

"Don't . . ." I hear Charlie say, but it's distant. Like she's not the one holding the phone.

"Oh, come on, I should talk to her, don't you think?" An unfamiliar female voice. A laugh.

"Tess, I asked you not to answer it . . ."

There's more shuffling, another laugh, then a click as someone ends the call.

I blink at the screen, trying to push back the prick of tears. I shove the phone into my back pocket and force myself up the stairs and into my house.

Mom accosts me the minute I close the door. She stands in the entryway hall, glaring at me with her hands on her hips and her curls twisted into a messy bun. She looks tired. Lately, it seems as if everyone looks tired all the time. Suddenly, I feel the same, all my elation from the river and Alex dissolved by that tinny little laugh on the phone.

"Where have you been?" Mom asks.

"Out." I move around her and into the kitchen. I fling open the freezer and grab the pint of cookies and cream I remember seeing this morning.

"Out?" she says, following me. "That's all you have to say? I've barely seen you in days."

"I was at Charlie's, that's all." The lie burns cold on my tongue, colder than the ice cream I'm spooning into my mouth. I dig up another scoop and head for the stairs. "I have homework."

She stops me with a hand on my arm. "Mara. What is going on? Talk to me, honey."

There's so much I want to tell her. How much I miss Charlie, how I just kissed Alex under the moon. Things a daughter should be able to talk about with her mom over mugs of hot tea. But there are too many other unsaid things that keep me from saying anything at all. How I feel my brother — my family, myself — splitting in two. How scared I am all the time. How, for the past three years, I have a nightmare at least once a week about losing my voice, Mr. Knoll's fingers ripping the vocal cords right out of my throat.

How, last night, I had the same dream, except this time it was Owen's fingers, my voice shimmering like a dull diamond in his palm. I was literally speechless, nothing but a broken heart.

"I'm tired, Mom."

She frowns but releases my arm and nods, her eyes sliding to my ice cream. "That's not a proper dinner. I could heat you up some leftovers."

"I'm fine."

She studies me for a few long seconds, eyes narrowed. Mom's always believed that a good staring contest will cause anyone to crack. When I was ten and broke a picture frame on the mantel while running through the house trying to snap a blanket at the back of Owen's legs, I blamed the cat we had at the time, Zipper. Mom crossed her arms and fixed me with *oh really* eyes until I caved. She's held to this tactic faithfully, even after it was no longer effective. The summer after Mr. Knoll, she'd watch me during dinner — the only time I ventured out of my room — a sort of hunger in her eyes as she waited for me to talk to her. I didn't break then and I'm not breaking now. This is no smashed picture frame.

"All right," she finally says. "But say hello to Owen, okay? He mentioned he hasn't seen you much lately. He misses you."

I pause midstep, a scream rising up my throat like a flash flood. I hate how calm she sounds, how normal she's acting, how sure she is that Owen is still the Owen I grew up with, the Owen holding my hand in the stars.

As though sensing my hesitation, she sighs. "Mara, please. He needs you."

My brother used to need me, I think. *Owen McHale does not.*

But then a sad lonely voice from last night filters through my head, delicate smoke from a candle. *Please. It's still me. I'm just me.*

Without another word, I head upstairs. Icy condensation gathers between my fingers, the cardboard pint growing soft. I stuff another milky bite into my mouth, but I can barely swallow it. On my way down the hall to my room, I drop the whole thing, spoon and all, into the bathroom trash can.

"Mar!"

His voice sends my stomach lurching upward. I didn't expect that, the way his voice is suddenly such a shock. I walk toward his meticulously neat bedroom, a flash of red snagging my attention.

A flash of red and another unfamiliar female voice.

I stop in his doorway. He's on his bed, his back pressed against the headboard, an open textbook in his lap.

There's a girl next to him. Her hair is stick-straight and nearly black, her cherry-red fitted T-shirt bright and peppy. The laugh on her lips dies when she sees me.

"Mar, hey," Owen says, grinning. "What's up?"

"Nothing," I say.

"You know Angie, right?" He nods toward the girl. "She plays flute."

"Yeah, sure." I study her, her name pulling up a memory from my history of music class last year, but that girl had hair so curly it seemed almost alive. "You straightened your hair."

"Oh, yeah." She laughs nervously, pulling at her locks. "I flat-iron it sometimes." She keeps twisting her hair, her gaze flicking from Owen down to her book and back again. He nudges her with his arm and she grins wider.

"We're studying for calc," Owen says. "Pain in the ass. You want to join?"

I hear him talking, but my thoughts are already gone, rising above the house and through the trees to the lake, finding Hannah crying on her bed.

"Mar?"

I flinch, my name bringing me back to Owen's room. There's something almost manic in his eyes. A feverish glow, some sort of expectation, like he's Mom hoping I'll crumble, like he's hoping last night fixed something between us. Answered some question. But I know it didn't. I knew it then and I know it even more now. Still, I feel myself mirroring his movements, like I always have. It's instinct. A twin thing I've always loved.

"No," I say. "That's okay, I'm good."

His hopeful smile dips, but he nods and tilts his head toward his window. "Gemini later?" Next to him, Angie furrows her brow, clearly curious, but he doesn't explain. Just watches me, his fingertips fiddling with the pages of the textbook.

"Um . . ."

"Come on, Mara. Our twins have been severely neglected lately." A soft smile moves over his mouth. "Please?"

"I'm . . . I'm really tired. I just . . . soon. We'll do it soon, okay?"

He slumps against the headboard but nods. "Yeah. Okay. Soon."

"Good night, Angie," I say softly. I feel myself shaking, *soon* a desperate hope thumping my heart against my ribs.

CHAPTER FOURTEEN

THE NEXT EVENING, the drive into Nashville with Charlie is full of lots of music and absolutely zero talking. School sucked, whispers trailing me in the halls like vicious ghosts. Every time I saw Owen's laughing friends, I couldn't decide if I wanted to cry in the bathroom for an hour or rip their heads off. I settled for neither, keeping my head down in the halls and my mouth shut in class. Owen's name was everywhere, but I could never quite catch sight of him, which was a relief.

And also lonely as hell.

In between second and third periods, Angie waved at me in the hallway. And smiled. And said, "Hi, Mara." Her smile slipped when I just stared at her, frozen by the soft look in her eyes. She looked away quickly, hugging her books to her chest. By the time I snapped out of it and realized what an asshole I was being, she was gone.

I ate lunch with Alex outside on the front steps, so I'm not sure if Charlie saw us. Not sure if she'd care anyway. Right now I have no idea what to say to her, a million questions about Tess on the edge of all my thoughts, but I have no right to those questions. I made out with a boy not even twenty-four hours ago.

And I don't regret doing it. I wanted to kiss him. But there's something else swirling around my chest that I can't get a grip on. It's not regret, but a feeling like something is . . . missing. It's probably why neither Alex nor I mentioned the kiss during lunch. We didn't touch. We didn't hold hands or even hug hello or goodbye. We just talked about nothing and ate our overcooked cafeteria cheeseburgers and it was good.

Now, after school, Charlie fidgets next to me in her truck. She adjusts the temperature, the fan speed, the song playing, the volume, and her rearview mirror over and over again. It's amazing how much a person can move while she's driving.

"Nervous?" I ask after she listens to about ten seconds of every song on an entire Silversun Pickups album before giving up and picking Fleurie's latest EP.

"No, of course not," she deadpans. "I'm just about to perform on one of the best stages in Nash-freaking-ville. No big."

"Sorry, dumb question."

She exhales heavily. "It's just . . . what if no one likes my stuff? What if I get booed off the stage? What if . . ."

"What if what? Everyone's going to love you."

Charlie runs her fingers over the hem of her lacy tank top underneath a slouchy T-shirt. "Do I . . . do I look like a boy?"

"You look like Charlie." I say it automatically, not because I'm trying to placate her, but because it's true. Charlie is beautiful and strong. She loves mascara and men's ties and big combat boots and skinny jeans and gloomy girl music and peanut butter on her waffles and Harry Potter almost more than life itself. She's Charlie, like I'm Mara and Hannah's Hannah. "Who do you want to look like?"

She shrugs. "Today I feel a lot more . . . feminine, I guess, but do I even look like that? I just want to look like me. You know, express *me*."

"You do look like you."

"I don't always feel like I do, you know?"

"I think everyone feels like that a little. At least sometimes."

She nods, and immediately, I feel like shit. "I'm sorry. I didn't mean to play it off like it's no big deal."

She relaxes, giving me a soft smile. "I don't understand how I feel half the time. Well, that's not true. I do. I know how I feel. I think I just get stuck between expressing how I feel and how I think I should feel. I mean, I was born a girl, right? So I should *feel* like a girl all the time. Shouldn't I?"

"Should you? Says who?"

She presses her mouth flat. "What does *feel like a girl* even mean, anyway?"

"Exactly."

She blows out a breath, releasing an *ugh* sound with it. I want to take her hand, want to tell her I love her. That's true no matter how she feels, regardless of any Tess or Alex.

So I do. I grab her fingers fluttering near the defrost button — even though it's sunny and nearly seventy degrees outside — and lace us together.

"I love you. You know that, right?" I try to keep emotion out of the words—or at least, any kind of *longing*—forcing strength and steadiness into my voice.

She nods and squeezes my hand, keeping her eyes on the road, and she doesn't let go until we pull into the 3rd and Lindsley parking lot.

"Mara," she says, cutting the ignition. Our hands fall away. "About last night. I didn't mean for Tess—"

"It's okay," I say, unbuckling and opening the car door. If we talk about Tess, we talk about Alex, and I don't want to talk about either.

"But—"

"You've got an audience to enrapture." I push her shoulder toward her own car door. "So let's go enrapture them."

She smiles, but it quickly wobbles, her nerves leaking into her expression.

"Enrapture," I say again, enunciating every syllable and tilting my head so she has to meet my eyes.

Nodding, she inhales a huge breath and takes my hand, squeezing it one more time.

★.

3rd and Lindsley is a dark bar and grill with black floors and servers with lots of piercings and tattoos. The second level has a bunch of tables and chairs, people eating dinner and slurping beer. The first level is where all the action is: a huge stage filled with a drum kit, several microphone stands, and a ton of wires. In front of the stage, a crowd waits for the show to start.

I'm jostled here and there as Charlie and I walk down the side of the room, following a guy named Grant, who has an affinity for the word *dude*, so Charlie can get a sound check. How they do that with a crowd full of people, I have no idea.

"The sound guy uses headphones!" Charlie yells behind her when I voice the question out loud.

"Okay, dude," Grant says, stopping at a door that leads backstage. His closely buzzed head glints under the stage lights. "Head on back and drop off your stuff, then set up your guitar on stage. You're on third, so you can hang out backstage until your turn. Sound good?"

"Yeah," Charlie says vaguely, eyes wide as she takes in the scene.

"Everything all right?" I ask. Or rather, yell.

She nods, swallowing hard.

"Can I come with her?" I ask Grant.

"Sorry, dude. Musicians only. We'll take care of her. You can grab a shady spot out in the audience."

"You'll be okay by yourself?" Charlie asks as Grant gestures toward the door.

"Yeah, sure," I say, but I already feel pressed, all the bodies behind me like walls shrinking inward. "Good luck. You'll be great, I know it."

She pushes her free hand against her stomach, her other hand tight on her guitar case. "Try to get a spot close, okay? So I can see you?"

"Of course."

"Okay. Okay, bye."

Still, she doesn't move, just stands there biting her lip. Behind her, Grant looks less than amused, mouthing something that looks a lot like *teenagers* while glaring at his phone.

I smooth my hand over the top of Charlie's hair—just once, and playfully—then turn her around and press my palm to her back, nudging her toward the door. She goes and I weave through the thick crowd, easing my way closer to the stage. By the time I find a spot a couple rows back from where Charlie now stands tuning her guitar, I'm out of breath and my hands are sweaty. Laughter bursts from the left, a scream from the right, and a slosh of something spills out of a nearby cup and splashes near my feet. I hook my hands around my elbows and hold tight until the lights dim even more and the first musician comes out on stage.

It's a guy about our age, shaggy hair, indiscriminate features, angsty emo song about grieving his lost love by wandering in the woods or something. He's decent and has a really smooth tone to his voice, but he doesn't hold the crowd for very long. Still, plenty of cheers rise up when he finishes, lots of fists in the air and *hell yeah*s.

The next performer is a girl with dark skin and gorgeous curly hair, and she launches into an aria I recognize from school but can't put my finger on the title. She's lowered the key and paired it with an acoustic guitar, and her voice is super folksy. Somehow, it works, the crowd a little more attentive than with Emo Boy.

Finally, Aria Girl strides off stage. There's a pause as a tech guy raises up the microphone a little and checks some pedal on the ground. Charlie's up next. Nerves tighten around my stomach like a fist.

And then she's in front of me, tall and elegant, all trace of nervousness gone. She greets the audience and says her name into the microphone, her voice clear and light. Perfect. As she talks, her eyes drift through the crowd, finding mine before her last name is even out of her mouth.

"This song is for you," she says, her gaze now wandering through the whole crowd.

Then she plays. The first few chords are enough to tell me that I've never heard this song before.

> *Come with me outside,*
> *you don't have to hide,*
> *our masks are crumbling to the ground.*
> *Crushing smiles beneath our feet,*
> *words curled with smoke and heat,*
> *a million girls who can't make a sound.*
>
> *Beauty and strength,*
> *it's a mask, it's a maze,*
> *it's a wonder we're standing up straight.*
> *Beauty and strength,*
> *it's a fight, it's a phase,*
> *don't tell me I don't know my place.*

Charlie doesn't look at me again, but I can't take my eyes off her. The room is a lot more hushed than with the previous two performers, everyone transfixed. Her voice is husky, but also smooth like river water over rocks. The song . . . god, this song. It almost hurts, it's so raw. So . . . Charlie. I can't even think straight as I listen, trying to memorize the words so I can roll them over and over in my head later.

"Damn, that's good stuff. She's fucking amazing," some guy next to me says. I don't know if he's talking to me or his friends or the universe itself, but it doesn't matter. My smile comes easily, hearing some stranger with no loyalty to me or Charlie praising her. Really seeing her.

"Yeah. She's magical, isn't she?" I say.

No one answers, but I don't need them to. I just need this. Charlie.

I spiral through the crowd, needing to get even closer to the stage, Charlie totally electric above me. The song rises, fevered as she repeats the chorus again.

> *Beauty and strength,*
> *it's a mask, it's a maze . . .*

She moves gracefully on the stage, not too expository but energized enough to rivet anyone watching her. Her short hair and lace tank top, combat boots and guitar. I have no idea why she wants to hide all of this from her parents. They'd love seeing her up there. They'd love everything about this.

When she sings, I can barely stay still. It's always been like this, something fluorescent and nearly radioactive lighting up my veins. And it's not only that I like her music, like her voice, like *her.* There's something that lights up in me when she plays, some fundamental part of me aching and fighting to get loose.

There's a reason Charlie is largely considered the best singer in the school. Her voice is like the love child of Adele and Halsey, ensnaring everyone within hearing distance and rendering them completely powerless. The first time I heard her, we were fourteen and had known each other a week, though it felt like longer. It felt like a lifetime. We were in her room, and I'd joked that she was like one of those Sirens from *The Odyssey*. She'd smiled, almost shyly, and started singing some old song from some old movie, her voice all silk and sultry folk.

> *Go to sleep you little babe*
> *Go to sleep you little babe*
> *You and me and the devil makes three*
> *Don't need no other lovin' baby*

I nearly died then and I'm nearly dying now.

I wanted to kiss her then and I want to kiss her now. Do something wild, anything, everything, to match what this song and her words are doing to my blood right now. Scream and run with my fingers catching the air until I collapse.

Her song wraps up, a vehement slamming of her pick over the guitar strings, and the rich sound echoes through the room.

The crowd erupts.

I mean, it absolutely explodes.

I raise my hands in the air, clapping along with everyone, bouncing on my tiptoes and willing her to look at me. She smiles and gives the audience the subtlest of bows, all elegant composure and heaving breaths. Right before she turns away to walk off stage, her eyes find mine. She winks. Actually winks and I can't help but laugh, something giddy and girlish bubbling into my chest.

The audience doesn't quiet down once she leaves the stage. They're not really cheering for her anymore, but there's this restlessness in the crowd now. An expectation or a wanting—I don't know. My own fingertips buzz with impatience and I crane my neck around bodies and toward the stage door, waiting for Charlie to come out.

Needing her to come out.

I head toward the door, barely noticing the blaring multitude. Finally, I spot her dark head and smooth shoulders, a smile on her lips. When she spots me, her smile widens and she waves, moving toward me. She stops every couple of steps to talk, everyone wanting to tell her how amazing she is.

"Hey, oh my god," she says when she reaches me, raking both hands through her hair, making it almost comically tall. "This is wild, right?"

"Yeah. You were amazing." My words seem so paltry, so small. But along with all of this energy, there's a shyness, too. I get it every damn time she sings. I'm not sure if it's awe or envy or a little bit of both.

"Yeah?" she asks.

"Oh my god, yes."

"You don't think it was too——"

I cut her off by taking her hands. Her hands always fit so perfectly in mine. "Seriously, Charlie. That . . . *you* . . . just blew me away. You blew everyone in this room away."

Color floods her cheeks.

"That song," I go on, and her smile grows wider. "Beautiful. No, *beautiful* isn't even the right word. I don't think there *is* a word for what that song was."

"Really?"

"Really. How did it feel?"

She sighs, her eyes fluttering closed for a split second. "Perfect."

"Yeah? It was a good voice day?"

She breaks into another huge smile. "It was. It felt so right, Mara. And it just felt so damn good that it felt right, you know?"

I nod, squeezing her hands. Charlie vacillates between loving and despising her voice. Some days, she says her voice feels like her, expresses what she wants, sounds beautiful and unique in her ears. Other days, it's too high or too clear or not gritty enough.

"It just doesn't *feel* like me," she told me one sunny afternoon in tenth grade. She was working on a song for her vocal teacher, frustration pushing tears into her eyes that she refused to let fall.

"I'm glad," I say now.

"It was fucking incredible," she says through a laugh. She presses both hands to her mouth, then flings them toward the towering stage, where the next act is setting up his electric guitar. "I mean, holy shit, I just did that."

"You did. And it *was* fucking incredible. *I* feel fucking incredible. This whole damn room feels fucking incredible."

She laughs and I laugh and we feel like *us*. We're happy, drunk with exhilaration, even, and I've forgotten how powerful that is — just being happy with your best friend.

"Will you teach me?" I ask, pushing my hands onto her shoulders. She's literally bouncing. Or maybe I am. I think we both are.

"Teach you what?"

"All of it. Guitar, writing songs."

She laughs. "I've been trying to get you to learn guitar for at least two years."

"Well, I'm ready *now*."

"Stubborn."

"Always."

We grin at each other and it feels as though there's more air in the room than before. This feels right. This is us, everything we should be.

"We can start whenever you want," she says, an excited lilt to her voice. "I actually just bought some beginner books because Tess wanted . . . to . . ."

I wait for her to go on, deliver the blow, but she doesn't. Then I realize she probably stopped because I dropped my hands from her shoulders. I can feel the surprised hurt on my face like a thick foundation, covering up anything nonchalant.

"Oh," is all I say.

"Mara —"

"It's fine." I shake Tess off. Tess isn't here on one of the most

160

important nights of my best friend's life. I am. And I refuse to give that up for anybody. "Of course. We can start next week."

She hesitates, but then breaks into another grin. "I can't wait to hear you write a song."

Something sharp and hopeful flares in my chest. It's small, but it's there. For the first time in a long time, I think I do have something to say. Maybe I'm finally ready to say it.

CHAPTER FIFTEEN

THE NEXT MORNING, I wake up ravenous. My stomach feels empty, but there's a different sort of hunger and it feels as though it's clawing out my insides. I can't decide if it's a good feeling or not. After Charlie dropped me off last night, I spent all night trying to sleep, all night failing, my head burning with too many thoughts, songs, words long buried.

After I shower, trying to wash off the energy seeping to the surface of my skin, I sit on the edge of my bed and towel-dry my hair. My feet bounce on the carpet, my chest filled with that sort of carbonated feeling I get before school concerts and the day an Empower issue comes out. The same feeling I had last night while Charlie played. I can't shake this need to do something, anything.

I focus on smoothing leave-in conditioner through my hair, dabbing on a little mascara and lip-gloss, feeling the press of my fingers against the cold bathroom counter. All the little ways I order my world, the ways I make sure I don't disappear. Lately, all of those ways have been slipping away.

I push myself to my feet and over to my closet, distracting

myself from this restlessness with menial decisions. Shirts, pants, shoes, hair up or down. I'm pulling an oversize sweater off one of the built-in shelves when my gaze catches on a pleated black skirt on a hanger. I run my fingers over the smooth cotton.

It's years old and too short for me now. I'd thought about it as an option for my dress code plan and tried it on a few weeks ago, but considering the fact that when I sat down, I felt the cold press of my desk chair on half of my bare butt, it doesn't exactly toe the line between acceptable and a violation.

On my nightstand, my phone buzzes. I let the skirt fall back into place among my clothes and slide my finger over my phone's surface to read the text.

I'm coming back to school today. Meet me at our lockers?

It's from Hannah.

Yes. You know I will, **I text back immediately.** Whatever you need, I'm here.

I stare at the screen as how much I mean those words soaks into my bones. My stomach clenches, wondering what Hannah's going to have to deal with when she sets foot in those halls. Halls loud with laughing boys and giggling girls, side-eyes and whispers. Halls filled with Owen McHale.

Walking back to my closet, I yank the skirt off the hanger.

※ ★ ＊ .

Alex's expression is almost comical when he sees me. After I got dressed, I'd texted him and asked him to pick me up. I didn't really want anyone else to see me, Owen and Charlie included, until I was already at school. I hid in my room, ignoring my mother's calls for breakfast, until I saw a flash of yellow turning up the driveway. I ran down the stairs, yelled a goodbye with my bag already slung over my shoulder, and flew out the door before my parents could catch a glimpse.

As I jog down the stairs, trying not to pull at my skirt, Alex gets out of the car. He blinks at me as I approach, his mouth slack.

"Hi . . . what . . . um . . . hi."

I laugh. "Good morning to you too."

His eyes trail down my body, lust and shock warring in his eyes. With the black skirt, I've slid on a dark-green Pebble-brook High School T-shirt from my freshman year that hugs my hips and boobs just right. My tall black combat boots finish the ensemble.

Alex is still speechless, and it's so tempting to press myself against him, look up at him through my lashes. I even sort of want to purr at him while I do it. These clothes make me feel sexy, make me want to touch and be touched, make me feel in control. But there's still that weird something between Alex and me, a gap I can't seem to cross, so for now I just smile at him and shrug innocently.

"What are you . . . why are you dressed like that?" he asks.

I shrug again and offer him a half-truth. "Just something for Empower."

"I mean . . . not that you don't . . . er . . . look nice, but you're going to get sent home."

"I know."

He tilts his head toward me. "Scheming?"

"Maybe a little." I laugh to cover up this mess of anticipation and anxiety and elation and fear I can't shake since getting dressed.

Alex's eyes darken on mine, the concern in them unmistakable, but before I can say or do anything else, the front door bursts open behind me.

"Hey, man," Owen calls. I don't turn around, but I hear his feet pound down the steps. "Did I text you for a ride in my sleep or something?"

"Uh . . . hey," Alex says. "No, Mara asked for a ride."

I turn around then. Owen's digging in his bag, attention on the contents. "Mara?" he says, pulling out his dark blue beanie hat. "Why—"

He sees me then. Really sees me, and his eyes expand, wider and wider until I'm sure his lids will split from the tension.

"What the . . . ?" His mouth stretches open as he takes in my outfit. "Um, no. Just no."

"Excuse me?" I ask.

"Seriously? There's no way I'm letting my sister go to school like that."

"I'm sorry— *let* me?"

"Yeah, *let* you. You think I want everyone staring at your . . . at your . . ." He waves his hand toward my legs. "Who are you supposed to be, slutty schoolgirl?"

My heart nearly stops at the disdain in his voice, at how quickly I can become someone else, a *certain kind of girl* to him, just because of what I'm wearing. Owen has always had a problem keeping his mouth shut when he's upset. When we were eight, the remnant of a hurricane covered our whole state in thunderstorms for days, canceling our swimming pool birthday party. He was so mad when Mom told him, he used every swear in the book and got sent to his room without cake. Our years are filled with these little moments, f-bombs dropped behind teachers' backs and in front of our grandparents, clipped tones and strained voices before auditions and finals.

But this is more than a snarky comment. This is *me* and he should know better. He should know better about a lot of things and I'm not going to be the one to calm him down this time.

I lean toward him, gritting my teeth to keep myself from screaming. "That's exactly who I'm supposed to be."

"Mar, come on," he says, rubbing at his forehead. "Alex, tell her this is a dumb idea."

Next to me, Alex radiates tension. He's never been very good with conflict. When Owen and I would fight over the Wii controller in middle school, he'd try to get us to play some boring game like Sorry! or something, just so we'd stop arguing.

"Please go change," Owen says, his eyes pleading.

"No."

"Then I'll tell Mom. You think she's going to let you go to school like that?"

"Again, there's that word *let*."

"She's our parent, Mar. She gets to *let* and *not let*."

Rage rushes through my veins, hot and quick. I'm delirious,

furious with this guy in front of me using words like *let* and *slutty*. Dizzy, I turn away from him, yanking open the passenger door.

A hand on my arm. "Mara."

I jerk back. "What's the big deal, Owen? Afraid someone's going to rape me?"

Immediately, I regret saying it. Not because he isn't wrong, but because *the word* slipped out of my mouth and it feels like a sharp knife lashed over my skin.

Alex sucks in a loud breath and Owen recoils as if I slapped him. We stare at each other and I can't decide if he's hurt or angry. I can't decide which one I want him to be.

"Seriously, Mara?" he finally says, but it's so quiet, I almost don't hear him. "What the hell?"

I don't say anything. I can't. Instead I turn away and fold myself into the front seat of Alex's car, eyes on the windshield. Outside, the boys talk and Owen's voice crescendoes, but whatever Alex says seems to mollify him. I don't look directly at him, but I see Owen walk away, hear *fuck it* on his lips as he heads toward our car. After a few seconds, Alex rounds TLB and gets in.

"He's pretty pissed," he says, pushing the ignition button.

"Good," I say, but it comes out in a whisper, the threat of tears strangling my voice.

CHAPTER SIXTEEN

BY THE TIME WE PULL INTO THE SCHOOL PARKING LOT, all my energy from last night has morphed into anger. My body zips and zings with it, as though an IV slowly dripped a drug into my veins the entire ride here. Owen's horrified expression as he looked at me in the driveway sears itself onto my brain, an indelible mark. There was no trace of the brother I've shared a roof with for the past decade. There was only a boy looking at a girl and not really seeing her.

Shame presses against all of my edges, *stupid little bitch* a hissing whisper in my ears. The words battle against my fury, and as Alex turns off the car in the school parking lot and sighs into the air between us, I'm not sure which one will win today.

"You okay?" Alex asks. He lifts his arm toward me like he wants to take my hand, but I guess he changes his mind because he rests his fingers on the gearshift instead. We still haven't touched since that night at the cemetery.

"Yeah," I lie.

"Owen can be an ass, you know?"

"I do." My inflection curls at the end like a question, because until a week ago, I would've laughed at that statement. Joked around at what an *asshole* Owen was, knowing that my adoration leaked through every single syllable. I mean, yes, he can be an ass, but it's always been the laughable kind, the kind that was fun at parties and cracked ridiculous jokes, the kind that quieted down when he was with me on the roof.

"He's just . . . worried," Alex goes on. "He doesn't want you to get in trouble."

"You think I'm a slut too? Because of my clothes?" I turn toward him in the seat, not bothering to pull down that little black skirt as it slides upward, so close to my hip I feel my entire thigh break out into goose bumps.

Alex's mouth falls open. "What? No, I—"

"You think dressing the way I want and looking for a little control is a bad thing? Guys love that kind of girl, don't they? They want her and secretly hate her and not so secretly treat her like she's not even human and—"

"Hey, stop," he says, his eyes focused on mine. "I don't think any of those things. I think you're smart and talented and you can do what you want and I could never hate you. We're friends."

I inhale a shaky breath and nod. "I'm sorry."

"Don't be. Owen really was an ass. Lately, he's . . ." Alex's words trail off and he shakes his head. "I don't know."

"I don't know either."

Alex grabs his bag from the back seat. Then he sweeps his gaze over me again, an appreciative quirk to his lips. "You're still going to get called to the office."

I roll my eyes but manage a smile.

As we climb out of the car, my blood cools a few degrees, boiling water slowed to a simmer. Eyes fall on us, whispers starting up as kids strolling in from the parking lot see us linked. I hear Owen's name a few times, hear the word *skirt* coupled with *holy shit* more than once, but I let everything roll off me.

Until I see Charlie.

Or, I should say, until Charlie sees me.

She's standing at the front doors of the school underneath a huge sign painted with red and orange letters advertising the Fall Festival on Saturday. Leaning against the stair railing with her ankles crossed, a few books clutched to her chest, she looks so casual, dressed in her quintessential plaid and black jeans, but her expression is a mess of . . . I don't even know what. She smiles, but it's tiny and nervous, her lips parting as she takes me in. Her face twists my heart into a million knots. I'm not sure what I expected to feel after last night, but right now I feel *everything*, and it knocks the wind out of me.

Then I remember Tess's voice on the phone the other night, a person I still know nothing about because my best friend won't tell me. And I remember last night with Charlie, how perfect it was. But was it perfect because we're better off friends, or because we'll never be only friends?

The question makes me dizzy. As the little green flecks in Charlie's brown eyes get closer, I don't know what else to do but smile and force my chin into the air between us.

"Hi," I say as brightly as I can manage.

"Hey," she says, her voice a scratch. She clears her throat. "Hi. Hi, Alex."

"Hey, Charlie." I can feel him glancing between us as we stare at each other. "Um . . . I need to go to my locker. See you later?"

"Yeah," I say. He nods at Charlie and disappears into the school.

"So . . . you're hanging out with Alex?" Charlie asks.

I shrug as if it's no big deal. It shouldn't be. But Charlie knows better than anyone that Alex and I have never hung out on our own. Still, that was before. Before everything.

"A little," I say.

Charlie frowns. "Since when?"

I open my mouth to answer, but nothing comes out. *Since when?* suddenly seems like a very complicated question.

"Why didn't you tell me last night?" she asks.

"I didn't think there was anything to tell."

She tilts her head, her eyes softly narrowed on me. "Okay."

"Okay."

And this is our new dance, a quiet movement of bodies trying to find the right position. Not quite best friends anymore, but not quite brave enough to say why. The truth is, I did mean to tell Charlie about Alex. I even wanted to tell her that we kissed, though I'm pretty sure the kiss was a one-time desperate grab for . . . something. But then Tess was on her phone and then Charlie was on a stage, her guitar and voice spinning magic and stars, and we were happy and I never thought of Alex again the entire night. Charlie eclipsed everything, and there's a tiny flicker in the back of my mind that knows that means something. Exactly what, I don't know and I don't care and I can't care right now.

"I brought you these," Charlie says, setting a few books into my arms.

Looking down, my stomach flips gently. They're guitar lesson books. "You're not going to teach me?"

"No, I am. Just thought you'd want to look at them before."

Tess doesn't need them? The words nearly fall from my mouth, but I shove them back behind my teeth.

"Thanks," I say instead. "When should we start?"

"Whenever you want."

"Okay. This weekend maybe?"

"Okay."

It's all so polite and tempered.

"What's with the skirt, Mara?" she asks.

For a second, I'd forgotten what I'm wearing. "Oh. Hannah's coming back today."

Charlie lifts her brow. "She is?"

"Yeah — we need to keep an eye out for her."

"Of course. But what does that have to do with your skirt?"

Her question rankles me. "Everything. I just . . . wanted to wear it, okay? For me. To do something, anything, I don't know.

And maybe if people are looking at me, they won't look at Hannah as much."

Charlie tilts her head, considering. Then she slides her eyes up from my feet, up my legs, and to my face again. It's not really a sexy look, more observation, but a ribbon of heat curls down my center anyway. No one can draw it out of me like Charlie. With her, there's no hesitation, no wondering if I'm safe, no looking for ways it might all turn ugly and dirty and wrong.

"Well, people are definitely going to look at you," she says. "That's not really a gray-area kind of skirt. You're going to get sent—"

"I know."

She raises her hands, surrendering. "All right. Fine."

Instinctively, we move toward the entrance, walking side by side just like normal. Our lockers are next to each other and we make our way through the throng. There are so many kids in the halls before homeroom, my skirt is hidden in the press of bodies.

For now.

I'm just throwing my British lit and music theory books into my bag for first and second periods when a strange hush sweeps through the crowd. I glance at Charlie, meeting her eyes for a split second before looking for the reason for the sudden quiet. Arcing to my tiptoes and craning my neck, I see a swath of strawberry hair weaving through the hall. Students part to let her through and it's so surreal, like a scene from a movie. Some kids keep walking and talking, oblivious, but most eyes are on Hannah, as though she's a bomb waiting to go off.

Her posture is a steel rod, her expression unemotional and blank, but her fingers are white around the strap of her bag. She wears gray leggings, a long-sleeved tunic dress in unassuming solid black, and boots. Her hair is soft around her face. Too soft. She looks like Hannah. And she doesn't look like Hannah at all.

I wave at her, and when she spots us, a small flash of relief flares in her eyes. Her pace quickens and kids start to move again, talk again.

"Hey, slut, welcome back."

The words slice through the air and Hannah freezes. So does everyone else, a few shocked gasps mingling with the laughs and *Oh, damn*s. Next to me, Charlie springs into action, shouldering her way through the masses to get to Hannah, who's standing like a hunted animal at the end of the barrel of a gun in the middle of the hallway. I look around for the source of the male voice, but there are too many guys, too many possibilities, as the scene unfreezes.

Charlie returns, her arms hooked through Hannah's.

"Jesus Christ," she mutters, trying to put her body between Hannah and everyone else. "Are you okay?"

Hannah swallows several times. "I don't know."

"Do you want to call your mom?" I ask.

She shakes her head. "She didn't want me to come today. But I . . . I had to. I have to . . . god, I have to get over this." She rubs both hands over her forehead, sliding them down and pressing them into her eyes.

"You don't have to do anything," Charlie says softly. "I

don't . . . I don't know, but I'm not sure this is something you just get over, honey."

"But I'm *fine*," Hannah says, and she sounds anything but fine. I notice the brace isn't on her wrist, but a few yellowed bruises still mottle her skin. "I've been out of school for almost a week already. That's long enough — I'm fine."

"It's okay not to be," Charlie says, but it only makes Hannah more agitated. She shakes her head over and over again. Tears build in her eyes, falling quickly, messily. She slaps them away.

"Hey, slut, welcome back."

A different male voice, this one quieter. Hannah startles, her back colliding with the metal locker behind her. I whip around, looking for the asshole, but everyone blends together in a mess of color.

"Hey, slut, welcome back."

Charlie tries to shield Hannah from view, but it's impossible to cover her completely. She grips Charlie's arm, clearly about to completely lose it.

"Hey, slut, welcome back."

The words keep coming, over and over again, different boy voices spitting venom, each verbal slap delivered so carefully I can't get an ID on the guy attached to it. I hear a few female voices mixed in as well. I spin in circles, my veins boiling, desperate to get a lock on the source, but there are too many people in the hall. Everyone's mouth is open, laughing or talking or joking around.

Hey, slut, welcome back.

Hey, slut, welcome back.

Hey, slut, welcome back.

The voices blur together. There are probably only fifteen or so, but it sounds like a chant in my ears, the exact same phrase flung into the hallway with the exact same tone, the exact same inflection.

As if it were planned.

"I'm getting her out of here," Charlie says. She takes Hannah's arm and heads for the nearest bathroom, Hannah looking totally shell-shocked. I watch them go, eyes still peeling for a perpetrator.

Finally, I find one.

As Charlie and Hannah move down the hall, pressed against the lockers to avoid notice, I see Jaden Abbot spot them and smirk. His mouth opens, lips curling around ugly words.

Hey, slut, welcome back.

The blood in my veins boils over.

I move toward him, cutting through other kids like a warm knife through butter. I don't have a plan, don't know what I'll do when I get there, but I keep going.

When I reach him, my arm lashes out. I feel the sting of my palm against skin, the barest hint of scruff scraping my fingertips.

"What the fuck?" He stumbles back, hand flying to his face.

I follow his movements. I shove his chest. I scream at him. I don't even know what I say. It's as though I'm outside of myself, floating near the ceiling and watching it all happen. Jaden's expression blurs in my vision, shimmering from his own to Mr. Knoll's. To Owen's.

A circle forms around us and I keep pushing him. Keep hitting him. Keep screaming. He keeps stumbling backwards.

"You bitch!" he yells, and my hand arcs through the air again. This time, he catches my wrist, flinging it away from his face, but I don't even care.

Because this. This is more than a skirt swishing at the top of my thighs. This is *doing* something.

"Mara!" I hear Alex's voice somewhere behind me, but it's not real, not really there. My throat aches from screaming, but I keep at it, words incoherently falling from my tongue, words for this asshole and every asshole.

My arms are wrenched behind my back. I don't even glance around to see who has me, just glare at Jaden, who's now straightening his clothes and glaring right back. A red handprint surfaces on his cheek, one eye all puffy and watery.

"Miss McHale, I think that's quite enough."

Principal Carr is at my side, Ms. Rodriguez next to him. Our on-site security officer, Deputy Russell, has my arms behind my back. I can tell he's trying to be gentle, but I'm not making it easy for him. I buck and snarl, something wild set loose inside of me. The fact that I'm probably flashing my underwear to half the student body is a dull *holy shit* in the far corners of my mind, but I don't even care right now.

The three of them drag me down the hall toward the office. Right before the door closes behind us, I see a mess of golden-brown curls near the first wall of lockers. Owen stares at me, mouth hanging open in shock. His expression clears my fevered vision and I want to shake off my captors, run toward him, grab at his shirt and make him tell me he didn't put his friends up to that shit show I just witnessed. That he didn't break Hannah into pieces.

But then all that feeling I think I see in his eyes flickers out and goes cold. His lower lip trembles despite his tightened jaw, but then he turns away from me and is lost behind a cluster of frantic freshmen as the late bell echoes through the hall.

CHAPTER SEVENTEEN

THEY MAKE ME SIT in a scratchy polyester-covered chair outside Principal Carr's office until my parents arrive. The secretary, Ms. Villanova, who's always been pretty nice to me, keeps throwing disapproving glances at me and my exposed legs, which does nothing to calm the hurricane swirling and building strength in my head right now.

The glass door leading from the office into the main hall swings open and my mother blasts through, hair loose and long and flying in her wake. My father trails behind, his hands stuffed into his pockets.

Ms. Villanova doesn't even greet them, just picks up the phone, presses a button, and says, "The McHales are here," before hanging up again.

Mom finds me vibrating in the corner and her eyes nearly fall out of her head. She blinks at my outfit, at my tense posture, my clenched jaw.

"Mara," Dad breathes out, angling around Mom to get a better look at me. "Honey, are you okay?"

I can't answer him. I don't want to lie, but if I say no, I know he'll kneel down in front of me and take my hands in his and then everything in me will break.

"Clearly, she's not, Chris," Mom says. "Mara, what in god's name are you wearing?"

I just glare at her, hating her for the disgusted look in her eyes. She flinches. My mother literally startles and I savor it. I wish I could take a picture of myself right now, so I can remember this fiery girl, hold on to her.

Before Mom can say anything else, Principal Carr's door opens and he steps out, all pinstriped suit and red tie and too much product in his graying hair. He and my dad shake hands like the manly men they are, and he offers Mom a gentlemanly nod. I roll my eyes so hard it hurts.

"Thank you for coming in, Mr. and Mrs. McHale," he says. "Why don't we all go into my office?"

"Of course," Mom says, sweeping past him as he gestures her inside. Dad hesitates, waiting for me. I stand on wobbly legs, the adrenaline still in control like a drug. Dad inhales sharply, my outfit on full display now, but he says nothing.

Once my parents are settled in the two leather wingback chairs in front of the massive mahogany desk—I'm perched on the edge of a plastic chair—Principal Carr launches into a very sad and sympathetic-sounding account of what happened in the hallway. Except it's full of holes and half-truths, leaving out Hannah and the vicious whispers snaking through the halls like a goddamned python. Instead it's all *Mara* and *inappropriate* and *violent* and *unprovoked*.

"And if that wasn't enough," he says, "Mara is in grievous violation of our dress code today."

"I can see that, Principal Carr," Mom says, "and we will talk with her about that, but right now I'm more concerned about this Jaden boy." She turns to me, her mouth a thin pink-lipsticked line. "I don't even know what to say, Mara."

"How about *why?*" I spit out.

"Watch your tone, young lady," she says, eyes narrowing.

"You really don't want to know why?"

"Of course I do. But I'm sorry if I'm a little irritated because I receive a phone call in the middle of a restoration informing me that my usually very well-behaved daughter has assaulted some poor boy."

"He's not *some poor boy*. He's an asshole."

"Okay," Dad says. "Let's all calm down."

"And isn't this what you wanted me to do?" I ask Mom, gesturing to my skirt. "Weren't you *so* excited about me taking on the . . . what did you call it? 'The institutional misogyny of the patriarchal system'?"

Her face flushes red. "That is not what I meant and you know it. This is too far. That skirt is inappropriate, and violence in any form and for any reason is unacceptable."

My teeth clench, the words I need to say fighting against me to get out. I hate these words—fear them, even—but they're strong and furious, shoving themselves from my mouth. "I think you're talking to the wrong twin."

Silence trails after my words. Principal Carr clears his throat, but no one looks at him. Mom stares at me, horror practically dripping from her pores. I relish that, too, while at the same time hating how quickly she's turned into some stranger I don't know, how I don't fucking recognize anyone anymore.

Team Owen.

Principal Carr hems and haws for a few seconds and then starts in on the details of my two-day suspension—one for the dress code violation and one for "behavior unbecoming of a lady." That's the actual phrase he uses and I want to spit it back in his face.

By the time my mother pulls me up from the chair by one arm, I'm so angry I can barely see straight. I'm speechless, boneless. Mom hauls me from the building while my father signs the office write-up.

We're halfway home before I realize I never explained *why* and Mom never really asked.

***

After we get home, my dad has to head back to the furniture store, but my mom stays, probably to make sure I don't try to escape. She declares herself too angry to look at me as she grabs a Diet Coke from the fridge.

"Change out of that costume and go think about what you did," she says. "We'll talk about it more later." Then she disappears into her room, slamming the door as she goes, just in case I didn't understand how pissed she is.

I feel like sticking my tongue out at her. Treat me like a child, and a child is what you'll get.

Before he leaves, Dad just stares at me as if he doesn't even know who I am. He probably doesn't. We don't know who any of us are. Years under the same roof and we're all strangers, circling one another and living with happy illusions about star-infused twins and the parents who love them so much that they let them adventure in the sky.

I wander around the house for a while, my skin and blood still buzzing too much to stand still, but eventually I crash. I end up in my room, standing in front of the full-length mirror, staring at my thighs and the tight stretch of the T-shirt over my chest. My arms come up instinctively, wrapping around myself, not to hide, but to hold myself together. I should feel empowered, proud, even. The skin on the palm of my right hand still smarts a little from slapping Jaden, and a dull scratch scrapes the back of my throat from telling him off.

But I don't feel empowered. I don't feel proud. I feel drained and powerless, tired and sad.

I lie down on my bed and curl myself into the comforter, burrowing deep. My sound machine sits silent on my night table and I can't even reach that far to snap it on. The quiet rings through me, bringing up memories.

A specific memory. The day a certain girl died and another was born.

CHAPTER EIGHTEEN

THE FINAL BELL SINGS THROUGH THE AIR and the class erupts, hands clapping and mouths laughing, an entire summer stretching out before us like an endless ocean along a shore. From across the room, I catch Alex's grin. The past three years in middle school have sucked for him, a constant barrage of pudgy jokes and squinty-eye slurs from jerks, and I know he's been waiting for that last bell for a long time. I smile at him, swiping a hand across my forehead in a whew gesture. He laughs and nods, then ticks his head toward the hallway.

Owen. He's going to find Owen, the need to celebrate and high-five with his best friend winning out over walking out with me.

I shoot him a thumbs-up and pick up my bag weighed down by the contents of my locker: worn-down pencils and filled-in notebooks, the little makeup case packed with fruity-flavored lip-gloss and roll-on perfume I convinced my mother I had to have at school.

Andrea and Callie, two chorus friends who cried literal tears the day I told them I was enrolling in Pebblebrook instead of the local high school just next door to Butler Middle, fall into step with me as I make my way toward the door. They chatter on about summer plans, sleepovers and beach trips and lazy days spent lying in the grass by the lake slathered in coconut-scented sunscreen.

A bright feeling opens up in my chest, all freedom and sunshine and friends and laughter.

"Mara?"

I turn, meeting Mr. Knoll's pool-blue eyes. My ears bleed red, just like they always do whenever my math teacher looks directly at me. He's tall, broad shoulders stretching wide under a cerulean button-up and skinny gray tie. His sandyblond hair falls over his forehead, all at once effortless and perfect. He smiles at me and my belly flutters.

"I need to speak with you for a moment," he says.

Andrea's and Callie's hands fly to their mouths, giggles trapped underneath.

"Okay," I say, shoving Andrea's shoulder playfully with my own as I walk around her.

"See you at my house at six, right, Mara?" Callie asks. I nod, promising to bring the M&M's and my collection of High School Musical movies to our sleepover tonight.

Mr. Knoll wishes them a good summer and cracks some joke about getting into trouble or staying out of trouble or something completely expected and inane. I'm too busy wondering why he wants to talk to me, my mouth drying out as I remember all the times my friends and I have joked about how cute he is. I shake myself and laugh, because gross. He's a young teacher, but a young teacher is still ancient.

He closes the door behind my friends and then makes his way to his desk. He rifles through some papers. Then, after picking up a few, he walks across the room and sits on the table he uses for small groups sometimes. I follow him, turning my body to face him, waiting. He sets the papers next to him and braces his palms on the table's surface, looking at me. There's a little smile on his face, the faintest quirk of one side of his mouth.

"Excited about the summer?" he asks.

"Yeah."

"Big plans?"

I shrug. "Just . . . the normal stuff, I guess."

"The normal stuff can be fun." He waves his hand around the classroom. "Anything's better than being cooped up in here any longer, right?"

I laugh. "Pretty much."

"I loved summer when I was your age. I still do."

I nod, shifting my bag's strap higher up on my shoulder.

"So," he says, that tiny smile taking its place again. "Mara."

I swallow. "Is . . . is everything okay?"

He sighs, concern spilling into his expression. He picks up the papers next to him again, the smile dipping into a frown as he flips through them. "I'm afraid not."

"What . . . what's wrong?"

He holds the papers out toward me. "Tell me about these."

I take them, my eyes scanning what look to be my last three tests, three As circled in red next to my name.

"What about them?"

"They're yours, correct?"

"Yes."

"And you worked hard on them? Gave them your best shot?"

My mouth twitches. "Yes."

He tilts his head, frowning, and my stomach flips and flops. I have no idea what he wants me to say, so I say nothing.

Finally, he sighs again and folds his arms. "Mara, a student — a student who will remain nameless at their request — came to me earlier today and informed me that you've been cheating off their papers for several months."

186

"What? I haven't——"

"They said you copied off their homework and their tests. They didn't come forward sooner because they were concerned they'd be in trouble. And you're well liked, Mara. I think this person was scared I wouldn't believe them."

My mind whirls, thinking about who could've said this. We sit in rows, one behind the other, and I've barely ever talked to the two people I've sat next to all semester. Gabriel something, who's so shy I've never actually heard his voice, and Jackson West, who, if I'm being honest, sucks at math.

"But I didn't. I swear I didn't cheat," I say. Prealgebra isn't my favorite subject, but I'm decent at it. I'm not great at tests in general, but I've gotten mostly Bs, bumping my grades up to As the past couple of months because I actually started studying my notes at home before tests instead of only paying attention during class. I've even helped Owen with a few of the harder concepts, and he has the easier teacher, Ms. Sparks.

Mr. Knoll holds his hand out for the tests. I pass them back, my thoughts in knots as he looks over them again.

"Mara, I'm sorry. But these grades are significantly higher scores than your previous tests."

"I know. Because I——"

He holds up his hand. "This is fixable. I won't fail you if you're willing to put in a little work."

"Fail me?"

"I can't pass someone who's been fabricating her test scores for more than half the semester."

I gape at him, trying to figure out what is actually happening. "I don't understand," I say, barely a whisper.

He nods, his expression sympathetic, but then his eyes travel from my legs up my body. I'm dressed in jeans and a baggy *Butler* sweatshirt. The air outside to-day is cool for May and it's raining. Plus, I feel safe in this sweatshirt, my already C-cup boobs hidden underneath the soft burgundy cotton. But the way Mr. Knoll looks at me now knots up my stomach. I feel suddenly naked, and a tiny warning flares in the back of my mind, but I don't know what it means. Mr. Knoll is a teacher and I'm in my school. What is there to be afraid of?

"It's really simple, Mara," he says. "I'm disappointed in you, but I know you're better than this. Regardless, you're at risk of failing this semester, and unless you're willing to work with me, you'll have to repeat the course in summer school."

"Summer school? But . . . I understand everything I've learned in this class. And it's the last day of school. Why—"

"Despite the cheating, you've been distracted, too focused on summer and high school. I think you'd benefit from repeating the course."

"But all my teachers have been telling me to focus on high school," I say.

Irritation flickers in his eyes. "Nonetheless, we still have a problem. Are you willing to work with me on this? I assume you don't want to spend the summer stuck in a classroom."

"No! I mean, yes, I'll work hard. What do I need to do?"

He inhales slowly through his nose. "Nothing too difficult, I hope." We stare at each other for a few moments and I'm not sure what to do. Something feels off, but I'm too freaked out by the fact that one of my favorite teachers thinks I'm actually a cheater and a liar.

"Come here," Mr. Knoll says, and I take a step closer. He watches me, a look in his eyes I can't name. "Good girl."

My heart slams against my ribs as my teacher's hands go to his belt buckle, his thumbs hooking around the silver rectangle and undoing it.

"I think we can fix this right now, don't you, Mara?"

"I . . . I don't know."

His forefinger goes to the button on his pants and my mouth goes dry, questions filling me up.

"What are you doing?" I ask.

"Be quiet," he says.

Tears spring into my eyes. His voice is still soft, just as nice as it always is in class, but something edges his words, his tone. Something too soft, like a secret he doesn't want anyone to know about. Goose bumps break out all over my skin, the bad kind. The warning kind.

His fingers flick the button free and it's then that I notice a telltale bulge in his crotch. The kind of bulge that boys laugh about during gym and girls giggle over in the locker room. Shock blasts through me in a cold rush. I try to take a step back, to run for the door, but I'm frozen, unbelieving eyes wide open and stinging.

Mr. Knoll unzips, revealing mint-green boxers. The color looks almost childish, like something in a baby's nursery. But there's nothing childish about this. I squeeze my eyes shut, willing this to be a dream, willing myself to wake up.

"You need to work with me, Mara," he says softly. "Open your eyes."

I shake my head, clenching my eyes so hard that fireworks explode behind them.

"Open. Your eyes."

His still-gentle voice sears through me and I obey. I glance toward the door, but it's closed tight, the black paper teachers have to roll down when we have intruder lockdown drills covering the rectangular window.

"This is an easy solution, Mara," Mr. Knoll says, leaning back a little. "Don't be stupid."

I don't know what to say, what to do. What does he want me to do? I just stare at his face, my breathing so fast and shallow I feel dizzy.

He waits, watching me gulp at the air. The quiet is deafening, a ringing in my ears drowning out the sound of my lungs contracting. The pungent smell of dry-erase markers and teen-boy sweat stings my nose. My senses are in overdrive, a bitter tang on my tongue, goose bumps rippling up and down my arms and legs, even under my sweatshirt and jeans.

"You're overthinking, Mara. It's not a big deal," he finally says. "I've seen the way you blush when I talk to you. You're a beautiful girl. It's okay. It's natural to be curious and to have a little crush."

"I . . . I don't . . . I . . ."

"Don't do that. Don't be coy."

I shake my head, at a total loss.

"Come closer."

"I . . . I can't——"

But he doesn't let me finish. His hand encircles my wrist and he pulls me toward him. I gasp, but instead of letting me go, he puts my hand on him. It's a complete shock and I try to pull back, but he holds tight.

"It's okay," he whispers.

He moves my hand, forcing my fingers to do what he wants. I feel like a puppet, a smiling master above me manipulating my limbs as though they're connected with strings.

"See?" he says, his breathing raspy. "We're just having fun, right?"

"I . . . I . . ."

He reaches for my face, trailing his finger down my tear-stained cheek before palming the back of my neck and pulling me closer. "Soon you can go and have the summer that you planned with your friends, with your family. You wouldn't want to ruin that, would you?"

Somehow I manage to shake my head and Mr. Knoll smiles.

"Good girl."

I'm sobbing silently now, tears on a mad mission to escape my eyes. All I can think about is how Owen wrinkled his nose the one time I told him I thought Mr. Knoll was kind of cute. Dude's a total creepster, he'd said. I'd rolled my eyes and defended Mr. Knoll. Mr. Knoll, who was always kind. Mr. Knoll, who was always patient. Mr. Knoll, who was always smiling. Mr. Knoll, who never touched anyone, girl or boy. Not even a pat on the shoulder.

Mr. Knoll, whose hand is buried in my hair and pulling me closer to him. His fingers massage my neck and bile rises up in my throat. He's busy with my hand on him, and his grip on my neck slackens a little. I sip at the air, too terrified to inhale deeply. Just when I'm about to wrench myself away, his hold on my hair tightens, fingers tangling in the curls.

I throw myself backwards anyway.

Pain lashes across my scalp and I trip over the bag I'd dropped on the floor, landing hard on the dingy tiles. I scramble to my feet, hooking my arm through my bag's strap, an animal-like sound escaping my throat as I move away from my teacher and press my shoulder blades into the painted cement wall. The pencil sharpener digs into my ribs, but it almost feels good. It feels like safety.

Mr. Knoll watches me impassively. There's a glint of anger in his eyes, but mostly, he just looks disappointed. He does nothing to cover himself, just flicks his hand out into the space in front of him. Several strands of my long hair cascade to the ground.

"You're a stupid little bitch."

I don't wait to hear what he'll say next. Eyes clouded, bones trembling, nothing but adrenaline pushing me forward, I manage to get the door open and stumble into the hall.

I walk fast, keeping my eyes down. I get myself home. I don't even remember how, really, but later that night my mother fussed at me for the mud that I'd tracked into the front hall.

I remember standing in the shower for more than an hour, water scalding hot, scrubbing my hands over and over and over.

I remember lying awake on my bed, playing music from my phone all night long because suddenly the silence of a sleeping house felt like fingers pressing down on the back of my neck.

I remember drifting into an uneasy sleep, Mr. Knoll's last words a sinister lullaby in my ear.

CHAPTER NINETEEN

I FLOAT THROUGH THE REST OF THE DAY in relative solitude. My mother remains so pissed at me, the *we'll talk about it more later* never actually happens. Around noon, she leaves a tray laden with grilled cheese sandwiches on thick sourdough bread and creamy tomato soup outside my door—my favorite comfort food—but doesn't even knock. It's as though she's trying to make peace without actually engaging with me, and I leave the food untouched in the hallway, feeding on the stash of Luna bars I keep in my school bag for rehearsal snacks.

Charlie texts me several times, benign inquiries about how I'm doing, all of which I ignore. She eventually stops. I try not to think about what that means or doesn't mean. I try not to think at all. Alex and I text a little, but it's about nothing, and the one time he calls, I don't answer.

There's a constant dull ache in my bones, a too-sharp brightness to my thoughts. I'm grounded indefinitely, but by the time Friday night arrives, I'm desperate to get out of my house.

Around dinnertime, I'm scheming ways to sneak out when

Owen knocks on my door. I know it's him before he even calls my name, his syncopated-rhythm knock giving him away. I debate ignoring him, diving under my covers and pretending to be asleep, but my light is on and my music is playing and I hear my voice call out "Yeah?" before I can stop it.

He cracks open the door and sticks his head in, making eye contact with me before he steps into the room.

"Mom told me to tell you we're going out to dinner. Pizza."

"Oh?" I sit up from where I'm leaning against the headboard, one of the guitar books Charlie gave me open on my lap. I glance around my room, dirty clothes everywhere, wondering what I'll wear and how I'll manage to sit through a meal in public without screaming at my entire family. How I'll pretend everything is fine.

"She left you some of last night's pasta in the microwave," he says, and everything goes quiet inside of me.

"Oh," I breathe out. It's amazing how quickly reluctance and anger can shift into disappointment and open wounds.

I settle back on the bed, hiding my balled-up fists in my comforter. Owen watches me, his brow wrinkling. He rubs the back of his neck and I keep waiting for him to leave, go have his happy dinner with our adoring parents, but he just stands there, gaze trailing from my darkened window to my eyes, as if he's trying to place me in the stars and can't quite picture me there anymore.

I look down at my legs and the pink and purple kiss-print pajama pants I changed into earlier. The emotions warring on his face are too familiar, too close.

"You really don't believe me, do you?" he asks, so quietly I almost don't hear it.

My head snaps up. Instinctively, my mouth opens to answer, because I always answer my brother. I've never had a reason not to. Before, my voice was always ready to engage with his, thoughts ready to share, ears ready to listen. But now I have no answer for him, no voice. I can't tell him *yes*, but I can't say *no*, either. I can't even say *I don't know*, because some part of me *does* know, but it's stuck, lodged inside the tangle of fears and facts in my head.

When I say nothing, he blinks rapidly and turns his head away, his jaw tightening. "The state attorney called Mom today," he says. "They're not pressing charges." And then he's gone, my door clicking quietly shut behind him as everything his words imply settles on me like a heavy snow—beautiful and painfully cold.

There's a girl inside me, a sister, who wants to leap out of her bed and fly from her room, hurtle herself down the stairs and into her brother's arms. She wants to cry, tell him everything, let him explain again why *charges* were even a possibility, because she knows him and she knows there must be some explanation, some way it's all a misunderstanding.

But there's another girl inside of me too. Tired. Scared. Lonely. Angry. Devastated. Wounded. She gets up from the bed, but she doesn't chase after her brother.

She doesn't have a brother.

She goes to the window and opens it. She hears the garage door rumble up and rumble back down, sees a charcoal-gray car drive away with her family, no doubt ready to celebrate Owen's freedom. The girl feels a stab of relief at the news too, but it fits all wrong on her skin, like a too-small coat stretched over widening hips. She climbs through the window and sits on the roof, staring at the black expanse above her. She doesn't look for the twins. Instead, she seeks out Andromeda, a girl made of stars whose mother wouldn't shut up about her daughter's beauty, so the daughter was punished. Poseidon secured her against the coastal rocks, leaving her to be ravaged by a monster. Now she lives in the sky, a memorial to the time she spent chained up and nearly sacrificed because of another's choice, another's obsession, another's selfishness.

I blink at the sky, feeling my own skin around my bones again. Andromeda's hard to find, usually too far south on the horizon to see. But she's out there somewhere, trapped and alone, awaiting her own release.

CHAPTER TWENTY

THROWING PIECES OF GRAVEL at a second-story window belonging to a family who probably hates me isn't my best idea, but Hannah isn't answering my texts and there's no way in hell I'm ringing the doorbell.

Sheer curtains frame the dimly lit window. I toss up another pebble and it plinks against the glass. A few seconds later, a shadow interrupts the amber light. Hannah's face appears. She stares down at me, expressionless. I gaze back, but eventually I manage to lift my hand in greeting, curling my fingers and waving her down. She disappears and I pace circles around her side yard, avoiding eye contact with the lake and breathing in the smoky leftover scent of burning leaves.

Too many minutes pass and I'm just about to head back to my car parked on the street when I hear the creak of the screened-in porch's door at the back of the house. Edging around some juniper bushes, I see Hannah's form inching the door shut carefully behind her. She holds a finger up to her lips and I nod as she freezes, listening. Then she tiptoes down the stairs and falls into step beside me. She's in jeans and a sweatshirt, her hair in a sleek and boring ponytail. I didn't even know Hannah owned a pair of jeans. Hell, I didn't even know she owned a hair elastic.

Wordlessly, we move away from the lake and down the neatly trimmed grass running alongside her driveway. We don't speak until we're safely closed inside my car.

"Are you going to get into trouble?" I ask.

She shrugs, sighing and leaning her head back on the seat. "I told my parents I was going to bed, then snuck down the back stairs. Doesn't matter."

"I think your parents would disagree."

"They disagree with a lot of things these days."

"I'm sorry." The words slip out, but they feel right. I *am* sorry, and I feel as though I need to say it to her, over and over, even if I'm not sure what I'm apologizing for.

"Where are we going?" she asks. Her eyes find mine in the dark, and I don't know why, but I feel myself relax as we watch each other. Truthfully, I didn't come over here with any sort of plan. I just wanted to see her, something in me reaching out for something in her. As we sit in the silence, exhaustion and power-lessness physical things lying heavy on our skin, I smile.

"I think I know a place we can go," I say.

We drive through Frederick's tiny downtown, all softly glowing streetlights and cobbled sidewalks, the air deceptively gentle and ac-cepting. I park on a side street near the centuries-old Presbyterian church and we walk south, staying off the main road, heading away from the city center and restaurant patrons out for dinner.

Finally, our destination looms before us, a white ghost against the black sky. A wordless marquee, save for the name THE MENAGERIE at the very top, wraps around the front of the old abandoned theater. The front façade is almost cathedral-like, whitewashed stone and turreted roof reaching toward the heavens.

I cup my hands around my eyes, peering through the darkened brass-lined doors. Inside, I see ragged red carpet covered in dust and littered with old movie tickets and popcorn cartons. This theater has been around since movies were called moving pictures, but it closed for repairs a few years ago, much to the town's chagrin. It housed one auditorium, which had curtains lining the screen, velvety seat cushions, and ushers dressed like fancy hotel bellhops. They used to show old movies and serve Italian ices and chocolate malts at the concession counter. I saw *The Wizard of Oz* for the first time in this theater, my excited feet swinging from the seat next to Owen's, my toes never even grazing the ground.

"What are we doing here?" Hannah asks.

I turn back toward her, expecting to find a mischievous glimmer in her eyes, like that first day I met her and she took off running with my hand in hers, hurling us into the lake.

But her eyes are wary, flitting from my face to our surroundings.

I walk back to her and lace both of my hands with hers. I do it slowly, reaching out carefully, making sure she sees my every move. When she doesn't pull away, I squeeze her fingers. "We're going to break into this theater and explore and remember being girls watching old black-and-white movies. We're going to do something stupid and wild and fun."

"Why?"

"Because we still can."

She stares at me for a few long seconds and I think she's going to say no. We can't. Maybe we never could. But then the tiniest smile lightens the tight set of her mouth, eyes flaring briefly with a bit of her old self. The smile grows, spreading to me and catching like fire until we're both laughing. We keep our hands linked as we run around to the side of the building, searching for a way in and giggling the entire time.

Finally, at the back of the building, in an alleyway piled with old trash bins and a dumpster filled with theater seats and rat-gnawed velvet ropes, we see a window that's cracked open about an inch. It's a couple of feet above our heads, but with the help of the dumpster's rim, I'm pretty sure I can reach it.

"Can you give me a boost?" I ask Hannah, and I step into her linked fingers. She tosses me up and I nearly overshoot the dumpster and land inside of the damn thing. I manage to hang on to keep my stomach on the edge and then hoist myself onto my feet.

"Oh my god." Hannah laughs. "Sorry."

"Yeah, sure you are." I grin down at her.

Balancing with my arms out, I make my way to the window. Dust and dirt and something that looks disturbingly like small animal bones line the sill. I brush it all aside with my sleeve and wiggle the window up. Peeling paint sprinkles to the ground, but I get the window open enough to crawl through. Hannah finds an old milk crate behind the dumpster and climbs up behind me. Soon, we're both tumbling into a men's restroom.

"Ugh," Hannah says, getting to her feet and smoothing her hair. "Smells like piss."

"Don't most men's rooms smell like piss?"

"Exactly how many men's rooms have you been in, Mara?"

"Oh, loads."

She offers a smile and it feels like a victory.

The city is supposed to be renovating the theater, so they keep the electricity running and there are already a few lights illuminating the hallways. I find a set of switches and flip the rest of the lights on, filling the lobby ahead of us with a sepia glow. We wander around for a while, stepping around unidentifiable crap all over the floor, looking at old movie posters I remember as a kid still attached to the peeling walls. There is even a smattering of personal items long forgotten—a tattered black and white polka-dotted umbrella, a faded Atlanta Braves baseball cap, one of those ancient flip cell phones. It's like touring the inside of a ghost, seeing all the things that used to make it a real live person. For some reason, it makes me sad, but a cleansing kind of sadness, a sickness that needed to get out.

Eventually we find our way upstairs. The ceiling in the auditorium is domed and textured, dark pink paint bleeding in between ornate cream-colored swirls of plaster, all of it worn and molting like a bird sloughing off its old feathers. We stand side by side at the balcony edge, the wide expanse of the theater spread out before us.

"Is it just me, or is this depressingly beautiful?" Hannah asks.

"It's not just you." I clap my hands once and the sound echoes through the space at least five times. "And tonight, all this depressing beauty is ours alone."

I say it as a joke, but neither of us laughs. Because this feels right, being here with Hannah. This place, hollowed out and still standing, full of history but nearly forgotten.

"I heard about what the state attorney decided," I say.

Hannah inhales a sharp breath. "Yeah."

"Are you okay?"

"I don't know. I didn't want a big mess, you know? But . . . the fact that some stranger gets to decide whether or not he thinks anyone would believe me, whether or not it actually happened? It's just . . . fuck."

"Yeah."

"They told me they found some pubic hairs during that god-awful examination, but you know what? The state attorney said they're not even going to test them because Owen used a condom."

"Oh."

"I told you I said no pretty far into it."

"No, I know."

"The attorney also said that even though the hairs could prove he had sex with me, the condom is problematic. That's what he said—*problematic*—like we're talking about some political opinion or something."

"That's fucked-up."

"Yeah. Everyone thinks that when someone gets ra—" She

swallows hard and takes a deep breath. "That when someone gets raped, it's this quick, spontaneous thing, always violent with bruises and black eyes. But I guess that's not always the case, you know? Even my wrist? *Problematic.* Because we were outside on a stone bench and hey, you know, awkward teenage sex."

"God."

She shrugs, but the motion is stiff, exhausted. "The fact that he was my boyfriend and we'd slept together before is a huge issue. Of course no one would believe me."

"I do."

Her eyebrows bunch together. "Why? He's your brother. You guys are close. He adores you, Mara. And you adore him, I know you do."

I don't answer right away. Instead, I sit down on an aisle step and lie back, eyes tracing the intricate patterns on the ceiling. Hannah joins me, linking her hands over her stomach.

"Sometimes, I don't know why," I say. "I even hate that I believe you. Like, he's my brother, right? He's my twin. I've felt sick since all of this happened and I can't help but feel that it's because *he* feels sick too. That any minute, he's going to sit us all down and explain what happened. Confess. Do *something* to make this anything other than what it is."

Silence fills the tiny space between us as tears clog up my throat, but then I just say it. I say it because I need to, because I have to, because it's the truth.

"I don't want to believe you."

A beat of too-quiet. "I don't want to believe me either."

"But I can't *not*. I tried, at first. Who wants to believe that about their own brother? But I . . . couldn't. I hate either option."

She takes my hand and squeezes. "Me too."

We sit there for a while, letting that settle around us.

"I still love him," I say, like a confession.

"Mara. God, of course you do."

"But you shouldn't have to say that." My throat aches, the wellspring of tears pushing at every cell. "You should be able to hate him and let all your friends hate him with you."

A million seconds go by before she speaks again. When she does, her voice is soft, almost a whisper. "Can I tell you something messed up?"

"Yeah."

"I miss him. The guy I knew before that night. The guy I think I loved. He was always a little spoiled, a little arrogant, but that was just . . ."

"That was just Owen."

"Yeah. It was sort of cute, you know?"

I nod, my mouth suddenly dry.

Hannah rubs at her eyes. "God, it's like he's two different people. And I should've known. Dammit, I should've known."

"How could you have known this would happen?"

"Well, not this. But he's a Gemini. I'm a Scorpio. Air and water, two different elements trying to blend. I thought we'd defied the stars, you know? I mean, I know a lot of people think astrology is silly, but I like it. I like the cosmic balance and purpose to it all. And I thought . . . I don't know what I thought. I thought we worked. Right up until the moment we didn't."

"It's okay that you like astrology, Hannah. I like it too." I think about Owen's and my stories on the roof. Twins adventuring in the sky. We've never paid much attention to our horoscope or how our sign might influence our lives like Hannah has, but the stars — the stars have always been a part of us.

"And none of this is your fault," I say. "Please tell me you know that."

She nods, fingers pressing into her eyes again.

"I don't think it's messed up that you miss him."

Brother and boy. Family and stranger. Friend and enemy. It *is* messed up, but not because we're splitting him apart in our minds. It's messed up because we have to.

"I can only say that about missing him to you, Mara. So, don't feel bad, okay? About feeling . . . the way you do about him."

I find her hand, twining us together and holding on as tightly as I can.

"Thank you," she says.

"For what?"

"For this." She holds up our hands and I squeeze her fingers.

"Would you have told anyone?" I ask. "If Charlie hadn't found you that night?"

She sighs heavily. "I don't know. I really don't. A huge part of me thinks I wouldn't have, even though I know that's the wrong answer. I should tell, right? It's a crime and I'll never be the same because of it. A lot of people will never be the same. My mom

keeps telling me I'm so brave, but I'm not. I'm just trying to sur-
vive, to get from sunup to sundown. But . . . I never got it before,
you know? All the stories I've heard other women tell about how
much shame there is in being the one it happens to. But there is.
There's this weight of responsibility, of . . . god, I don't know. Of
just existing. Like somehow, if I'd just stopped breathing at some
point, everyone would be better off. And I don't mean that like I
want to not exist . . . just like . . . I don't know. Like I *shouldn't.* Like
I feel stupid because I do exist. It's messed up."

Stupid little bitch echoes inside of me, an old companion, too
close and too sharp. And then I can't help it. Sobs leak out of me,
ugly and wet and loud. They reverberate through the empty theater. Hannah props herself on one elbow and I can't even look at
her. I cover my face, shuddering into my palms.

"Mara. What is it?"

I shake my head because this isn't her burden. She shouldn't
bear the weight of my story — she has her own, fresher, more raw,
more invasive, her abuser's sister lying right next to her. But there's
that something inside of me — stardust and silent tears — reaching out again for that something in her, something we share, something only the two of us in all the world can really understand.

And that's why everything that happened with Mr. Knoll spills
out of me. Not only to gain some comfort, but also to give it.

She doesn't speak when I'm done. I don't even think she breathes.
The silence is oppressive, so loud I'm about to scream. But then
Hannah curls into my side, her arm slung carefully over my stom-
ach. She lays her head on my shoulder and starts humming gently,

softly, beautifully. It's so perfect, water keeps streaming down my face, mingling with the tears I can hear in her own voice. Until this moment, I didn't realize how much I needed this, just someone to listen.

Soon, I blend my alto voice with her sweet soprano. We hum "Sing Me to Heaven," an a cappella song our choir performed last year at the spring concert. It's gorgeous and poetic and sad and powerful. Words form and wrap around the notes and soon we're sitting up, standing, though I don't remember getting to my feet. Our fingers wrap around the balcony railing, our voices finding the perfect tones as they fill the abandoned room.

In my heart's sequestered chambers lie truths stripped of poet's gloss . . .

The lyrics flow out of us, surreal and too real all at once. The sound is beautiful, our voices perfectly blended until I can't tell who's singing melody and who's harmonizing. Our fingers are knotted together, refusing to part as the emotion of the song — of unspeakable things — finds this strange release.

It's such a serious, sober song, written for perfectly controlled and trained voices, firm whispers and prayers.

Sing me a lullaby, a love song, a requiem . . .

But as Hannah and I sing, our voices grow louder and bolder, smiles lighting across our faces. A few gulps of laughter mixed with tears begin to escape every few notes, and soon our song is anything but reverent.

It's a battle cry.

We sing it again and again, our arms lifted above our heads, our bodies raised up on tiptoes and nearly bouncing, a musical echo swirling around us as if we've woken the dead.

And I can't help but hope that maybe we really have.

✸★✲.

On our way back to the car, Hannah pulls the hair elastic from her ponytail and flicks the rubber band to the asphalt. She never breaks her stride, but she slides her fingers through her shiny strands and tousles them into something slightly less smooth and tame.

It's not the beautiful, tangled mess it usually is.

But it's close.

CHAPTER TWENTY-ONE

THE NEXT MORNING, I blink my eyes open and stare at my ceiling fan, waiting for the familiar blanket of heaviness to settle on me like it has for the past few mornings.

Well. For the past few years, really. I'd gotten so used to it, so distracted at times by Empower and Charlie—almost happy—that I stopped noticing how much the weight scratched at my skin and hung on my shoulders, curling me in on myself.

But this morning . . . there's none of that. Instead, there's this clarity that almost scares me. The soothing hush of the sound machine and the hazy autumn sunlight filtering in through the slats in my blinds try to blur my thoughts, but they won't dull. Last night with Hannah sharpened everything, set loose a tidal wave of relief inside me. Finally *telling* someone. Finally knowing someone would believe me.

Last night, Hannah seemed okay when I dropped her off. We were both still teary and our throats were raw from singing totally improperly, but there was a sort of calm surrounding us both, as though we'd finally shaken off something heavy and old from our shoulders. Right before I drifted off to sleep, she texted me.

Thank you.

That's all she said, but in those two little words, I recognized her relief, to have someone to cry and scream and laugh with, to break into an old theater with just to prove we still had it in us.

I push my covers back and pull on a pair of jeans and my Pebblebrook Choral Singers sweatshirt. Last night, right after Hannah texted, Mom popped her head inside my door and informed me that she and Dad still expected me to attend my school's Fall Festival this weekend and work the "Guess That Song" booth.

"It raises money for the school," she said, "and neither Principal Carr nor I think it's appropriate for you to shirk your responsibilities. Especially considering I know you went somewhere with the car and you're technically grounded."

"Okay," I'd said. We looked at each other for a few seconds. I wasn't going to apologize for leaving the house and going out with Hannah. I wasn't sorry. Eventually, I rolled over in my bed and faced the wall. She lingered in the doorway and I could feel her eyes on me. I waited for her to come over and sit next to me, rub my back until I fell asleep.

She didn't, but I also don't remember her leaving. I must've fallen asleep with her still standing there, the stale smell of The Menagerie still clinging to my skin.

Now my hands shake as I pile my hair into a messy bun and slick on some mascara and lip-gloss. It's as if I've downed an energy drink on an empty stomach, all my nerves buzzing.

The Fall Festival is usually one of my favorite events at our school. It's hot cocoa and burning leaves and gold and russet cloths draped over bales of hay and silly games that make me laugh and act like a little kid. Last year, Charlie and I ran the boring bake sale booth, which we spiced up by requiring patrons not only to pay a dollar for their brownie but also to guess the song Charlie strummed on her guitar and I hummed loudly and obnoxiously. We pissed off so many chocolate-deprived parents, Ms. Rodriguez suggested simply running a song booth this year, sans baked goods.

My stomach flips at all the texts from Charlie that I ignored yesterday, followed by her silence. The Fall Festival equals normal, and if there's anything Charlie and I really need right now, it's normal.

Downstairs, my parents circle each other, preparing eggs and bacon and laughing like any other Saturday morning. My dad is drinking tea and my mother is probably on her fourth cup of coffee. She fills a plate with golden-yellow eggs and then hip-checks Dad away from the sink so she can rinse the pan. He responds by flicking a kitchen towel at her butt. I watch them for a minute, taking a deep breath. Something about the scene feels wrong, like trying to squeeze into a pair of jeans long too small.

Then Owen walks in the front door, sweaty and red-cheeked from a run, and my entire body locks up, fight-or-flight ratcheting up my pulse.

But something else edges out the panic. Something new and bright.

"Hi, honey," Mom says to him, setting two plates on the breakfast counter where Owen and I usually eat on school mornings. "Oh, Mara. You're here too. Dad and I have to go to the store, so you two are on your own at the festival."

"Wait," I say. "We're riding there together?"

Mom lifts an eyebrow at me. "Of course you are."

"I'll shower, I promise," Owen says, nudging my arm as he passes to grab a bottle of water from the fridge.

Frozen, I just stare at him. He moves like he always has, gracefully and strong, comfortable in his own skin. For the past week, something's been off a little, his body wearing a tension I was never used to seeing on him, and it helped divide him up in my mind. But now he simply looks like my brother, and I find I can't stop studying him as he uncaps the bottle, as he takes a few gulps, as his eyes meet mine and I see a familiar softness.

Gemini.

But then he looks away, and it's a crack of thunder. It's a song echoing through an abandoned theater. Nothing is the same. Nothing will ever be the same again.

Mom must see the conflict roiling in my expression, because she puts her hands on my shoulders and guides me out of the kitchen and into the living room, where she turns me around to face her. She squeezes my arms and looks me in the eyes for the first time in days.

"Sweetie. I know everything that happened with Owen was scary. But he's okay. They're not pressing charges and we need to move past this. For us. For our family." She tucks a lock of hair behind my ear. "We miss you, honey."

Hannah's tears from last night flash in my memory, a firework blasting into the dark sky.

But last night was more than sadness. It was more than anger. It was the way we curled into each other. Our song. The way my confession blended with her own story and it became something more than just what happened to me and what happened to her. It became what happened to *us*. Together. Last night, after I told Hannah everything and then we threw our voices out into that old theater, peeling walls and littered carpets and all, there was this hint of something I haven't felt in years.

Freedom.

Release.

A sort of falling apart that felt like letting go. And maybe that's what I've needed all these years. That's what she needed. Just for someone to hear us. There's a warmth in my blood from that, from Hannah, but I worry it's just a drop of fire in a frozen ocean.

I look down at my bare feet, green nail polish that Charlie painted on weeks ago receding away from my cuticles. The truth is, I miss the hell out of my family. Not only Owen, but my parents, too.

And I know Hannah's tired. We're all ready for this to be over. Really, I've been ready for three years. Everyone wants to move on. Problem is, I think everyone has a different idea about what *moving on* actually is.

I don't know what to say to my mother, so I sort of fall forward, hooking my arms around her waist and pressing my face against her shoulder.

Mom lets out a surprised *oof*, but wraps her arms around me immediately. She runs her hands over my hair, down my arms, all the ways I've wanted to let her hold me for the past week. For the past three years.

"I love you, honey," she says.

I squeeze her tighter, inhaling familiar hibiscus lotion and Dove soap. I do it for comfort, for connection, because I so want this moment with my mom to feel like a victory.

A change.

Even when everything in me knows there's still so much to say.

CHAPTER TWENTY-TWO

OWEN AND I DRIVE to the festival in silence. He keeps inhaling sharply, then clearing his throat, then picking a new song on his phone, then starting the whole routine over again. It reminds me of Charlie, both of them habitual fidgeters, so I know he wants to say something. I can't decide if I want him to or not.

That moment with my mom at home was the truth—I'm ready to move on. Criminal charges for Owen aren't a possibility now. Mr. Knoll was too long ago, too hard to prove. What else is there to do? What else is there for any girl to do, when everyone but her can just forget everything like a random bad dream? I have no idea what *moving on* sounds like, looks like. I've spent the past three years trying and decidedly not getting over anything.

"So," I say, swallowing hard. "How's first chair stuff?"

I feel him glance at me and I make myself meet his eyes. "Good," he says. "It's busy with the fall concert coming up. You know, I have to walk out there all by my little lonesome and lead the tuning. It's weird."

"Oh, please." I force a laugh. "You love it and you know it."

He shrugs, a smile touching the edges of his mouth. "What can I say, I was born to make grand entrances . . . *before everyone else.*"

"You did not just compare first chair to our birth."

"Birth certificates don't lie."

"Are you kidding? Of course they do. It's called human error. Some overworked and exhausted nurse clearly got our birth times all turned around and . . . maybe . . ."

My words slow and trail off, my throat tight. This feels wrong, this banter back and forth between us, as though these words are not the ones I should be saying.

"Mar?"

I don't answer him.

A few minutes later, Owen pulls the car into the school's parking lot, and we walk over to the grassy field next to the stadium where the festival is already in full swing. He hesitates near the booth he's manning, a cakewalk set to recordings of the school orchestra's best concerts.

"So, this is me," he says.

I nod but say nothing.

"Mara. What's wrong?"

"Nothing. I'm fine."

It's a lie and he knows it. He lifts his eyebrows, waiting for me to go on, but I'm already walking away before I can say anything else. What my words would be, I don't even know. They're formless in my head, dark swirls and sharp corners. They're not pleasant or witty or loving.

Not fine, not fine, not fine.

As I walk across the field, the words swirling through my head, my legs swishing through the grass, I feel dozens of eyes on me. I haven't seen anyone from school except Hannah since I tried to scratch Jaden's eyes out, and honestly, the memory almost calms me down a little. I jut my chin into the air as a few of Jaden's orchestra buddies glare at me. But then I remember that they're Owen's friends too, that the whole shit show with Hannah was *because* of Owen, whether he egged it on or not.

Not fine.

My walk slows a bit, but I force my jaw to tighten, my eyes fixed on the red-topped tent I see a little ways off, a GUESS THAT SONG sign fluttering in the breeze.

"Mara!"

I turn toward my name, bracing myself for some asshole, but nearly crumple to my knees when I see Alex weaving through a family laden with bright puffs of pink and blue cotton candy.

"Hi," I say, so relieved to see him that I actually manage a smile.

"You okay? I feel like I haven't talked to you in a while."

"It's been about a day."

He waves a hand and smiles, but it fades quickly. "I'm sorry how things went down at school."

Now it's my turn to wave a hand. "It's done. I'm fine."

Not fine.

"So, your parents set you loose?"

"Only to *work.*" I hook finger quotes around the last word. "But I'll take it."

"So will I. Hey, you want to come over tonight?"

I lift my brow and he actually blushes.

"Just to hang out," he says. "My parents always make dinner and we can . . . I don't know. Play Wii or something?"

"Wii? As in Mario Kart?"

He grins. "As long as I get to be Princess Peach."

I can't help but laugh at that. Owen always chose Princess Peach whenever the three of us played Mario Kart when we were younger. "She's badass!" he'd say, and I always loved that he picked her. How cool was it that my popular brother wasn't afraid to be the girl and make damn sure that she always won?

The thought is a sharp punch to the chest. Everything that's been simmering and boiling in me since last night surges, and for a second, I can't breathe.

"Hey." Alex steps closer. "You okay?"

I nod, pressing my hands against my stomach, trying to force air into my lungs.

Alex reaches out, and soon he's touching me for the first time since we kissed. It's not a huge deal, just his hands lighting gently on my shoulders, but it shocks me enough that I gulp a big breath and then another and soon feel calmer.

Until I see Owen watching us from a few tents down, open-mouthed, cakes stacked like a fortress on the table behind him. His forehead is wrinkled and his eyebrows bunch together like when he's confused. I call it his old man stare. Consequently, he calls it my old lady stare, because I do the exact same thing.

"Have you talked to Owen lately?" I ask Alex.

He frowns. "Not a lot, no."

"Yeah. Me neither."

"I know — I'm sorry."

I shrug, and his hands fall away from my shoulders. Unsaid words hang between us — *charges, belief, Hannah* — but I can't bring myself to say any of them.

"I've got to go find Charlie."

He nods. "Okay. Sure."

"Hey." I catch the sleeve of his navy sweater. "I'll see you tonight."

"Really?"

"Yeah. If my parents will let me."

He smiles, a tiny thing. "Six thirty?"

I nod before walking toward the song tent. I don't look back at Owen, but I can't help but picture us sitting on the roof, faces turned toward the stars.

You know you pretty much have to marry Alex now, right? he'd say.

Why's that?

He touched your shoulder — that's like a marriage proposal in my book. Plus, I can't divide my loyalties. Very unfair.

Ah, yes, I forgot that my friendships are all about your comfort.

Damn straight. Plus, then I can just live with you guys in your basement and you can take care of me for life.

Dreams do come true.

That's how it would go if all of this weren't happening. If there weren't all these lies and a stranger wearing my brother's face between us.

The ache in my chest is so sharp it steals my breath. I want that imagined conversation to be real. I want a lifetime of teasing smiles under the stars. Our stars. But I'm starting to think that life is gone forever. Maybe it never really was. Maybe I lost it the second Mr. Knoll asked me to stay behind. Maybe that's when I lost everything.

I keep walking, a million different thoughts and wishes trailing after me. Charlie comes into view and I pick up my pace.

She doesn't see me at first. She's perched on a stool behind a table, bent over a ball of gold yarn and brandishing her knitting needles, weaving the wool into a crimson lump. Her bottom lip is caught between her teeth and I see her mouth form the f-word as she unravels some unintended knot. She's so damn cute that the fact that we haven't talked in twenty-four hours fades to the back of my mind.

"Hey," I say as I duck under the tent's awning.

She startles, her knitting needles clattering onto the table, and her ball of yarn drops and rolls a few feet away.

"Hi," she says. Then she's in motion, picking up the needles and yarn and cramming the whole whatever-it-is she's knitting into her bag. She stuffs her hands into her pockets and tries to smile. "Hey."

"You okay?"

She nods. "Yeah. Just . . . I'm glad you're here."

Her gaze on me is so intense, her thoughts pretty much bleed out of her eyeballs.

"I'm fine," I say before she can ask. "Really."

"Yeah?"

I nod.

"You never texted me back," she says.

"You stopped texting me."

"Yeah, because you never texted me back."

I push my hair out of my face. "I was grounded and I needed to think."

"You had to know you'd get suspended for hitting Jaden."

"I didn't really think about it at the time. And Principal Carr suspended me for the skirt, too."

"For real?"

"Yep."

"Asshole. Though you did look . . ." She trails off, biting her lower lip.

"I did look what?"

A smile ghosts over her mouth. "Sexy as hell. But you look sexy as hell in anything."

My stomach handsprings down to my feet.

"Sorry," she says, lacing her hands together. "I shouldn't have said that."

"You're not allowed to think I'm pretty?"

She frowns. "No. I just . . . I don't know."

"Oh, right. *Tess.*"

"I didn't say that."

"Who the hell is she, anyway?"

Charlie sighs, dragging both hands through her hair. It sticks up everywhere, dark mountains and valleys, and it's so adorable it makes my teeth ache.

"I met her at that pizza night I went to a few weeks ago for my dad's school. Her mom's a math teacher there."

"Cute. Are you together?"

"Don't do that."

"What?"

"You know what. Talk to me like you're interested when you're actually pissed."

"I'm not pissed—I just want to know who she is."

Charlie fiddles with the peeling plastic rim of the table and shakes her head. Only when her eyes are off me do I register the throbbing in my fingers from balling them into tight fists, trying to hold all these different threads of my life together. But they're all coming unraveled.

"You wanted this," she whispers. "And you have Alex."

"I don't have him. We're just friends."

"You something him."

Hurt blankets her words, but I don't know what to say. When I broke up with Charlie, it seemed smart and safe, for both of us. I didn't think I could ever be a good girlfriend to Charlie. So I did want this. But I didn't want *this*. I brush my hand over her back, feeling her breaths push against my fingertips.

Romance and friendship blur with Charlie and me. Always have. It's hard to tell the difference. It's hard to tell which is more important. It's even harder to tell if one actually has to be more important than the other with us. But Charlie and me, we'll always be more than something.

"So do you have a list of songs with which to stump our patrons?" I ask, leaning against the plastic table. I need to stop thinking about this. I need to stop thinking about everything.

She stares at me for a few long seconds, a thousand emotions playing over her face. Finally, she presses her lips together and looks down at her feet, nodding.

"Songs?" I ask again.

"Yeah." She reaches under the table and pulls out a glass fishbowl filled with folded-up pieces of paper. After setting it onto the table, she grabs her guitar from its case on the ground and strums a little, twisting the tuning pegs. "They're all pretty basic. Shouldn't be too hard."

I sift through the bowl and pull out a slip of paper, unfolding it and rolling my eyes.

"'Let It Be'? If you can't guess that within three notes, you don't deserve the glow-in-the-dark bracelet or edible necklace or whatever crap we got donated as prizes this year."

Charlie pretends to be affronted. "Everyone deserves a fair shot at a temporary *Wicked* tattoo, Mara." She grabs a wicker basket full of quarter-size Elphabas and Galindas and sets it next to the fishbowl. "Everyone."

I laugh, so glad to be joking around with my best friend again.

Soon, we start getting a few customers and Charlie strums the tinny strings while I hum "Hotel California" and "Billie Jean." In between customers, she shows me a few chords on the guitar.

"It looks like I'm flipping someone off," I say as she places my fingers on the frets.

"It's a G."

"Still looks like I'm flipping someone off."

"Well, they probably deserve it."

She releases my ring finger and it immediately pops out of place.

"Dammit," I say. "My fingers don't bend that way."

She laughs. "Yes they do. They just have to learn how." She scoots her stool behind mine and my insides flop when I feel her breath on my neck. Her chest presses against my back as she wraps her arms around me so she can manipulate my hands on the guitar, her legs wide on either side of me. I clear my throat as she concentrates, peering over my shoulder as she pushes my fingertips to the strings.

"Ow," I say, but it's a whisper.

"You need rougher fingers. They're too soft."

"My fingers are plenty rough when they need to be. Besides, what's wrong with soft fingers?"

When she doesn't answer, I turn my head toward her and nearly collide with her face. I didn't realize how close she was, but my mouth is inches from her reddening cheek, which completely confuses me until I retrace our conversation in my head.

"God, way to make it awkward, Mara," I say, feigning conversing with myself to cover my embarrassment.

Charlie laughs and her flush deepens. She's so pretty, I have to take my gaze away, remove my hands from under hers. I wish this would go away, this constant desire to go back on what we said we wanted, what we said was right for us.

I feel Charlie's hair against my cheek, as if she's shaking her head, and she inhales deeply. She's still the color of a beet, but she takes my hand back and runs her fingers along mine, setting them on the frets again. "This is G." She folds my fingers into a new position, gentle and careful. "C." Her voice is soft in my ear and her callused fingertips glide over and under my own, moving them easily. "D." Another bend, another feathery touch. "And E minor."

I hold my breath and my blood pounds out a rhythm in my veins. I'm not sure what Charlie's doing, but it's not just a guitar lesson. There's a Tess out there somewhere, but in here, there's just a Mara and a Charlie.

And that—*us*—is my normal.

"Learn those four and you've got a song," Charlie says, her mouth still close to my ear.

"Okay." I'm out of breath, out of thoughts. "I'll practice those."

"You do that." Her voice has a flirty lilt to it and I don't know what to do with that.

Charlie and I separate when a tired-looking mother ambles up to our booth with two little kids in tow. I hum "You Are My Sunshine," and we pass out a few more tattoos. Several more parents and students visit our tent, all of them easily guessing the songs. Even Principal Carr comes by and leaves with a Galinda, though

I'm almost positive he leaned over the table to check the length of my skirt. He pretty much *harrumph*ed under his breath when he spotted my jeans.

Around five, we start closing down the booth. Everything in me feels like kindling. I'm placing the fishbowl into a cardboard box full of stuff that needs to go back into the school, but I can't stop thinking about Charlie's fingers on mine over the guitar, guiding me, helping me. Her voice in my ear. A voice I've always trusted.

My favorite voice in the world. My favorite person in the world.

I rub my eyes to keep the tears back, to keep all the *fine* in place, and then, just like I knew she would be, Charlie's right there.

My back is to her, but she taps my elbow.

"Hey," she says softly. "What's wrong?"

Because there is no hiding with her. There never really has been. It's only because she met me after Mr. Knoll that she never knew I was keeping something from her. But now that *something* doesn't want to stay hidden. It's tired of the dark. I fed it a bit of light last night with Hannah and it's hungry, this something. It's ravenous. Distracting it with guitar lessons and dinner with Alex isn't enough. Those things are a penlight when it wants the sun. It needs light and air and maybe, maybe, maybe if I tell Charlie, my *person*, it'll be satisfied. Maybe then it can finally lie down and sleep.

"Hey," Charlie says again. My shoulders are shaking. My hands. My legs. My heart. My lungs.

I turn and settle on a stool, my breathing so loud and deep that I'm dizzy.

Charlie sits next to me. "Mara, you're scaring me."

She sounds totally freaked out, so I grab her hand. Breathe. Breathe.

"Whatever this is, let me help," she says. She leans closer to me, her cheek on my shoulder. It's so natural. So safe. So right. So us.

I rest my head on hers and look out at the festival winding down. Little girls with sticky cotton-candy fingers. Tween girls with freshly glossed lips, casting shy glances at the high school boys. Girls my own age in jeans, in skirts, in running shorts, in flannel, long hair and short hair and dyed hair, walking through the grass, searching, hunting, needing connection and belief and validation and *something*.

Something to feel worthy. To feel like ourselves.

"Mara," Charlie says. She lifts her head and wipes the tears off my face with her thumbs. "Is it Owen?"

I think about this, because everything has felt like Owen lately. But then I realize this isn't. This isn't Owen at all. This is me. This is mine.

And then I open my mouth and give myself a little more light.

CHAPTER TWENTY-THREE

CHARLIE'S FINGERS TIGHTEN AROUND MINE, her eyes dark with worry. But she doesn't say a word. She just waits, stays close while I tell her everything.

It has nothing to do with bravery or strength. It has to do with nothing left to lose. No matter how much I've tried to make it all work, I don't have Charlie. I don't have my brother. I don't even have myself anymore. Now that day with Mr. Knoll tumbles out of me in a messy rush, tears and snot, trembling and embarrassment and shame. It explodes into the light, carnivorous and determined, and I let it have its way.

"Oh my god, Mara," Charlie breathes out when I'm finished.

"That's why I could never . . . when we were together, why I didn't let you . . . didn't touch you . . ." A sob gets stuck in my throat and all I can do is wave my hand between the two of us, hoping she gets what I'm saying.

"No, no, no," she says. "Shhh, don't even think about that. It's okay. You know that was always okay with me."

"I wanted to," I say, my voice broken wide open, light spilling into all of the cracks. "I really did want to."

Then I'm in her arms and she's holding me so close that I can feel her heart beating an erratic rhythm, feel her softly shaking, register the hot splash of tears that aren't mine against my cheek. I cling to her, feeling hollowed-out and full all at once, hunger replaced with nourishment.

"That's why you seemed so sad when I first met you," she says.

"I did?" I ask.

She pulls back so she can see me and nods. "I wanted to make you smile so damn bad."

"You did make me smile. Every day."

Tears race down her cheeks, matching mine, and she swipes them away. "God, I'm sorry. I'm so sorry," she says.

I don't know what to say to that. Don't know what to say to anything. I just want to stay here, where Charlie knows my secret and I don't have to think about anything other than the spicy scent of the boy deodorant she uses and the press of her fingertips on my back.

We stay like that for a while, close breaths and light caresses. I feel that hungry *something* retreat and I sigh in relief. I feel it start to lie down. I feel it getting drowsy, satiated by my confession.

"Why didn't you tell anyone?" she asks softly, and everything wakes up again. The *something* leaps to its feet and prowls.

I untangle myself from her.

"Didn't you have proof that you didn't cheat?" she asks. "Did he name the person who said you did? When he had to file the paperwork about you failing?"

I blink at her, *stupid little bitch* echoing in my head.

"He . . . I don't know," I say. "Administration called in my parents a few days later, told them what happened."

"And your parents never questioned it?"

I swallow. "I . . . I don't . . ." But I can't get it out. I can't say *I never gave them a reason to*, even though it's true. In Empower, Charlie has seen me speak out for so many issues, so many girls and queer kids. But never myself. Not directly, at least. I've lumped myself in with my labels—*girl, bi, queer*—but I still can't seem to really apply any of it to the person I see in the mirror every day. That girl is still voiceless, still scared.

"Mara, you have to tell them now," she says.

"What? No."

"Why not? You need . . . god, Mara, you need to tell them. They need to know, get that asshole fired and locked up."

"I—"

"Oh my god, does he still work there? Does he still teach?"

I press both hands to my forehead, trying to calm my thoughts.

"Does he?" Charlie asks, and all I hear is *stupid stupid stupid.* The fact is, I know he still works at Butler. He teaches prealgebra and coaches the boys' basketball team, and I caught a glimpse of him through the velvet curtains last spring when all the middle schools in the county were bused over to watch Pebblebrook's production of *Guys and Dolls.* He looked exactly the same and was talking with a smiling female student as they filed into the auditorium. During the show, I lost him in the crowd and lights, and I'd never been so glad to be denied a principal role in the musical as I was that day.

Now all I can think about is that smiling girl. His student. I'm sure she trusted him, liked him, thought he was cute. She had wavy brown-red hair. It was long, coiling more than halfway down her back. Just like mine.

I wonder if she was in summer school this past June and July.

"Mara."

I wonder if she was scared.

"Mara, look at me."

I wonder if she fought back.

"Mara, you have to—"

"Charlie, shut up!"

She blanches, her mouth falling open. A mom and her young son walk by the tent, shooting us alarmed glances, their arms piled with stuffed animals and buttery bags of popcorn.

Charlie leans in closer, lowering her voice. "I'm just trying to—"

"To help. I know. To do the right thing. I know that too. But it's not that easy—it's not black and white."

She frowns. "I'm sorry. I'm just . . . Mara, I'm worried about you. This is huge and you've been dealing with it alone for three years. And yes, it *is* black and white. He's a scumbag and a child molester."

"I know he is. And I know he's the asshole here. What he

did is black and white, yeah, but *dealing* with it isn't. Did you know he was awarded Teacher of the Year that spring? Teacher of the fucking *Year.* It never even entered my parents' minds that he might be lying about my cheating. Because why the hell would the teacher of the year lie about a stupid little girl's tests? No one would believe me. They wouldn't have then. They sure as hell won't now."

"I believe you. And I believe Hannah. Belief *does* happen."

I know she's right. But no matter how much I try to convince myself otherwise, my own belief is so mixed up with my brother, I can't see the situation clearly. Can't see what to do about it. Can't help Hannah, can't hate Owen, can't say anything that matters. Anywhere I turn, I'm betraying my own—my friend, my brother, myself. Belief isn't easy, it isn't black and white.

"I just want to move on," I say. I shove my hands through my hair, fingers tangling in my curls. "I just want to let it go. I can move on."

"Not like this. I'm sorry, Mara, but I don't think you can."

"Why not? I told Hannah. She gets it. She can help me. I can help her. I told *you.* That's all I need. You two are all I need—it's enough."

Charlie's lower lip trembles. "I get that, but that doesn't change the fact that your parents have no idea that this happened. That he's still out there, working with kids. You can't get any closure because of that."

"So Hannah can't either?" I shoot back, and Charlie pales.

"Owen's going to walk away from all this like it's nothing but a bad breakup story. She doesn't get to move on?"

"That's different. She tried. She told the truth. And she's going to start seeing a therapist—she's trying to work through it."

"So I'm a piece of shit because I just want to forget it and move on?"

Charlie's eyes widen. "No. Of course not. I didn't mean that at all."

Tears run down my face, desperation in every single drop. Desperation and anger and exhaustion. So much exhaustion.

"Just tell the truth," Charlie says softly. Too softly and it pisses me off. "That's all you have to do, and I'll help you."

"Oh, because you're so damn good at truth telling—just ask your parents."

The words are out before I can stop them. She visibly flinches. "I—"

"They've got a perfect daughter, don't they? Their daughter would never go play on some Nashville stage behind their backs. Their daughter would never feel like a fucking stranger in her own body sometimes, would she?"

"Holy shit, Mara."

I know I'm being an asshole, but I can't stop, can't seem to shut up. "Have your parents ever even asked why all your friends call you *Charlie?* Oh wait. I forgot. Of course they have. But you lie *with loving care.*"

She gapes at me, and one thick tear plummets down her

cheek. She brushes it away before I can decide if it was really there or not.

"That's not the same thing," she whispers. "They already know I like girls. And I can come out to my parents about my *own fucking body* when I'm ready. I'm not hurting anyone."

"Neither am I."

"You're hurting yourself. And who knows if that asshole—"

"I need some time," I say without looking at her. I can't stand to see the disappointment in her eyes, the anger, and I hate her a little for that, for taking away my safe place. For taking away this moment where I thought the confession would be enough. "Can you just leave me here?"

"Mara—"

"Please."

"Shit. I know you're upset and I don't mean to pressure you. I just—"

"Fucking *go!*" A few festival-goers passing by startle at my scream, wide-eyed and whispering.

Charlie rears back as though I slapped her. The space between us grows thick with this *need* to do something, be something, change something. But eventually, Charlie does what I ask, leaving me on the stool with nothing but the too-gentle press of the evening breeze to calm me down.

Eventually, I stand up and find my way into the parking lot, half blind from silent tears. Our car is nowhere to be found, but I barely register its absence. I start walking, the movement distracting and welcome. But it feels as if the miles between here and wherever I end up will never be enough to silence the voice in my head.

Because there is no way to really move on. No song or empathetic friend or all the love I have for my brother will ever change that, and I was *stupid stupid stupid* to think that I could. There is no going back.

CHAPTER TWENTY-FOUR

STUPID LITTLE BITCH.

Stupid little bitch.

Stupid little bitch.

The words are loud, impossible to silence, even as cars fly past me as I drift down the sidewalk in a daze. I'm not even sure where I am, how close to home, what street is coming up or why I didn't just call Owen to come get me.

That last idea sends a shiver twisting up my spine. I'm not even sure why, whether it's the fact that he left me at the festival without telling me or the thought of him at all—just existing and sharing my blood and the stars above us and a birthday—so close to me but somehow lost. I can't tell what anything means, can't sift through my cloudy thoughts.

Next to me, a car slows and I stiffen. Immediately, I realize the sky is dark, and my eyes peel through my surroundings for some place to run or hide.

How? I think. *How did I get like this?*

"Mara!"

Hearing my name only increases my speed, tightens the ball of panic in my chest.

"Mara! Are you okay?"

The female voice makes me pause, makes me take a deep breath. I turn toward the dark-green SUV rolling slowly next to me. The passenger window is down and I see Greta leaning over the center console, her blond hair almost glowing in the dark.

"Do you need a ride?"

I stare at her for a moment before answering. She pretty much kicked my ass out of my own club, but her voice is soft right now and she's putting off whatever her Saturday night plans are to make sure I'm okay.

"All right. Thanks."

I slide into her car just as a massive black truck slows down behind her and lays on the horn.

"Yeah, yeah," she mutters. "Hold your wad, asshole."

Something about this makes me laugh. Greta smiles at me and rolls her eyes at the huge truck that seems to me more than a little horn-happy.

"Compensating for something, are we?" she says.

I laugh again, buckling my seat belt as she pulls away from the curb, but then suddenly I just feel so damn tired. As though that laugh was all I had left in me. I rest my head against the window as she drives through town — apparently, I somehow ended up on Fourth Avenue near The Menagerie — and will myself to fall asleep or disappear or whatever comes first.

"You okay?" she asks.

"No. Not really."

She says nothing to that. It's probably not the answer she expected. Hell, it's not even the answer I expected to give her. Greta and I aren't exactly the kind of friends who offer up more than the obligatory *I'm fine* or *Doing well* to the *How's it going* question.

"Look," she finally says. "I've been meaning to talk to you."

"Oh yeah?" I ask blankly. "About what?"

"About Empower. I'm sorry how that went down. I feel bad. I just didn't know how to handle the whole situation. God, it was just awkward." She pulls onto my street and keeps talking. "But you were totally badass, yelling at Jaden and everything."

I snort a laugh. "I did more than yell at him."

"I know, and that had to be hard."

"Are you condoning my violent acts, Greta?"

She smiles. "That's bad, right? I shouldn't be, but yeah, I guess I am."

"Well, Jaden's a dick."

"Such a dick."

In front of my house, she throws the car in park, but I don't get out. Owen's car — *our* car — isn't in the driveway, but the house windows glow warmly, beckoning deceptively with love and acceptance and faith. "You were right."

She shifts toward me. "I was?"

"About Empower. I was in no position to lead. Maybe I never was."

"I don't think that's true."

"It is."

"Mara, you do a great job. You have really great ideas, and your articles for the paper are amazing. They're important and you're a really good writer. People actually read them. Like, most of the school, in fact. That's pretty huge."

A couple of weeks ago, I would've lapped up her words, beamed and turned a delicate shade of red, shy and proud all at once. Especially hearing them from Greta, who I always felt saw through me anyway.

Now I just feel ashamed.

"Can you take me to Alex Tan's?" I ask her.

I feel her hesitation, so I tack on a *please.* She agrees and we drive the few miles in silence.

When she pulls into Alex's driveway, Owen's and my car is right there, parked so casually and benignly, there's absolutely no reason for this wave of dread to wash over me.

No reason whatsoever.

☀★*.

Alex's house is a Victorian-style home that looks like something right out of a ghost story. It's three levels high and bright white, with a huge screened-in front porch and tall columns in front of a long circular driveway. Next to Alex's sun-yellow TLB, my own car is parked crookedly, as though Owen was in a hurry when he got here.

I tell Greta goodbye, thanking her with as much sincerity as I can muster through my trembling voice. Then I wait until she drives away to walk around the side of the house, hoping I'll find the boys playing basketball near the garage. The net hangs above the doors, tattered with age and undisturbed. Hands buried in the pocket of my sweatshirt, I round back to the front, heading for the porch stairs.

I've just put one foot on the bottom step when I hear my brother's voice.

". . . asshole about this."

"I'm not. I just—"

"You are. You've been acting like a douche for a week and now my sister? Really, Alex? She's my fucking *sister*."

"We're just hanging out."

"Yeah, right. You've never wanted to hang out before. Not without me."

I freeze, my heart huge and loud in my chest.

"I would never hurt Mara," Alex says.

"That's not the point. My best friend boning my sister is just weird."

"Holy shit, dude. We're just friends!"

"You know she's bi, right? Can't make up her mind."

I suck in a breath, my hand clapping over my mouth to keep in the sudden sob strangling my lungs. Did my brother really just say that about me? Owen gets mouthy when he's stressed, can't shut up. I know this. But all his talk has never been directed at me quite like that, and his words feel like a knife dividing us into two.

For a few seconds, there's nothing—no sound, no air, no light.

Then, quietly, Alex says, "Do you even hear yourself right now? This isn't you."

A beat. "You don't know what's me or not, because you don't give two shits anymore."

Alex says something I can't make out. The porch swing lets out a groan — someone getting up.

"Fine," Owen says. "Fuck you."

"Owen, come on."

"No, no, it's fine. Good to know you pretty much think I'm a lying asshole."

"That's not—"

But the door leading into the screened-in porch flies open, banging against the stair railing. My brother storms out, Alex on his heels. Owen freezes when he sees me. There's a flash of sadness in his eyes. Regret. But then something hard glosses over his face, and his jaw tightens.

"Fucking figures," he mutters, then brushes past me at the bottom of the stairs, nearly knocking me over. I grip the banister, shocked as I watch my brother and his best friend of more than ten years fall apart.

Alex squeezes my arm, but it's a flash of comfort, because then he's running through the grass after Owen. He catches up with him at our car, pulling Owen's shoulder around.

"Get the hell off!" Owen yells. His tone feels like knives in my stomach because it's not just anger in his voice. It's fear and sadness and panic and loneliness. Maybe it's a twin thing, but I can almost taste his emotions, a bitterness on the back of my tongue. I sure as hell feel them.

"Don't do this, man," Alex says. "Just talk to me. Tell me the truth—that's all I'm asking. All I ever asked."

My fingers dig into the white paint of the handrail, a little sliver cutting under one of my nails.

Because they're not talking about me anymore.

Owen glares at him, his chest heaving up and down. "You don't want the truth. You just want to pretend like nothing's changed. Like you didn't totally crap out on me when shit got hard."

His glance moves to me. There's a sheen to his eyes that makes me move away from the stairs and closer to him. The stars are out and I want to put my brother into our car, drive him home and sit next to him on the roof, spinning tales.

Spinning lies.

I stop in my tracks and he visibly flinches. He locks his jaw into place, but I see it trembling and I feel paralyzed. Unmoored and floating through space.

Then he gets in the car, engine rumbling and tires squealing as he backs out of the driveway. Alex stumbles back and shoves both hands through his hair, watching Owen leave.

He stands there for a few seconds, hands still on his head, staring at the street. Finally he turns, wordless, and takes my hand. He leads me up the stairs and into his house. We step into a big open space, the foyer leading into the kitchen leading into the living room. His parents are cooking and the whole house is filled with savory smells and bubbling sounds, but when they see us, they freeze, concern etched all over their faces.

"We'll be down in a minute," Alex calls. I barely have a chance to wave before he's pulling me up another set of stairs and into his bedroom.

"Sorry," he breathes as he releases me and sits on the bed. He drops his head into his hands. "I need a minute. I just . . ."

His shoulders shake and he makes a wrecked sort of noise. I stare at him, totally transfixed as everything I feel pours out of him. I've known him my whole life and barely know him. He's falling apart right in front of me and I can't help but feel a wash of relief, because now I'm not so alone while all these pieces of myself fall away one by one.

I walk over to him, barely making it before I sink to my knees. I don't care about this uncrossable gap between us, I don't care who I love and who I need. I don't care. All I care about right now is making all of this go away. Everything I just told Charlie. Everything that just happened between Alex and Owen. All the days, all the minutes, all the seconds, wondering *why* and *how* and *what now.*

I need it all gone.

And Alex needs it gone too.

I press close to him, his legs on either side of my hips, and run my hands up his arms to his shoulders. He's still trembling, and a tear slips down his nose and darkens a spot on his jeans. I glide my hands up to his neck, then cup his face before slipping my fingers into his hair. I can't stop touching him, mingling his loss with mine.

His breathing calms and he lifts his head, red and tired eyes searching my face. He opens his mouth to speak, but nothing ever comes out. Instead, he grips my hips and pulls me closer.

Our foreheads press together. I feel the tears on his face and it feels so good that I move my mouth to his. He opens to me, desperation and hunger colliding. My thoughts go hazy, dreamlike, and the feeling is a drug, morphine to a broken heart. I flick open the first few buttons on his shirt, sliding my hands across his skin. He shivers, his hold on me tightening. I push myself to my feet, but only so I can crawl onto his lap, my knees closing around his hips.

I'm shaking and I can't tell if it's the good kind or not. Everything is skin and adrenaline. Sounds and spit and teeth, the gentle scrape of fingernails as our shirts hit the floor. Alex's lips are on my neck, my collarbone, everywhere. My hands pull at his hair and he rolls us onto the bed so he's above me. His fingers fumble with my bra clasp and I reach behind me to help him.

"This is okay?" he asks.

"Yes."

The word explodes through me, empowering and sexy, and I can't get my bra off fast enough. His parents are downstairs but I don't care. My heart is dissolving in my chest, but the rest of me is alive, finally. The rest of me needs, wants.

Then his hips roll into mine and my vision goes dark. I feel him through his jeans and I can't breathe, the hard jolt through my center too much, too foreign and familiar all at once.

Hannah. Lying cold and shocked on a trail bench.

Me. Trembling and wishing I'd just disappear.

My entire body goes cold and then numb, my chest so tight I can barely get a breath as memories flood in.

My hand where I never wanted it.

My tears pulling at his smile.

My voice too shocked and scared and small to say no.

To say stop.

To scream.

"Stop," I manage to whisper. "Stop, stop."

Alex is off me and on the other side of the bed so quickly, it's almost as though he were never there.

"Shit, I'm sorry," he says, breathing hard. "Fuck, I'm so sorry."

I shake my head but I curl up, wrapping my arms around my knees to cover myself and stop the shaking. I'm dizzy, too much oxygen, not enough space in my lungs.

"Alex," I choke out. "You didn't . . . you didn't do anything wrong."

"Yes, I did. Shit. I'm such an asshole."

I want to crawl over to him, but I can't move, can't make my thoughts stop screaming at me.

Stupid little bitch.

Stupid little bitch.

Stupid little bitch.

I squeeze my eyes shut and pull one of his pillows to my chest, trying to get a damn grip. I've never been with a boy like this. Never even been with Charlie like this. We only ever went to second base, and even that took months, and then it was only over the bra or Charlie's chest binder for even more weeks after that. I've never touched anyone my own age below the waist. And it's not that I don't want to — I do. I wanted to with Charlie. God, I wanted to, but every time my fingers brushed the button on her jeans, I'd freeze and it was as if some force I couldn't control was moving my hand away. Her hands would drift south too, and she'd always ask if it was okay, and every single time, I'd lock up and move her hand back to my waist. She was fine with it, her kisses just as gentle, the sigh she released whenever I pressed my lips to her collarbone just as happy and content as ever.

Right now I want this with Alex, even though it's for all the wrong reasons. But my body and mind are at war, fear and memory shredding through the desire.

"I'm sorry, Mara," Alex says, and he sounds totally destroyed.

"Alex, look at me."

He does, but I still can't make myself go over to him, and when I speak, I don't even recognize my voice. Or maybe I do. Maybe that scared little girl is finally tired of being tucked away and hidden. "You're fine. I just freaked out."

"This is not fine, Mara. This is anything but fine. I can't do this . . . I can't."

I stare at him, thinking back on him and Owen in the driveway, his tears on this very bed just minutes ago, and something shifts inside me. Another memory of a different night, a different Alex, a different Mara.

Did you find Owen?

Yeah. He's fine. He's fine, he's with Hannah.

"Alex. Why did you ask Owen to tell you the truth tonight? What did you mean?"

He lifts his head to look at me, but he can't hold my gaze. He squeezes his eyes shut and takes a deep breath.

But you saw him and Hannah at the lake, when you went back to tell him you were taking me home?

Yeah, I saw him.

And he was fine, right? Hannah was fine?

They . . . they were pretty wrapped up in each other. I didn't want to interrupt them.

"Alex."

"I just want him to talk to me. Really talk."

"What—"

"I saw them. That night. At the lake, I saw them."

"You already told me that," I say. But he didn't. He didn't tell me like this. With fear and guilt in his eyes, with tear tracks still on his cheeks.

"What did you see?" I ask.

"I . . . I don't know. They were on the bench and it was dark and I could tell they were kissing, but when I got closer . . ."

"What? What happened?"

"It just didn't look right. They weren't . . . totally naked or anything, but Hannah's dress was pushed up and Owen was . . . sort of . . . holding her arms down." He gasps a breath, literally gasps, and drags a hand down his face. "Her face was turned away from me. So was his. I couldn't . . . I couldn't tell. I got out of there pretty fast and I thought they were just . . . you know. But the more I thought about it, it just didn't look right. It didn't look right at all."

"I thought you just saw them kissing."

"I—"

"That's what I thought you told me."

"I told the state attorney what I saw. The day after it happened, he called my parents and me to his office because he wanted to talk to all of Owen's friends. I told him because I just couldn't . . . I couldn't get it out of my head, you know?"

"Yeah, I goddamn do know, Alex."

He winces and takes a deep breath. "The attorney didn't bat a fucking eye, Mara. You know what he said? He said it didn't prove anything. He said the defense would just claim that some girls like it rough and drag Hannah through the mud to prove it. He said it was a classic he said—she said scenario."

"That's because people are assholes, Alex, not because you didn't see something important."

"It didn't make a difference, Mara!"

"It makes a difference to me. To Hannah. Shit, maybe even to my parents. How could you not tell me? Even after knowing how devastated Hannah is? Even after you could see how broken up *I* am, all that shit Owen and his friends pulled at school?"

Alex shoves his hand into his hair but yanks it out just as quickly. "He's my best friend, Mara. He's the kid who told off those jerks in middle school when they made fun of the way my eyes are shaped. He's the guy who actually cared about *me* and asked me stuff about my heritage instead of treating me like I was some exotic story. You think it's easy to believe he raped his girl-friend? You think that's an easy thing to just admit?"

"How fucking dare you." I get off the bed, pillow pressed to my chest. All my limbs are shaking as I find my shirt and throw it over my head, dropping the pillow. I don't know where my bra is, nor do I care. "He's my twin brother. You want to talk *easy?*"

He presses his eyes closed. "I know. Shit. I'm sorry. I didn't know how to handle it."

"You sure as hell didn't." I scour the room for my bag and find it near the door, half of its contents spilling across the floor from where I dropped it in my desperation to hold on to this boy who's a fucking liar just like every other boy.

"Please don't go."

But I'm already opening his door.

Stupid little bitch.

And I am. I am so, so stupid.

"At least let me take you home," he says, getting to his feet.

"I'm fine."

"Mara, *please.*"

The crack in his voice stops me. I turn to meet his eyes and everything in me deflates. He's not a threat. He's not smirking at me or manipulating me. He's standing in the middle of his room, shirtless, stomach and shoulders looking almost shriveled as he folds in on himself.

He's just as broken as I am.

"I'm sorry," he says, fresh tears falling. "Please. Fuck, I'm so

249

sorry. I'll talk to Hannah. I'll tell her I'm sorry too. I just didn't know what to do."

My breathing is tight and fast in my lungs, but god, I can't walk away from him. Because I don't know what to do either.

I drop my bag to the floor but keep hold of the strap. "I'm sorry too. This is . . . I didn't expect this."

"I didn't want to keep it from you. It was shitty."

"Not that. I mean, yes, you should've told me, but that's not what I'm talking about." I look down at his floor, following the tiny fissures all along the decades-old hardwood. I wave my hand between us. "This."

His expression falls, and with that subtle drop of his eyes, I know he didn't expect it either.

"We should probably just call this what it is, Alex."

"And what is it?"

"Two really lonely people in a lot of pain."

He sighs and rubs at his forehead. "That's not true."

"Really? Then why have you never asked me out? Why have we never hung out without Owen or Charlie? It's not just because of them. It's because it's never crossed our minds before right now. Until we were all each other had. Even after we kissed at the cemetery, we didn't know what to do about it. Didn't *want* to do anything about it."

"I've always thought you were beautiful and talented. I've told you that."

"That doesn't equal wanting to be with someone."

"I'm not using you," he says, his voice strained.

"Yes, you are. And I'm using you. It's okay to admit it. It doesn't make you an asshole."

"Yeah, well, what does it make me?"

"Fucking human."

He presses his mouth together, his chin all wobbly, and it claws at something inside me.

"I knew he was lying," he says, staring down at his feet. "And I knew you knew it too, and I . . . didn't know what to do. It just . . . it helped. Being around you."

My throat aches. "I know."

"But that's not all it is," he says.

"No. But that's how it started. And it's not enough. You know?"

He nods, chewing on his bottom lip.

"I don't want to lose you as my friend," I say. "That's meant a lot to me, but I'm not ready for this. I don't think I'll ever be ready for this. For you and me. For a lot of reasons."

"Mara—"

"I need to go."

"Seriously, let me take you."

I shake my head, lifting my bag from the floor. "I'll call a ride."

"Are you sure?"

"Yeah. Bye, Alex."

He lifts a hand, sadness and regret like a winter coat around his shoulders.

Downstairs, I find his parents and offer some halfhearted excuse about too much homework. They're super nice, smiling and inviting me back some other time. I think I smile back, but something in me is cracking, the memory of how Alex's body felt on mine so welcome and so horrible at the same time. I just need out, need air, need away from Alex, who I like and want but for all the wrong reasons. Who I don't like and want enough.

I manage a civil goodbye and get myself out the front door. Every nerve hums and tears blur my steps as I walk through his yard and spill onto the sidewalk down the block. I collapse on a bench half covered with low-hanging magnolia branches, my lungs heaving, tears falling, too many fears and thoughts swirling in my head.

I take my phone out and send a text. Ten minutes later, Hannah finds me crying on the bench and takes me home.

CHAPTER TWENTY-FIVE

I KNOW HANNAH WANTS TO WALK ME TO MY DOOR. I also know she physically can't get herself out of the car. She came to a complete stop on the street before she was finally able to turn into the driveway, and now we're just sitting here, both of us staring at my house while I try to calm down.

My face feels cracked from dried tears and I'm still shaking. Can't stop shaking. "It's okay," I say, when I think I have enough breath. I'm far from calm, but it'll have to do.

"I can't go any farther," she says, her eyes fixed on the top floor windows of the house, my brother somewhere behind them. Her fingers wrap around the steering wheel. "I'm a shitty friend."

"You're not. You're amazing and I love you." I hug her, as much as I can while my bones rattle together, and press a kiss to her forehead. "Thank you for coming to save me."

She laughs, but it's soft. "I didn't save you. I can't save anyone."

"You can. You did."

"I just hate that we hurt like this, you know?"

"What do you mean?"

She grabs my hand and squeezes. "I think about the things we've talked about in Empower. Articles we've read about all the girls who were thrown away by boys like they meant nothing. All the times a girl's voice seemed to mean less than a boy's. All the times the courts sent out a shit ruling on a rape case. It never really hit me, you know? I mean, it did, but not like this. I never thought it'd be *my* story. Or yours. I never wanted to let this be our story."

"You didn't let it happen, Hannah. You trusted Owen. There's a difference. And with me . . ." I inhale a deep breath. "I didn't let him either. He just took."

She nods and squeezes my hand tighter.

I want to tell her about Alex, about what he saw, and I will, but right now there's this feeling inside me that I can't explain. I'm either dying or being reborn, joints coming apart or melting together, all my blood leaving me or swelling my veins. I kiss Hannah's cheek and manage to get out of the car, promising to text her later, and make it inside my house.

The TV mumbles in the living room, but I head straight for the stairs. I need my room, my bed, my sound machine emptying my thoughts and singing me to sleep.

"Mara, is that you?" Mom calls, but I don't answer. I've just reached the second floor, nearly running, when I ram smack into Owen in the hallway.

Holding hands with Angie.

His other arm reaches out to steady me. Instinctively, I shrink away. He sees my retreat, and some desperate part of me wants to apologize. The other part wants to scream and slap and claw.

"Hi, Mara," Angie says, but he's already pulling her down the stairs. He calls something to our parents I can't make out and then they're out the front door. I hear our car start up, but I don't move toward my room. That *something* growls and stalks, still hungry, still unsatisfied.

Angie's hair was curly, wild and thick, her cheeks flushed and her hand tucked so trustingly into Owen's. She loves Mozart's flute concertos—I remember that from History of Music. One time freshman year, I forgot my lunch and couldn't stomach the cafeteria's Salisbury steak, and she split her peanut butter and honey sandwich with me. I don't even know why we were sitting together. Charlie must've been absent or maybe her lunch sucked too. It's all hazy, but right now, standing in the hallway, all these little moments from going to school with Angie for the past three years come trickling back into my mind.

She suffers from major stage fright and never auditions for solos.

She has a 4.0 GPA.

She has a baby brother. He's only about six months old, and I remember that every member of the symphonic band brought her a green balloon the day he was born last spring. She left school that day with a ton of balloons, several of them escaping during dismissal and drifting off into the sky.

She came to an Empower meeting once or twice. She said she wanted to come to more, but the time conflicted with her private flute lessons.

Angie is not stupid.

She is *not* stupid.

Mom calls my name again, and something snaps in my chest. Or maybe it's in my head, my arms, my legs. Everywhere, something breaks and separates, like the stars splitting apart.

I nearly trip down the steps in an effort to get to my mother. She must hear the frantic pace of my feet, because she meets me in the hall, her reading glasses pushed into her hair.

"Honey, what's wrong?"

She moves toward me, alarm owning her expression. I don't even realize I've moved closer to her, too, but I must have because we sort of collide, my arms gripping hers and her hands on my face, wiping at tears I didn't realize had started to fall.

"Mara, you're scaring me."

"Where is he? Where did Owen go with Angie?"

She frowns. "He just took her home, sweetie."

"You're sure? He's coming right back?"

"I . . . I think so. That's what he said."

"Can you call him? I need you to call him and tell him to come home."

"Mara, what——"

"Please!"

"What's going on?" Dad says, coming into the hall from the living room. "What's wrong?"

"I don't know exactly," Mom says. Her hands have moved to my shoulders and she presses down on them gently, as if she's afraid I might float away at any moment. And I think I might, because that hungry *something* isn't anything apart from me.

It *is* me.

"I need Owen to come home. He's . . . he can't be with her. He can't do that. I don't want him to be that person. She's not stupid. She's not. And he's . . . he's my brother. He is."

I'm sobbing, molecules exploding, stardust covering the earth.

"Honey, you're not making any sense," Mom says while Dad smoothes my hair back from my face.

"Yes, I am. You know I am, Mom. Why wouldn't you believe me? Why couldn't you do that?"

Her eyes widen, but more with confusion than shock or knowledge. Because I said *me*. I meant to say *her*, but I said *me* and I'm not sure why or how to fix it or what it means.

"I'm not stupid," I whisper, and Mom flinches. "Hannah. She's not stupid. She's not a liar."

"We talked about this. It's over, honey."

"She's not stupid!"

Mom's color drains away as my scream echoes through the hall, her shoulders slumping. She takes my face in her hands, her fingertips gentle. "And your brother is? It's not that simple, sweetheart."

"No, Mom. You mean it's not that *easy*. Because what happened is that simple." And I know in that moment that I'm right. It's a tangled mess of simple facts, a kaleidoscope of right and wrong. The aftermath—that's what's complicated.

Mom searches my face, and her eyes are wet and wide and round. But before she can say anything, the front door swings open and my brother walks through, tossing the keys onto the hall table with a casual flick of his fingers. Relief assaults me, but not as much as anger. Sadness. I'm delirious with it all, with *lies* and *men* and *girls* and *daughters* and *stars*.

He stops in his tracks when he sees the three of us, a little knot of tears and panic in the hallway.

"What's going on?" he asks.

I break free of my mother and shove my brother in the chest. He stumbles backwards, mouth falling open as he collides with the door.

"Mara!" Dad calls and Mom cries out, but I don't really hear them. I keep shoving, my fingers ricocheting off Owen's shoulders only to return again, pushing and pushing even though he's already against the door.

I scream at him. All the words I could never seem to say to anyone.

Believe. Valid. Scared. Hurt. Space. Body. Mine.

No.

No.

No.

The words flow out as I hit him in the chest, as I cry and shake off my parents when they try to pull me back. I unleash the energy behind every star in the sky onto my other half.

And Owen lets me.

He just stands there, absorbing my fury, until all the light and fire blink out.

When I finally back off, he breaks. A strangled sound rolls out of his throat and his face crumples, eyes bleeding tears. He slumps against the wall, sliding down until he's sitting. My mother covers her mouth with her hands, but she doesn't go to him. She doesn't wrap her arms around him and rock him while he cries. Dad just stares at his son, shock stealing all the color from my father's face.

I watch Owen break apart, everything he'll probably never say so clear in every body-wracking sob. I wait for something to break in me, too, but there's nothing left. My fracture already happened. Exactly when, I'm not sure, but I know it's done. I feel loose and unmoored.

Half of a constellation.

Because this boy crying on the floor, burying his face in his hands, shamed and silent and guilty, is not only Owen McHale.

He is my twin brother.

CHAPTER TWENTY-SIX

"*Once upon a time . . .*"

Instinctively, my mouth bends into a smile as Owen settles next to me on the roof. He's been on my heels constantly lately, asking me about summer school and how I feel about starting Pebblebrook in the fall and trying to get me to laugh. Last night at dinner, he risked our parents' wrath and spelled out swear words with his rigatoni. I actually did laugh when he substituted the u in the f-word with a chunk of tomato.

"*A brother and a sister lived with the stars,*" Owen goes on. "*They were happy and had wild adventures exploring the sky. But lately, Sister Twin was super sad and she felt lonely, like she was in the sky all by herself, but luckily for her—*"

"Oh, here we go."

"Shut up. *Luckily for her, she had a charming, handsome, debonair—*"

"Debonair—oh my god."

"Hey, my story here."

"I'm just saying, accuracy matters."

He nudges my elbow and I can feel his grin trying to mirror itself on my face.

"Anyway," he says, "she had a charming, handsome, debonair twin brother who only wanted to make his sister happy."

"So, yesterday, when you ate the last piece of our birthday cake, that was for the sole purpose of making me happy?"

"Yes. I saved you a filling at the dentist's office."

"Ah. Thank you so much."

"Anytime. So one day, Brother Twin decided to collect a bunch of stars and make his sister a crown, to remind her how pretty and nice and amazing she was."

I stiffen at the word pretty, but if Owen notices, he doesn't let on.

"They flew through the sky together while she pointed out all of her favorite stars. Some were blue and some were green and some were purple, and when she touched them, they flew into her crown."

"I'll bet Brother Twin was jealous of that awesomeness."

"He totally was. Anyway, when her crown was full, they kept flying around for a while, but something weird happened."

"Brother Twin stole her stars?"

Owen rolls his eyes. "No. He's not that big of a jerk."

I snort-laugh.

"Shut up, and let me tell the story!"

"Okay, fine."

"Anyway," he says, cracking his knuckles, "stars kept attaching themselves to Sister Twin. Soon, she had a necklace and a bracelet and a belt and shoes and a shirt and it was like she was glowing."

"Glowing?"

"Yeah, because she's made of stars. Get it?"

"But if I'm made of stars, then where am I? Where's the real me?" The questions slip out before I can stop them. I love Owen's stories and I can't help but love him even more for trying to distract me, even if he doesn't know from what. Still, I have to wonder about his story, about the girl buried in stars.

"See, that's the thing," Owen says. "When they got home, she was so happy, but when she tried to take off the stars to go to sleep, she couldn't. The twins thought the stars were just covering her up, but that's not what was going on."

"Why not?"

"Because when they thought the stars were sticking to her, really all the loneliness and sadness were falling off. The stars were underneath."

"Underneath what?" My face turns toward him now, my voice a reverent whisper.

"Everything else. All the bad stuff. She just had to remember who she was underneath everything. She glows — she'll always glow. Of course, she needed Brother Twin to help her because he's awesome."

I laugh at that, but tears form quickly and slide down my cheeks and into my hair. In the dark, I don't think Owen can see them, but even if he can, all he does is take my hand as we stare up at the sky.

"It's you and me, Star Girl," he says seriously. "Always will be, no matter what."

I squeeze his hand. "No matter what."

CHAPTER TWENTY-SEVEN

TUESDAY MORNING ARRIVES hazy and heavy. My mind
wakes, but my eyes stay closed, desperate for a few more minutes of oblivion. After Owen fell apart—after we all did—the
rest of the weekend and all of Monday, the final day of my suspension, was a blur. He never explained his breakdown or why
he let me hit him over and over again, not that I really expected
him to. But my parents seemed totally freaked out. When he got
up off the floor and stumbled wordlessly to his room, they let
him go. My mother kept her hands pressed over her mouth, as
though she was trying to keep a scream inside. I'm not sure what
they thought. What they suspected. I didn't ask. I was scraped
empty. I fell into bed and didn't wake up until late Sunday afternoon.

When I opened my eyes, my mother was in my room, sitting
on my bed and rubbing circles on my back. Neither one of us said
anything. She just kept smoothing her palm and fingertips over my
shoulders until I fell asleep again. In my dreams, I told her things.

Why I'd been so distant for the past three years, why her lack of faith in Hannah felt like a lack of faith in me.

What happened to her daughter in a quiet classroom.

Now my room is empty and I force myself out of bed and into the shower. All the motions of a normal girl with a normal family whose only cares are how much homework she has and college applications and best-friend drama.

But I'm not that girl anymore. She was taken from me a long time ago and I'll never get her back. But I have to be someone. I have to be some type of girl. I look at myself in the mirror—the dusting of freckles over my nose, hair wild around my face and falling over my shoulders, a deep darkness under my eyes. The reflection looks right. It looks like me. Exhausted and sad, but still *here*.

I almost laugh, thinking of all those epitaphs I've hunted down in Orange Street Cemetery. What will mine say one day? Such a clichéd thing to wonder, but the question is a fist in my gut.

Mara McHale, Some type of girl

Maybe I'm the type of girl who likes short skirts.

Maybe I'm the type of girl who likes boys and girls and those who sometimes feel like both and neither.

Maybe I'm the type of girl who slaps a boy in the face when he does something shitty.

Maybe I'm the type of girl who hides and cries in her bed alone, remembering a terrifying day that took away all of her control and trust.

264

Maybe I'm the type of girl who's tired of hiding and crying alone.

Maybe I'm the type of girl who realizes she's not alone.

Maybe I'm the type of girl whose favorite person in the world did something unforgivable.

Maybe I'm the type of girl who finally accepts it.

Maybe I'm not a stupid girl.

Maybe I'm just a girl, plain and simple and real.

★.

I'm staring into my closet, my heart still a huge raw lump in my chest, when a knock sounds on the door.

Tap. Tap tap tap.

It's not his knock.

It's hers.

Charlie appears, her eyes searching and finding me in less than a second.

"Hi," she says.

"Hi."

"May I come in?"

I nod and push my hair back, even though I sort of want to cover my face with it, hiding every expression and thought and fear and need.

She clicks the door shut behind her, then sets her messenger bag on the floor by the desk. All of her movements are slow and careful, perfectly planned and executed.

"Hannah told me she had to come get you the other night," she says. "Are you okay?"

"I'm . . . I don't know."

She nods, her teeth pressing over her bottom lip.

"Charlie," I say, "I'm sorry for what I said to you at the Fall Festival. I was an asshole and I understand if you're mad at me. What you tell your parents and when is up to you, and you know I support you in that. I always will, whatever you decide."

"I know," she says softly. "I'm not mad."

"Oh. Well, good."

She cracks a sardonic smile. "At least, not anymore."

"I guess I deserve that."

Her smile dips a little and she tangles her fingers together. "Will you sit down?" she asks, motioning toward the bed.

"We have school."

"I'm aware," she says. "This won't take long."

She pulls out my desk chair and sits, threading her hands together and then sticking them under her legs. Her posture is tense, her shoulders hugging her neck.

My knees feel weak and I back up until I hit the bed, then sink onto the mattress. Charlie's chest rises and falls slowly with deep breaths.

"I invited my parents to my next show," she says.

"What?"

"My next show. It's in Nashville, at this tiny coffee shop in the Gulch. No big deal, really."

My eyes widen. "Charlie. Wow. It is. It's a gigantic deal."

She shrugs. "Anyway, I told my parents about it, about writing songs and . . . well, how everything I want to do with music has very little to do with four-part harmony and chorales."

I laugh. "And?"

"They were excited. My dad even . . ." She grins. "My dad even ran upstairs to my room and grabbed my guitar. Asked me to play him and my mom something I wrote."

"Did you?"

She nods. "But I didn't sing it. Just hummed."

I smile. "Well. Baby steps, right?"

"Yeah. Anyway, they're going to come to the show."

"Charlie." She lifts her head to look at me, her expression all nervousness and eager for approval. "That's awesome."

"I'm still kind of freaking out about it. I mean, you know my songs. They're—"

"They're you."

She sighs and drags a hand through her hair, but nods.

"I'm proud of you," I say quietly. "Really proud of you."

Her gaze meets mine. "I knew you would be. And I'm going to talk to my parents about"—she waves a hand down her body, covered in plaid and black jeans—"well, all of this. Me. I just need some time."

"Of course you do. That's a huge thing."

"Yeah, it is, but I'm ready to do it. Or I'm getting there. And there's something else I need to tell you."

"Okay."

She blows out a long breath. "I lied to you."

"What?"

"I asked you to tell the truth, to be brave, but I haven't told the truth and I haven't been brave. I guess talking to my parents about my music was a step, but there's more."

"What . . . what did you lie about?" A cold rush of fear fills my veins, because I don't think I can take any more lies. I don't think I can handle another person I love more than anything telling me they're full of shit.

She doesn't answer at first. In fact, she doesn't answer for a long time. Just breathes slowly and evenly. Finally, she gets up and comes over to the bed, tucking one leg underneath her while she sits and takes both of my hands in hers.

"I love you, Mara."

"I know you do."

"No, you don't. I really love you. I'm *in* love with you. I never wanted to break up. I only agreed because I could tell you were freaking out and I didn't know what to say to change your mind. And, yeah, part of me thought that if I fought you on it, I'd lose you as a friend, too. But, Mara, nothing can change this." She waves her hand between us. "We know that now. It's okay to be both best friends and together. It's okay to not be together too, but that's not what I want."

I open my mouth, but I can't tell if it's to say something or simply a shocked reaction. Either way, Charlie presses one fingertip to my bottom lip, stilling all my thoughts.

"You don't have to say anything right now. I didn't come here to get back together. I know you're confused and feel lost right now and I don't want to add to that. I just came here to tell you the truth, because you deserve it and because I can't ask you to do the same if I won't. I know it's not the same as telling your parents about what happened to you. It's not even in the same universe and I can't really compare them, but I wanted you to have this. This part of me, no matter what you need to do with it. I feel as if you might like Alex and I don't want to—"

"I don't like him. I mean, not like that." I take a breath, my thoughts whirling. "He's a good friend, that's all. We did kiss, but . . . we're not together. We won't be."

She presses her eyes closed and nods.

"What . . . what about Tess?" I ask.

Charlie laughs lightly. "Tess is a friend. She wanted more and I couldn't do it."

My fingers tighten around Charlie's. But before I can say anything, she untangles herself from me and moves toward her bag. Reaching a hand inside, she pulls out a scarf bright with Gryffindor burgundy and gold. It must be what she was knitting at the Fall Festival, except now it's complete, long and soft and perfect. Stepping back toward me, she loops it around my neck.

"For me?" I ask, running my hands down the velvety thread.

"For you."

"But . . . I'm a Ravenclaw."

She laughs and smoothes one hand over my hair. "Beauty and strength," she whispers.

My eyes widen. "That . . . that song is about me?"

"That song is about us. All of us."

And then she bends down and kisses me on the lips, a whispery and familiar brush of her mouth that's gone before I can lean into it. She backs away from me and I know she's trying to give me space.

But I don't want space from Charlie. I never have, even when it was scary, and it'll probably be scary for a long time. I don't know when I'll be ready for more than kissing, with anyone, and I know I need help, need to talk to someone about all of this. But ever since I met her, I've wanted as little space as possible from Charlie. And right there, I see another type of girl, the type who breaks up with the person she loves because she's scared.

Scared of giving her trust away.

Scared she's damaged, never enough.

Scared of giving someone else power to hurt her, to touch her, to lie to her, to do something so shocking and unexpected that she'll never recover.

And I'm not sure I ever will recover from what Mr. Knoll did. Not fully. It's changed me forever, but *changed* doesn't have to mean *broken*. And I know my family will never be the same either. My brother's and my connection has been altered, never broken but twisted into something I never expected, never wanted. We're no longer the twins in the sky, and I have to figure out how to live with that. How to be his twin sister and hate what he did all at once.

But I can have this.

I can be honest about this.

Charlie's back is to the wall as she watches me roll all of this over and over in my head. I wonder what I look like to her, a fractured girl piecing herself back together. This process of becoming whole again isn't because of Charlie and the fact that she loves me, but it's not *not* because of her either. Because she takes care of me. Just like she takes care of Hannah, and I want to take care of them. That's what friends do.

Charlie's eyes never leave mine as I walk toward her. I cup her face in my hands and a little tear slips down her cheek. I smile as I brush it away with my thumb. My own eyes are dry—I've never seen Charlie cry alone. But maybe, after everything she and I have been through, together and separately, she's a new type of person too.

"I lied too," I say. "About us."

She heaves a shaky breath and nods, more tears spilling out of her. But her shoulders round forward a little, letting go of her neck. For the first time in weeks, I realize how heavy my lie was. My fear. Charlie wore all of it like a wool scarf around her neck in the heat of summer. I hurt her. My best friend in the world. I hurt her and I hurt myself.

"I'm so sorry," I tell her. And I'm not sure if I'm talking about us or something else entirely. I'm not sure if I'm talking to Charlie or talking to myself or talking to some girl with wavy hair I don't know smiling up at her teacher.

Charlie shakes her head and tucks a lock of my hair behind my ear. "Don't. You weren't ready. I get that."

I lean my forehead against hers, not sure exactly what or who she's talking about either. "Thank you."

"For what?"

"For believing me."

"Always."

She presses her nose against my neck. Her breath is warm and her hands are on my hips and it feels perfect and gentle and safe. Even with all the other bullshit going on, there's this little space in the universe where everything is right. Everything is made of stars.

"Will you teach me how to write songs?" I ask.

She smiles against my skin. "I'll help you. But you already know how, Mara. You do."

And the wild thing is, in this little sliver of time, I believe her.

"I'll write myself a sappy love song," I say. "And then I'll write one for you."

She pulls away enough to grin at me. "You're a girl after my own heart, you know that, right?"

Her words send a sweet pulse of energy through my veins and I kiss her then, smiling against her mouth. It's not even that sexy of a moment. We're both sort of crying and our bones are fragile under our skin and I have no idea what sort of shape I'm in to be a girlfriend again, or even if I can be one right now, but she's here.

She loves me and I love her and it's not some way to deny every-thing else. It's a small step, but it's the truth. It's acceptance.

Mara McHale, Girl after Charlie Koenig's heart

Without a doubt, that's one type of girl I absolutely know that I am.

CHAPTER TWENTY-EIGHT

WHEN CHARLIE AND I COME DOWNSTAIRS, Owen is sitting at the breakfast bar, slurping cereal. I move through the kitchen, filling up my water bottle and grabbing a couple of granola bars, but my eyes keep finding him. I take in every single part of him —the parts I love, the parts I hate. Even these new parts of him, parts I never knew existed, that make me afraid. I can't avoid that fear anymore.

So I look.

Eventually, he feels my eyes on him and lifts his head. His gaze is so soft, I sense Charlie squirming behind me. Because this tightrope of love and anger, compassion and hate, is awkward and precarious. Maybe it will be for a really long time.

As I walk past him toward the door, I reach out — it's instinct, like lifting our heads toward the sky whenever we're together — and let my fingers drift near his back. I reach out, but I don't touch. Instead, I whisper goodbye and then choke on tears as we drive to school, Charlie holding my hand the entire time.

Hannah is waiting for us by the front doors. Her hair is wild and unbrushed, a mass of gorgeous waves and random little braids around her face. When I see her, I can't help but gulp her into my arms. She laughs quietly and then pulls back to look at me, her eyes roaming up my body as I do the same to her.

We're both wearing very short skirts. Not so short that Principal Carr could find any violation, but short enough to raise an eyebrow.

Short enough to make me feel sexy and empowered and in control of my life. It's such a little thing, this skirt. For other girls, maybe it's makeup or a sport or having sex or not having sex or writing or music or kicking ass in school or wearing your hair so it looks like the sun's unruly rays. I think every girl has a thing or two, tiny details in her life that say *This is me. I'm done hiding. I'm done feeling ashamed.*

And maybe I'm not there yet. Maybe Hannah isn't either. But we're trying and we're doing it together. We're making it about us and not them.

"Oh my god, finally," Hannah says, clapping her hands and jumping up and down.

"What?" I ask.

"What? Are you serious?" She flails her hands at Charlie, who's sort of pressed against my side and whose fingers I didn't even realize had slipped between mine again.

"Right?" Charlie says, and moves her other hand to circle my hips.

"What do you mean, 'right'?" I ask.

Hannah rolls her eyes. "Who the hell do you think Charlie's

been lamenting to for the past month?" She clasps her hands together and flutters her lashes. *"Oh, Mara. My Mara. My baby. Oh, my heart. What will I do?"*

"I was not that pathetic," Charlie says.

"You sure as hell were!"

"Well, I sure as hell never said, 'Oh, my heart.'"

Hannah waves a hand. "Close enough. Plus you're a Libra. A Gemini and a Libra are pretty much a match made in nauseatingly sublime heaven."

"Well, that explains everything," Charlie says dryly, but she's grinning.

"Aw, you were pining," I say, and pull Charlie toward me so our hips are aligned. A few kids stare at us as they pass, their jaws reaching for the ground. I flip them off behind Charlie's back. Because if there's one thing I'm not afraid of anymore, it's my arms around Charlie.

"I was not," she says. Then she sticks out her tongue at me. "Okay, maybe a little."

"Well, maybe I was too. Just a little."

She smiles and I smile back and it all feels so goddamned good, I never want to leave this spot outside the school, the rest of the world swarming around us.

"Ready?" Charlie asks, breaking the spell, her eyes flitting between Hannah and me. Immediately, my smile falls and Hannah audibly sighs.

"No," she says.

"Not even close," I say.

But Charlie takes Hannah's hand and holds mine a little tighter. "You are."

We walk into the school like that, skirts and plaid and interlaced fingers. Eyes and whispers follow us, but I try to ignore them.

Until I see Alex waiting by my locker.

"Um . . . give me a minute, okay?"

Charlie follows my gaze and stiffens, but I squeeze her hand before releasing her.

"Sure," Hannah says, and then she wraps her arm around Charlie's shoulders and leads her toward Hannah's locker down the next row. "It's okay," I hear her say to Charlie, and it all makes my throat tighten, how much we need one another, how much we try to take care of one another and be honest with one another now, no matter who's more damaged or hurt at one time or another. Last night I even called Hannah to tell her what Alex thought he might have seen that night at the lake and what the state attorney said about it.

I was shocked to hear Alex had already called her.

She was pissed, but I don't think it was about Alex. It was about our world, about the ways it ignores us every day. Still, it was the kind of angry that we both welcomed. The kind that made us feel solid and visible.

"Hi," I say as I reach Alex. He shifts his bag higher on his shoulder and looks at his feet.

"Hey."

Then we just stand there, a cloud of awkward and mistakes billowing around us.

"I don't . . . I don't know what to say, Mara. I'm just really sorry."

"I know."

"I didn't mean to use you. But you're right. It was fucked-up."

I look at him, so gentle and earnest. He comforted me when no one else could. "It wasn't. It was what we needed. Both of us."

He nods and takes a deep breath and looks out at the crowd of kids running to their lockers and classes, his lips mashed together so tightly I'm sure he's holding in some tears. He's lost a lot too. His lifelong best friend and, maybe on some level, his ability to trust another person, just like Hannah and I. I don't want him to be another casualty of Owen's fuckup. I just don't.

"You and Charlie?" he asks.

I swallow, my mouth suddenly dry. "I think there might always be a me and Charlie."

"Yeah." He takes a deep breath, nodding at the floor tiles. "I get it. I do."

"Hey," I say, reaching out to take his hand. "You helped me. You did. And I still need that and I still want to hang out. Whatever we were to each other, it was something, you know? And I don't want to lose that something, that friendship part of it. Would that be okay?"

He finds my eyes, watching me while a tiny smile lifts one corner of his mouth, there and then gone. "Hell yeah, it would."

I hug him, then press a chaste kiss to his cheek. When he releases me, he smiles—real and hopeful—before offering a little wave and weaving in between the bevy of students, joining up with a few of the less despicable orchestra kids. He disappears around the corner and I feel this weird amalgam of relief and sadness. Hannah comes up next to me, her shoulder pressing into mine.

"All good?"

I nod. "All good."

The first bell rings and I look around for Charlie.

"She had to meet with her guitar teacher. She'll see you in class."

"Oh."

"She's all right."

"Am I a shitty best friend?"

Hannah smiles. She's still gorgeous, even with the purple pockets underneath her eyes. "I think you're a very human best friend who's been through some shitty things."

I hook my arm through hers, pulling her close to my side. "You're too good to me."

She lays her head on my shoulder as we start down the hall. "We're good to each other. Have to be, right?"

"Yeah," I whisper weakly because it's all my voice can get out.

Up ahead, I see Owen. I almost forgot how tall he is — nearly an entire head and a half above me, all of our father's height pressed into his bones. He's walking with Jaden but he's not smiling, his eyes glazed over as Jaden babbles on about something stupid, I'm sure.

I feel Hannah tense as he gets closer, her breath audibly

catching in her throat. I want to pull her through the crowd, press her face against my neck so she can't see him, can't hear him, but there's no time. Suddenly, he's right there, inches away from us, and there's this violent tear inside of me.

Because I want to pull him through the crowd too. Hide him away. Hold him while he cries.

Hannah's entire body shudders as he passes, but she keeps walking. He's the one who looks away. The whole moment lasts only a few seconds, but I feel literally crushed by Hannah's strength and beautiful anger, by the brother I know I've lost, in some ways, forever.

But I was wrong, thinking that I can't move on. I can—we all can. I just won't move through the world like I did before. Some parts of me are gone. Some others have come alive, woken by the need to fight, to matter, to be heard. Some parts are wary, others angry, others heartbroken. But I'm still me. I'm still moving. We all are, in some way or another.

Charlie was right. I wasn't ready then. Not three years ago. Not three weeks ago. I'd learned to ignore that hunger, that prowling *something*. But I can't ignore it anymore and I don't want to.

I'm ready now.

CHAPTER TWENTY-NINE

A FEW DAYS LATER, Owen is on the roof. Earlier that night, as soon as I pushed away from the virtually silent dinner table and retreated into my room, I went to the window. Swept the curtains back to look at the stars.

But I saw my brother instead, dark form against the dark sky.

Now my hands open the window, my body crawls out, my mind screams at me to stay inside, my heart aches for my other half.

It's amazing, all these parts of me, all this love and hate tangled up and coexisting.

I make my way over to him. He turns to look at me and I meet his eyes for a split second before gazing up at the tiny pinpricks of light dotting the sky. I feel him turn away, his chin lifting to the stars just like mine. We're not even saying anything, but the tears come fast and hard and silent. There's simply no way around this. No magic words to make it better. He can't take back what he's taken away.

"Once upon a time," he says, and my breath stutters in my lungs. I don't say anything and he goes on, his voice a cracked whisper. "Once upon a time, a brother and a sister lived with the stars. They were happy and had wild adventures exploring the sky. One day—"

"One day the brother broke his sister's heart."

He falls silent, but not for long. Owen never could shut up. "I didn't—"

"Don't. Don't you dare."

He sniffs and folds his arms, shaking his head at the ground. "I want things to go back to normal."

I look at him. Finally look at him, his face and features so familiar, so like mine. "There is no normal, Owen. Not anymore. There's only making it something other than this."

He frowns. "How . . ."

"Tell the truth."

His hand drifts up to his lip, fingers poised. But then his whole body stiffens as he drops his arm, pressing it against his side. "I did."

"You don't know what you did. What you're still doing. Don't you get it? You raped a girl, Owen."

He flinches, but I don't. I can call it what it is now. What it'll always be.

"You took her choices from her," I go on, "her body, her power. You took her ability to trust, her ability to be with a guy, maybe for years. And do you see what's happening? Do you see how quickly the world turns against her? Do you see how strong she's been at school, despite all that? You're not going to ruin her. I won't let you. *She* won't let you."

Tears course down my cheeks and I know I'm not just talking about Hannah anymore. I'm not just talking about Owen.

"But you'll let it ruin you and me?" He waves his hand between us, his voice shaking just as much as mine. Matching breath for breath.

"I love you so much, Owen." And I know it's true. He's my twin, my other half, forever. Nothing will ever change that. I'll always love him. "But right now? I don't know. I wish I did, but I don't. You can't take back what you did—"

"I didn't. Goddammit, I didn't do any of that." He rubs at his forehead with both hands, hiding his face from me. Then his shoulders start shaking. "I didn't do that. I didn't."

I step away from him, my arms aching to hold on to him. Even now. Even after everything. And I can't do that.

"I can't be the one to fix us," I say. "I have to fix myself first."

He glances at me, a question in his red-rimmed eyes.

I take a deep breath and I tell him a story.

"Once upon a time, a brother and a sister lived with the stars. They were happy and had wild adventures exploring the sky."

Owen inhales . . . exhales. I feel him relaxing, as if this story somehow symbolizes the two of us getting back to normal.

It doesn't. This is an entirely different kind of story.

"One day," I go on, "someone Sister Twin admired, an important man in their starry community, asked her to stay behind after lessons. She did. Everyone respected him and Sister Twin believed in his protection, in his good intentions. She believed he would never hurt her."

Owen stiffens. "Mara. What——"

"The man smiled and told her not to worry, but that he had to talk to her about a serious problem. Something that could ruin her future, disappoint her parents. To fix it, he asked Sister Twin to . . ." Here my voice knots up, but I swallow a few times, running through the story the way I've rehearsed it in my head for days. Next to me, Owen breathes loudly and I know his hands are curled into fists.

Because mine are too.

"He asked Sister Twin to do things she didn't want to do. Things no grown man should ever ask of a girl."

"Mara, stop."

"When she didn't comply, he forced her to do what he wanted."

"Mar, holy shit. What *is* this story?"

"Sister Twin managed to get away from the man. She ran home and cried and never told a soul. She never thought anyone would believe her. The man punished her for running away, convincing her parents that she deserved it. And still, Sister Twin never said a word."

"What is this? Are you . . . are you talking about . . . what are you talking about? Mara, please."

He's crying now.

I know he is, because so am I.

"She never said a single word about it to her family," I go on, pushing through the tears. "Until right now."

Owen reaches out and takes my hand, his fingers trembling as they curve around mine. Instead of yanking back, I let him hold on to that little part of me because I need him to hear this. I need him to hear me. To hear all of us.

Inhale.

Exhale.

I turn to look at him and I make sure he's looking at me. Our faces mirror each other's — eyes red and wide, tears wandering down cheeks, and noses sprinkled with freckles.

"This," I say to him, and he frowns. I bring our twined hands to my face, pressing the back of his hand to my cheek. "This is a girl who thought no one would ever believe her. This is a girl who is not lying."

He's sobbing now, his cries rising between us to settle in the sky.

I untangle our hands and step away from him.

"Eventually, Sister Twin realized that she had to tell her story. Because that story was *hers*. Because she was worth the telling."

"Mara . . ."

But he doesn't go on. Just buries his face in his hands, a tiny boy made of stars.

And in that moment, Sister Twin breathes in a universe full of constellations, taking them with her as she leaves. Because she knows it's time for the brother and sister to leave the sky for good.

CHAPTER THIRTY

ANDROMEDA WAS CHAINED TO A ROCK by the ocean and left to be devoured by a monster. Only she wasn't. She was saved by a man, Perseus, but he rescued her only because her parents promised to hand her over to him in marriage.

Even girls made of stars are captives, bound at the wrists and traded like property. Even girls made of stars aren't asked, aren't believed, aren't considered worth the effort unless they can offer something in return.

Even girls made of stars buy into those lies sometimes.

My skin feels electric as I knock on my parents' bedroom door that night. I'm not sure if it's nerves or adrenaline or stars waking up, rising to the surface and escaping.

But I'm not a girl made of stars.

I'm just me, just a girl, just Mara.

Charlie waits in my room. I called her after I came in from the roof with Owen and she was at my house within ten minutes. We spent the rest of the evening curled up on my bed, curtains shut tight against the sky, her fingers plaiting little braids into my hair, our limbs tangled, quiet whispers and a few tears and kisses. Never more than that, always exactly what I need.

"You can do this," she said to me after the house quieted, everyone inching toward sleep. I listened for my mother's soft footsteps in the hall outside my room. She's been retreating to her bed pretty early for the past couple of nights, armed with a cup of tea and a book. Sometimes my dad joins her and I hear the gentle murmur of their voices late into the night. Everyone's been so hushed lately, all of our movements around one another careful and wary.

"I still don't want to," I said to Charlie.

"I know."

"And I do. Want to, I mean."

"I know that too."

"I just never wanted to be that girl, you know?"

"What girl?"

"The cautionary tale, I guess. The victim."

"You're not a victim. You're a survivor. You and Hannah both. There's a difference."

Survivor. The word sank into my skin and settled on my bones. "I'm glad you're here," I told her.

"Will you come with me, when I come out to my parents?"

I raked my hand through her hair, making it stick up even more than usual. "You know I will."

She smiled and I brushed my mouth over her forehead, then her eyes and her nose, and then we kissed for what felt like hours, safe and hidden in our own little world.

But eventually, we had to come out.

Now the *tap-tap* on my parents' door echoes through the hall and I just want to crawl into my bed again, circle myself around Charlie and disappear.

Maybe a small part of me will always try to lock myself away, yelling about everything except what I really need to yell about. I'll always try to chain myself to a rock. But then I think about a classroom full of fourteen-year-old girls, wide-eyed and open and trusting. I think about Hannah at school, devastated and strong all at once.

"Come in," my mother calls.

I open the door and find my parents on the bed. My dad lies on top of the covers still in jeans and a sweater, *The Atlantic* open on his lap. Mom curls in close to his side, looking small and vulnerable bundled under the sateen quilt.

"Hi, honey," she says, sitting up. There's a hunger in her eyes as she looks at me and I almost back out of the room right there, because I'm about to feed her a plateful of shock and sadness.

"Everything okay, honey?" Dad asks.

I can't answer, a sob cutting off my voice. Shaking my head, I crawl onto the bed and wedge myself in between my parents. My mom inhales sharply, but her hands come around me, smoothing my hair. My dad rests his cheek on top of my head. We used to do this all the time. Saturday mornings in my parents' huge bed, giggles and lazy yawns and hands rubbed over backs, a happy foursome with a day to waste.

Except Owen's not here and his absence is a shock all over

again—what he did, how powerless we are to do anything about it. We can't go back, and going forward seems so bleak. Maybe Owen will tell the truth. Even if he does, I have no idea what that means legally. Any option is terrifying. Either way, I'm not sure if we'll ever be that happy foursome again.

The thoughts come in waves, rolling over me, the salt water leaking out of my eyes.

"Sweetheart," Mom whispers, and presses her lips to my forehead. It feels so safe here, and for a few blissful seconds, I forget why I knocked on their door in the first place. That there's another truth circling us, one that belongs to only me.

"Mom . . . Dad . . . I need to tell you guys something."

For Hannah.

For Charlie.

For all the girls whose names I'll never know.

For me.

Girl made of flesh and bone.

Acknowledgments

First, to you. I began this book for you and I'll end it for you as well.

Infinite thanks to my agent, Rebecca Podos, without whom I would not be half as functional as I am. You inspire me daily and I'm lucky to have you in my corner.

Thanks to my editor, Elizabeth Bewley, as well as Nicole Sclama, Alexandra Primiani, and everyone at Houghton Mifflin Harcourt for their passion and faith in Mara's story. I could not have told her story alone, and I'm glad I didn't have to. Thank you, Susan Buckheit, for your amazing copyediting skills and discerning eye.

To my inimitable critique partners, Lauren Thoman, Paige Crutcher, Sarah Brown, and Alisha Klapheke. You believe when I don't and I thank you from the bottom of my queso-loving heart.

To my beta readers, Dahlia Adler, Keiko Furukawa, Becky Albertalli, and Ami Allen-Vath, I cannot thank you enough for your time and insight, especially when offering that insight was painful. Thank you for helping me see not only Mara and Hannah and Charlie, but you as well.

Thanks to Court Stevens for listening to me rant while we walked under the trees.

Thanks to Carla Schooler for writing Charlie's song with me. I could not have fully captured what I wanted her to say and how I wanted her to say it without you.

Thanks to Christa Desir for answering my procedural and legal questions.

Thanks to Lily Anderson, who, when I tweeted "What's something unique two girls could do together at night?" responded with the perfect answer. Mara and Hannah find a lot of comfort in that abandoned movie theater, thanks to you.

Thanks to my family at Parnassus Books and Stephanie Appell for being a tireless advocate of stories and kids.

To Benjamin and William, my little stars. I hope that one day, you read this book and are angry. I hope that one day, you read this book and are hopeful. I know that one day, you will be men who listen, who champion, and who ask.

And to Craig, thank you for listening, for championing, for asking.

Author's Note

WHEN I FIRST DECIDED to write this book, I was angry. I was ready to burn the world to the ground. In all honesty, I'm still angry and still ready to burn the world to the ground. But as I wrote Mara and Hannah's story, I realized I could not write the book I really wanted to write, one in which all foes are vanquished and justice is served and every wrong is made right.

That is not the world we live in.

However, Mara and Hannah taught me something invaluable, something precious, something that helps me sleep a little better at night. They taught me that there is always hope. They taught me that there are always people out there willing to fight for you and with you, that there is camaraderie and comfort in shared pain, that there is power in speaking our truth and letting others love us.

In letting others value us.

This may not be the book you wanted. In many ways, it was not the book I wanted. The book I wanted never had an Owen or a Mr. Knoll, and if it did, it had an Owen and a Mr. Knoll who paid justly for their crimes.

However, this is the book I needed, and I hope, in some ways, it's the book you needed too. This is the book that reminded me that despite a system and a culture that is perpetually against us, that lets our oppressors go free, that disbelieves our words, there is hope. There is love. There is comfort. There is healing.

There is life after abuse. A good life. It's not an easy one. It's not the same one we had before. But it is still *ours*. And nothing and no one will take it from us.

We are worth the telling. We are worth the fight. We are worth a good life and love *after*.

RESOURCES

National Sexual Assault Hotline: 1-800-656-HOPE (4673)

RAINN (Rape, Abuse, and Incest National Network) www.rainn.org

Take Back the Night Foundation: www.takeback thenight.org

The Voices and Faces Project: www.voicesandfaces.org

Yes I Can Chat Room: www.yesican.org/chat/chat room.htm. This chat room is available for those who want to discuss issues surrounding surviving child abuse and parental and domestic abuse. Chats are moderated by trained facilitators.

Pandora's Project: www.pandys.org. This resource provides support for rape victims and families and also offers a chat room and message board.

MaleSurvivor: www.malesurvivor.org

It Happened to Alexa Foundation: ithappenedto alexa.org. This organization specifically provides support to victims dealing with the trauma of a criminal trial.